About t

Ivy Ngeow was born and raised in Johor Bahru, Malaysia. A graduate of the Middlesex University Writing MA programme, Ivy won the 2005 Middlesex University Press Literary Prize out of almost 1,500 entrants worldwide. She has written non-fiction for *Marie Claire*, *The Star*, the *New Straits Times*, *South London Society of Architects' Newsletter* and *Wimbledon* magazine. Her fiction has appeared twice in Silverfish New Writing anthologies, in *The New Writer* and on the BBC World Service. Most recently, her story was published by Fixi Novo in an anthology, *Hungry in Ipoh.* Her first novel, *Cry of the Flying Rhino,* was the winner of the international 2016 Proverse Prize and was published in November 2017 in Hong Kong.

Ivy won first prize in the Commonwealth Essay Writing Competition 1994, first prize in the Barnes and Noble Career Essay Writing competition 1998, and was shortlisted for the David T.K. Wong Fellowship 1998 and the Ian St James Award 1999.

Ivy has been a highly accomplished multi-instrumental musician since childhood and won fifth prize (out of 850 entrants) in the 2006 1-MIC (Music Industry Charts) UK Award for her original song, *Celebrity*, when she formed her own band, Satsuma (2005–07). Her songs are funky, modern and eclectic, with strong urban grooves and lyrics. Satsuma has played headlining gigs at top London venues such as: The Marquee Club, The Troubadour Club, The Water Rats, The Betsey Trotwood, Plan B and Clockwork.

About the Author

Praise for *Cry of the Flying Rhino*

"When reading this vivid and vibrant novel, I am immediately thrust back into the jungles, the small towns, the sweaty heat, the barrage of animal noises, the pungent smells and tropical odours, Ngeow has so well depicted throughout."

– Vaughan Rapatahana, poet, literary critic, essayist and novelist

"...the dogged doings of vastly unique characters – personages from a large scope of social and ethnic spectrums, individuals whose stories we increasingly crave as we speed toward the at once incredible and inevitable intersection of the novel's five main arcs. Anyone impressed, anyone imprinted upon and inspired by Lalwani, Roy, Chatterjee, Burgess, Lowry or Orwell, will be correspondingly affected by Ngeow."

– Jason S Polley, Associate Professor, Department of English, Hong Kong Baptist University

HEART OF GLASS

HEART OF GLASS

IVY NGEOW

This edition first published in 2018

Unbound

6th Floor Mutual House, 70 Conduit Street, London W1S 2GF

www.unbound.com

ISBN (eBook): 978-1-911586-65-4

ISBN (Paperback): 978-1-911586-64-7

Design by Mecob

Cover image:

© Shutterstock.com

Printed and bound in Great Britain by Clays Ltd, Elcograf S.p.A.

Dear Reader,

The book you are holding came about in a rather different way to most others. It was funded directly by readers through a new website: Unbound.

Unbound is the creation of three writers. We started the company because we believed there had to be a better deal for both writers and readers. On the Unbound website, authors share the ideas for the books they want to write directly with readers. If enough of you support the book by pledging for it in advance, we produce a beautifully bound special subscribers' edition and distribute a regular edition and e-book wherever books are sold, in shops and online.

This new way of publishing is actually a very old idea (Samuel Johnson funded his dictionary this way). We're just using the internet to build each writer a network of patrons. Here, at the back of this book, you'll find the names of all the people who made it happen.

Publishing in this way means readers are no longer just passive consumers of the books they buy, and authors are free to write the books they really want. They get a much fairer return too – half the profits their books generate, rather than a tiny percentage of the cover price.

If you're not yet a subscriber, we hope that you'll want to join our publishing revolution and have your name listed in one of our books in the future. To get you started, here is a £5 discount on your first pledge. Just visit unbound.com, make your pledge and type LIAN18 in the promo code box when you check out.

Thank you for your support,

Dan, Justin and John
Founders, Unbound

Super Patrons

Siti Shahwana Abdul Hamid
Zozan Abrams
Anisah Adnan
Mine Albertyn
Zalina Aldenborg
Romi Arman
Ann-Marie Balatoni
S. Bernd
Ritu Bhatia Kler
M. Birch
Helen Bradshaw
Scott Brandon
Sarah Buck
Nigel Buckie
A. Buegener
Brett Burkett
Linda Campsey
Emma Chase
Jane Chee
Feona Man Shan Cheng
Mary Cheong
Siang Chin
Andrew Chin
Shera LM Chok
Shera Chok
Fiona Chong
Sophie Chong
Marina Chung
Natasha Coleman
Alice Crawford
Michelle Crosby
Vanessa Cullip

Cathy Davis
John Davis
Olive Davis
Sydney Wen Ying Davis & Melody Wen Yan Davis
Stephanie Dennis
Mihori Erdélyi
Adrian Esdaile
Penelope Faith
Siew Fong Monk
Tina Foo
Eleanor Forrest
M. L. France
Sue Gee
Alex Gordon
Shen Guinnepain
Nicole Hammond
Shirley Hartley
Brian Hawkins
Janice Hawkins
Tina Hene
Amy Hill
Karen Ho
Richard Howard
Tracey Husbands
Azlina Ibrahim
Elly Sabrina Ismail
Sweet Johnny
Aaron Johnson
Brian Jones
Dan Kieran
Patrick Kincaid
Rufus Knight-Webb
Sunita Knight-Webb
Tiang Son Kong
Yeu Huan Lai
Joon-Nie Lau

Ewan Lawrie
Florence Lee
Eng Seng Lee
Alexandra Lewis
Alasdair Lewis
Yanyu Li
Su May Liew
Phillip Lim
Jane Littlejohn
Wayne Loh
Yvonne Lyon
Hamish MacFarlane
Monica Mackenzie
Stuart Mason
John Mitchinson
Emmy Moran
Michele Morgan
Nicola Morris
Man Fah Ngeow
Kong Dee Ha & Dr T F Ngeow
Irwin Ngeow
Dr Ivan Ngeow & family
Sandy Noble
Rebecca Ollis
Fiona Parker-Cole
Johnny Patney
Cissy Piercy
Justin Pollard
Peter Quek
Gabrielle Radiguet
Michael Rawlinson
Rachel Robson
Isabelle Roux-Gregson
Melonie Salam
S.B.M. Sani
Philippa Smith

Stella Soh
Nick Spicer
Michelle Tan
Allan Tan
Tot Taylor
Karen Teo
Lynette Topham
Sari Trisulo
Deanne Tyrrell
Anne Walker
Isabel White
Clair Whiteman
Kin Chan Wong
John Wong
Susie Woods
Melvyn Yap

With grateful thanks to Joon-Nie Lau, who helped to make this book happen.

'Wherever you go, go with all your heart.'
— Confucius

To my family and friends

1980

Picture This

I woke up. I was dreaming of music, and it's free to dream. I was going to get caught very soon and I could feel it. My nose was tingling. Things were on the decline. No, seriously. Only that very afternoon I contemplated selling my wine-red Gibson Les Paul deluxe guitar in its silver padded bag, in order to live.

Last night, I met Paolo. I was 23 years old. I had 24 dollars left in my black patent clutch and some belladonna tabs. Four, if I remembered right. It was freezing cold, and just like the night in Blondie's 'Picture This'.

It was November 4, 1980. The streets were celebrating the former Hollywood actor, Republican Reagan beating Democrat Carter in a landslide. TVs in bars were showing the firework displays. My throat was also on fire. Outside I was ice but inside I was baking. I was dying of thirst and I hadn't eaten for three days. It took an hour to do my Maybelline makeup to look just like Debbie Harry. Dallas would be proud. I wore my red-framed plastic glasses. I was more Warhol than Debbie.

I headed straight for the Drake Hotel, open every night since Prohibition era ended. I eyeballed a guy who was a little on the short side, perhaps five seven. He was at least 40. He looked smart, sexy if you were into that kind of guy, skinny. The three Ss. He had small neat hands, like those of a teacher. He was dressed immaculately in a sharkskin suit with an unbelievably pointed collar and I assumed he was Italian. His face was tanned and chiseled like a doll. If I was speaking Dallasese, I would call him an Italian pimp-dog, a know-it-all *émigré* sonofabitch. After a couple of drinks at the bar, I asked him if I could have a cigarette. I only had six dollars left, after cabs, tips and so on.

'Join us,' he beckoned and called, 'We're celebrating.' I assumed he meant the elections, but Dallas said to always answer with a straight question. This way you kept the conversation going. If you said,

'Yeah, how 'bout that, huh?', then what would they or you be able to say next?

So I played the ingénue. 'Really? What are you celebrating?'

'We're goin' into partnership to open the first and the best pizza restaurant in Asia — in Macao.' He said McCow. Wow, I thought to myself, but I wasn't about to act like some dumb broad.

'If you're the first, then how can you be the best?' I said.

He squinted and looked at me. 'Waiter, can we have another glass?' He snapped his fingers real quick and twice. The waiter came back with a champagne flute. Paolo rolled his eyes and shut them, as if he had been sent a message from the Heavenly Father in Naples.

'Gentlemen, this young lady is a mathematical genius,' he said. 'Dja think we oughta drink to dat? Huh?'

They each raised a glass and laughed. He poured me a glass of bubbly and I tentatively took a sip.

'What are ya? Who are ya?'

I shook my head. I put on a real serious look. The three guys roared with laughter.

'Italian?' said Paolo, when the laughter died down, only he said it more like Eyetalyun.

'Well, no, actually my mom is Chinese from Singapore and my dad is from here, from Chicago. Irish.'

'*Bella*,' he said, looking at me approvingly, '*bella*. That's why I thought you were Italian.' I kicked myself under the black shiny tablecloth with a real red rose on it, just lying there as if a gardener from a country mansion somewhere had cut and left a single rose before running off. Why did I tell him the truth? I feared the three things that all immigrants feared: cops, hunger, truth. Something about him, his voice, his hands, made me tell him the truth. Dallas would kill me if she knew. The deal was a different story each night: we were the Queens of Magical Journeys into the Unknown, whatever that meant. I felt I was too old for this game and the stories had run out.

Paolo was with a couple of friends or distant relatives I didn't know yet, who ran Johnny's pizzeria on West 35th. Originally it was Gianni's but somebody, probably a Johnny, changed the name. It was Paolo's family business, but he had a huge family. 'Johnny's. Is famous.

Is a block from the big Walgreens. You never been there?' They were proud of their pizzeria. I had heard of it, though I was not exactly a regular in the 60609 neighborhood. 'There's always a line round the block. Ya get a pizza, fries and two cans of coke for about 12 bucks. Johnny's is great for toppings.' They were super-selling it to me. If they said any more, I reckon I'd hit the floor I was so starved. 'Pretty cheap date, huh?' They had no idea. I was given a not-so-top secret: the trick was that the pizzas at Johnny's were baked. 'We know everythin' there is t'know about pizzas and we ain't sayin' nothin'.' Huge guffaws. I made sure I was listening. In Dallas's rulebook, listening was number one.

The conversation unavoidably drifted to 'less regulation of business activity', 'direction of government policy', 'consumerism'... *Stay out of politics*, said Dallas. *You never heard nothin'*.

'Ya play?' Paolo asked, tossing his head toward the piano as only Italians could, without looking like they were doing neck stretches.

'Sure,' I said.

I thought I wasn't ever going to get an audience again.

I went to the piano when the pianist was on his break. I asked him if I could play. He balanced his unlit cigarette on the top edge of the piano as though he was about to perform some magic trick. He gestured with his palm as if to say be my guest, and just when I was about to sit down, he said, 'You gotta coupla bucks?'

'No,' I said but I continued to sit down. 'Jerk,' I said under my breath.

I played 'On the Sunny Side of the Street', Fats Waller stride-style, big pouncy crab chords in one-two. Paolo came over bearing our drinks during the middle eight, leaving the two guys behind at our table.

'This is incredible!' he yelled. 'Guys! She plays! We have found her!'

I didn't know what he was talking about. Found who? Paolo cried, 'Bellissima!' and started singing. His hands burst in the air like an orchestral conductor's. He knew all of the words. He had a kinda showbiz voice, smooth, deep. But after the song was over, he wanted to sing about some shark with pearly teeth and I knew I wouldn't get out of it. He was a big fan of Bobby Darin. I changed the mood and started playing something more apt: 'Dreaming' by Blondie, with its wonderful descending scalic melody, about meeting in a restaurant when one wasn't a debutante. Were truer words ever spoken? No. He shook his head. How could he not dig that tune?

During Stevie Wonder's 'Higher Ground', with its pulsing ascending blues bassline, I lost my fan. At first he politely nodded his head in time, but he didn't know any of the words and wasn't singing along with me. Then he was looking back at the guys. He jokingly mouthed to them, 'I'll call ya', and made the universal gesture of the phone call, fist to the ear. It was just as well. The real pianist came back from his break, winked in that cocktail pianist way and said, 'Hey, thought that was neat.' We headed back to our table but my legs folded over.

I passed out.

Dallas used to assign 'jobs' for me to do, but now she was in MCC prison in downtown Chicago. Not only did I want to quit my day job, I wanted out from the 'night-time enterprise' too, which was scoping. Sure, she recognized that I had my Catholic hang-ups. *Scoping and teaching were the only options for me*, she said. Scoping was spiking guys' drinks with belladonna, our beautiful lady, or scopolamine, and when they surrendered to the peaceful nightshade of twilight she robbed them, or, as she liked to call it, 'taxed them'. All the time I would be saying my Hail Marys. *You're a class act*, she told me, *at least you do good your wrongs.*

Luck only gets better when it runs out. That was what my mom said. And for all her Singaporean–Chinese wisdomisms, she had not an ounce of luck in all her life. It was the early '50s when she married my daddy, when mixed marriages were so rare in Singapore people secretly took my parents' wedding photos and sold them to the tabloids, as though it was the discovery of an illegal gambling den; so rare my mother was disowned, so rare she became a kind of local legend. Despite all this she loved him, but she didn't trust him. It was a pretty kaboom combination. Actually, it was her mother, my Ah Por, who told her not to trust him. The white man cannot be trusted. Ah Por had more wisdomisms than teeth.

Dallas said there was no such thing as luck. It was just a feeling. If you feel lucky, then you are. Like feeling skinny or crummy or chunky. But I said, *Yo? Like put down the Cheetos if you're feeling chunky?* Dallas only said everything was a feeling because she was already in the can. I'd been in once and it was enough for me. She said I'd better get out of town fast.

Didn't think it would be that fast. When I opened my eyes, I thought I was in heaven. Dallas said that no way were the bouncers gonna turn us away from heaven's door. We got into every club that ever was.

It was free to dream and maybe I was still dreaming. I was in a beautiful clean room with yellow-striped wallpaper and Versailles-type gilt furniture. And a real red rose in a drinking glass on a fancy carved octagonal table. A painting with a heavily ornate gold frame hung on the wall in front of me. It was of a man pushing an old-fashioned cart full of flowers, somewhere in Europe. The flowers were intensely colored. Intensely tacky. Perhaps I had become a Queen after all, of Magical Garbage. 'Dallas?' I called out, though I didn't really mean her; it was just the first word I thought of.

Paolo was next to me, unshaven and black quiff ruffled like a bird. He crowed softly, '*Bella, bella,*' shaking his bird head. He held my hand and from the way he held it and the strength that flowed through me then, I knew I was awake. 'You're gonna be just fine, hon.'

I didn't want to be called 'hon'. It was the worst word I had ever heard. I cringed and had a spasm under the sheets.

Paolo said that all this happened because I had nothing to eat for three days, after which I drank a bottle of champagne on my own. I'd failed to tax him. *Niente*, zilch, diddly squat, *nada* from his sharkskin pocket. Never mind the pockets of the others. I squeezed my eyes shut in pain.

'You're gonna be eatin' lotta pizzas from now, hon. You're one bad kitty.'

Yeah. And he's Top Cat. 'But wait. One, I don't know anything. And two, I don't know anything about you.'

'Well, for a start, one, you're smart and two, ya know my name is Paolo Giametti Russo. Three, dat's all ya need t'know. I promise.'

I slept, ate, slept. When I woke up, I was exhausted. I slept some more. It seemed no more than a few hours, but later Paolo said I had been recovering for six days. I was no longer exhausted. He said I got the 'jawb' and was 'good to go'. Dallas said to get out of town, didn't she? So now I got a great job abroad and I had a ticket and a passport in my real name, Li-an Donohue, and the clothes on me. I was no longer Madison. This was my chance. From starvation to starting anew.

Paolo was whistling the mesmeric two-note opening of 'We are Siamese' from *Lady and the Tramp*. I went back to my landlady and said my sayonaras. 'I always thought you were going up in the world,' she said. 'Now you got a job abroad. Well, make sure you gonna come back for my sushi pie.'

I didn't know what that was, but it sounded disgusting. Before she could offer me any to take on the trip, I grabbed my wine-red Gibson Les Paul, and hastily left with all the possessions I had in three Wieboldt's shopping bags, from when Dallas and I went on a spree at Harlem Irving Plaza. Those were good days.

But better days were waiting for me. And nights. Crime-free early nights after honest work, like a regular girl. And how. Paolo's taxi was downstairs, purring. He was alone. I couldn't think. I felt so proud I could hear myself laughing internally. I wore my striped leggings, an oversized sweater with ventilation holes and my big, bad thrift-store coat. As I clattered down the black rusty iron outdoor staircase, I waved and smiled to Paolo. I wore my red-framed glasses as he seemed to like them. He trusted me, for some reason. Being trusted was greater than being loved. I said my *Ciaos* to the world of taxing and teaching. I was too old for this business. This was the beginning. I was new. I hadn't a dime but I had my own teeth, my real name and a passport. Screw you, Dad, and screw you too, Sherylanne.

'C'mon, c'mon!' Paolo waved impatiently, grinning.

I dumped the three bags into the nearest trash can at the bottom of the staircase.

'I'm coming right now,' I said, and got in the car.

'Jeet yet?' he asked. I was so excited I hadn't even thought about eating. I shook my head.

We stopped by a stand and Paolo said, 'Gimme a dog wid everythin'.' He looked at me. 'Make dat two.'

As we drove through the City of Big Shoulders and onto the Kennedy Expressway, I felt terribly sad. Sad that I was eating a Chicago-style hotdog for the last time. That I would not see Dallas or this town again. But before I knew it I was trying on Ray-Bans at Chicago O'Hare's duty-free lounge.

I met Dallas six years ago, in the summer of '74, and that was when things were beginning to look up for me. She saved me from being a toothless hobo. I was 17. My father and my stepmom Sherylanne threw me out. By then I'd already got all the education I needed. I'd gone to a proper Catholic school, majoring in music (Catholic to please my stepmom and music to please my mom).

I dropped out of high school altogether. I emptied Sherylanne's purse when she wasn't looking (and, boy, she never looked) and I got 140 bucks. I packed up all I could fit into two rucksacks and I grabbed my acoustic guitar. I could name every chord that ever was and play any tune by ear. I could pick up any instrument and pretty much work out how to play it in an hour. But I'd not worked a day in my life before. I hadn't a clue even how to work. I most definitely would have been on the streets had I not met Dallas. I'd already spent the first night in some dump, for which I had to part with some of my cash. Day two of leaving home, I was pounding the sidewalks west of Chinatown at W. Cermak and S. Canal St and knocking on doors, begging for anything that anyone could give me — a job, food, music tapes, anything.

I stayed close to Chinatown because, I reminded myself, firstly I was an immigrant. Secondly, I was Chinese. Chinese people stay close to Chinatown to meet other Chinese people. That was what I was supposed to do. And if that failed, there were also Irish, Jewish, Lithuanian, Italian, Greek, Mexican and other *émigrés* in Chinatown.

Dallas was in a fluffy dressing gown and had just stepped out for a smoke from an artist's studio on W. 34th, real close to the railway line.

She offered me a cigarette but I declined. She then knew I wasn't in for the short term. 'Whatdya want, kid?' she said, blowing smoke in my face. She was a striking broad. All hair, lashes and lips. Even had a beauty spot, right where it should be.

'I'm real good at… at work,' I said. 'I can do… um… anything?' Except that it sounded more like a question to myself. 'Even play guitar!' I added with a triumphant flourish that was way uncool. And childish.

'Anything,' she said. 'Huh.' The thought of my desperation made her smile. She was like somebody who would play a bimbo in a caper film as a decoy for the baddies. I never found out how old she was but she must have seen just how young I was. My appearance must have been pleasing to her. 'Your luck's in,' she said. 'You can move in with me.' But, in exchange, I had to work with her. I agreed to anything. Didn't care, nup. I was only 17 but I'd just got a job the day after I left home. My mom never had such luck. I missed my mom so much. It wasn't her fault she got depressed and couldn't handle us, life in the States, the food, Daddy's drinking and, the worst of it all, winters. It was a lot. She was an immigrant with high expectations and high hopes. They all had. Well, they all started off that way, anyway. She was lonely. She got sick with no one to care for her. Couldn't even call home as the international calls to Singapore cost more than a hundred dollars each time. Two dollars per minute; more if you went through an operator. Each minute to speak to someone back home was like a fleck of gold dust.

Dallas fed and clothed me. She was more a mother than a sister or a friend. She totally 'got it' when I spent evenings telling her about my mom. She wept. Dallas said she was a mom once. It was sad. She couldn't speak about it. Not then, maybe another time. But she never wept long as she was vain and didn't want to ruin her perfect makeup, and crying was the daddy of all wrinkles anyway, she said. She always called me 'kid', 'girl', 'sweetheart'. She was so happy to see me. No one had ever been happy to see me. Sherylanne didn't speak to me and, if she did, she said, 'Now, scram.' Daddy went along with her and said nothing. When Dallas said, 'Good morning', 'Did you sleep well, kid?' and 'I'm so happy to see you!' every day, I knew I owed her big time. She loved me, and I her.

Dallas wasn't her real name. She christened me Madison. 'You need to be christened,' she said. 'You're Catholic, right?' I asked her how she knew. She said, 'The hair.' I hadn't laughed for years. I thought I had forgotten how to laugh.

She thought names of places was a good start, since we never went nowhere.

For my day job, Dallas suggested that I gave guitar and piano lessons. I stuck ads on lampposts and Walmart bulletin boards, on her advice. In school I was a brilliant student, but since I had no qualifications, formal or informal, I was making $10 an hour teaching. *Not bad for a 17-year-old*, I thought. I didn't get work all the time and I was better at piano than guitar. My students often left as soon as they could, for a better qualified teacher or more formal lessons. This left me feeling hopeless. A little part of me died every time a student left. It was like I was trying to pet a small animal that kept writhing and twisting until it finally jumped off my lap. I desperately wanted to leave my day job before it left me but there was nothing I could do. Dallas's day job was modeling for art classes. So you can imagine the patience she had.

And since we never went nowhere, what I wanted to do was to go somewhere. Someone had now given me a ticket. It was as far from Chicago as you could get without going to space. It was '(Just Like) Starting Over' by John Lennon. There is so much joy and optimism in that song and when I thought about it, it made me want to weep. He was my songwriting hero. It was the pentatonic scale in his melody lines giving them the Chinese sound, a moving, heart-tugging, melancholic feel even if they were happy. None of this was a secret. I would not be the first person who knew this, yet I also tried using the same technique. It just worked.

I had never been to Portugal or China. Macao was both places. I was born to arrive here — it was crawling with Eurasians. Like them, I was mixed, hail Mary. My first impressions of Macao were of cobbled streets, 400-year-old Mediterranean churches and thousand-year-old

Chinese temples. Like me, Macao looked best at night. It was full of neon and gold-dipped fun palaces. There were exotic Chinese seafood restaurants and several glitzy casinos with Vegas-style buffets. I was East-West, and so was Macao.

I was shown my 'room'. It was a pavilion-like turn-of-the-century private apartment in the grounds of Paolo's villa. It was pink and green. There was something fairytale-like about its frilly neatness and carved timber details. It must have been a hunting lodge at some point, or a keeper's pavilion. I could come and go as I pleased. I had my own gate access to the beach and another to the road. In the distance, a hazy sky hung over mist-shrouded hills. Two women wearing cotton gloves and headscarves cleared trash into bags. Further toward the horizon were fishing junks. Busloads of school children were offloaded from the road onto the beachfront, kept in line by teachers with megaphones. Each group had its own bright uniform, including matching hats and daypacks in yellow or blue. The children ran off to hunt or poke at crabs in the sand.

And, oh yeah — I was allowed to use his villa facilities if I wanted to, if I had to make a call or a sandwich, or use the pool or if I could really do with a big glass of Gewürztraminer. It was all good. Gewhat? I thought, but said nothing. Looks like my knowledge of European languages would be coming along nicely. 'Ya want anything, ya know who to ask.'

He introduced me to the housekeeper. I asked her name, but she said I could just call her Auntie. That would be OK. She frowned at me as though she wanted to say something else, but she didn't. She reminded me of my childhood servant, my *amah-cheh.* My mother said that my first word was 'panda', in Cantonese. I had learned Cantonese from my 阿媽姐, *amah-cheh*, though I remembered not a word, not even 'panda'. After a few days in Asia, I could feel it coming back to me, like swimming, or cycling. I just knew what people were saying, and soon I'd be able to reply.

The Cantonese are made of steel. They are the Scottish of Asia. They live hard and they talk harsh. They spit. There is no terrain or climate too severe. In fact, nowhere is tough enough for them. Often they were pioneers, laborers, servants or bondmaids, sold to families to perform domestic chores.

On my first day, after a nap and a quick touch-up of my hair and makeup, the jet lag seemed to melt away, temporarily anyway. Paolo had hired me a Thai driver, Thaew, who knew Macao inside out and his air-con, blue-tinted glass, light gold Mercedes Benz 300SD better than his own wife. I wanted to barf when he called it his 'blue-eyed babe filled with diesel'. He'd hung an assortment of plastic flower garland charms from his rear-view mirror and on his dashboard he'd stuck a tiny gold Buddha and a mosaic elephant, using foam-backed double-sided tape.

Thaew took Paolo and I to a temple. I was Catholic; maybe Paolo thought that I needed my eyes opening. Wasn't for him to be aware that I was brought up in Asia and needed no 'grand tour', no sir. Actually, the visit was for the monks' blessings. For the restaurant business, for us, for the music I was bringing to Macao. Devotees were buying prayer tiles and wooden bead bracelets. For centuries, monasteries had taken in small boys to receive religious education, with freedom to leave if they chose not to become monks. We crossed sandy courtyards, puddles, a stone pagoda and the White Lotus Hall, a traditional building with long tiled roofs, eaves painted in delicate pinks and greens, decorated with animal and flower carvings. We studied serious-looking wooden pillars and trellised doors, while frogs croaked in the ponds. For a couple of hours we hung out but then Paolo had all these meetings to attend to so I was dropped off back home.

I spent the late afternoon swimming in the sea. I'd forgotten I was quite good at swimming when I lived in Singapore as a child. When it started to rain, I stopped swimming. I got back in the early evening. Paolo was home. We had a lobster dinner, served by Auntie, with a bottle of chilled Semillon blanc. We ate in Paolo's darkened, peaceful study, all casual, with our dinner trays on our laps like old people or students. It was a room where you couldn't tell what time of day or evening it was. We finished with the plates and left them on the floor on their trays. He showed me his treasures. The records, his paintings on the walls.

'OK, while we're here, Li-an, let me show you the safe,' he said.

It was under the desk. He gave me the combination number. 'Not gonna do something stupid like write it down.'

'No,' I agreed. I made sure I paid attention. All of it was part of the job. Listening was number one. Every lesson that you ever taught me — thank you, Dallas!

'I want you to know it in case of an emergency,' he said. 'Like a fire, or in case something happens to me.' He'd put our passports and tickets in there and told me I could put my valuables in there if I wanted. 'Now, this being Macao, you don't know anyone. So you could write down the telephone numbers and addresses of anyone close to you. So if anything happened to you or me, the numbers are in there.'

'I could write down my folks' addresses and phone numbers. And Dallas's. Though she has no phone number. I have no valuables but my mother's pendant and necklace, which she left me.'

'Well, where are they now?'

I said in my pavilion, in my drawer.

'Well,' he said, 'you oughta bring 'em here.'

'I will later,' I said.

I took a mental note of the numbers, which was easy because they played a six-note sequence in my head, based on 'On Green Dolphin Street' (but without the flat).

'OK. Now,' he said. 'Whatdja wanna play? Take a look.'

I went through his tea chest. We found and played the Bee Gees. I had a sappy side. I didn't just play '11:59', 'Ziggy' and 'Disco Inferno'. When I saw these albums, I got quite emotional. I was both happy and sad, best summarized by the poignancy of diminished chords progressing to major nines in 'How Deep is Your Love'. The Bee Gees wrote phenomenal songs, no matter what the naysayers claimed.

We found a classical album with a painting of a man pushing an old-fashioned cart in Italy, called *Il Siciliano*.

'Oh, that!' he said. 'I accidentally found the album in a flea market but had to buy it for the cover, which I just love. You know, Li-an, part of collecting is the look of something. You might not understand that. Women don't collect anything but memories. And then they'll come back and use 'em as ammunition!' He laughed.

I had seen the original painting somewhere, but I couldn't recall when or where.

'I know you don't want to just listen to my boring old jazz,' he said, seemingly reading my mind. 'From now on, there will be my collection, your collection and ours. They are our friends.'

Fair enough. Other people shared books, but Dad used them to bust me about. I loved reading but I preferred library books to my own. I didn't want to see them at home. But music. It was my weakness and my strength. I would buy new albums whenever I was flush. There was no sound that didn't make me smile.

'Why don't you play me something on the piano? Would love to hear some Strayhorn.' It wasn't my strong point, straight ahead jazz, sad bastard stuff. I had to be drip-fed Southern Cees to play those well. I gave him a bit of what he asked for but quickly changed the mood to something more exciting, some of my favorite rags like 'Sweet Georgia Brown'.

I looked at the calendar in my room and marked the day. It was now Wednesday. Day Two. I found an envelope slipped under my door. Paolo had typed up a note that said he was in last-minute urgent meetings with lawyers and the local authority. He would be away all day and maybe evening. The envelope also contained 30 US dollars. He said I could get that changed. It was enough to do a few sights. I lost track of time. It felt like I had been here for a grip, when it was actually a day. This was the slow release of jet lag; nobody tells you that.

On my own, I cabbed it to and walked round the Grand Prix circuit, which started in 1960 and according to Paolo was better than Monaco's, visited a couple of museums and tried the Macanese cuisine — Portuguese-Cantonese fusion food that paired fried rice with salt cod. Days of going without food meant I wasn't a fussy eater. I took a cable car to the top of the Macao peninsula to see the Guia Fortress and lighthouse.

It all sounded kind of fun, but there was a down note: fellow visitors and tourists were middle-aged. Paolo-aged. Or downright ancient. They were foot-tapping jazzers, big band swing time foxtrotters.

Some even needed casino diapers. I could see there was going to be a serious clash of cultures, and I don't mean the salt cod on rice with Sambuca dressing.

What was a nice pizzeria doing in a place like this? That was an easy one. Food was king in Macao. Johnny's was the chance of a lifetime, Paolo said. The restaurant was to be on Estrada de Cheoc Van, off Praia de Hac Sa (Beach of Black Sand), which was deserted and in a shallow bay. It would be a relaxing, rather rustic place, modestly furnished, nothing fancy and all with Italian-style, intimate dining balconies facing the sea. Hac Sa was the best beach in Macao, two and a half miles long. Sun seekers could head to the beach bars, picnic spots and places to hire water skis.

I sat down in a local café for lunch. Macanese cuisine was a perfect and unique concoction of Chinese, Malay, Indian and Portuguese. Utmost importance was given to providing tourists with variety and quality, which, I now understood, was why Paolo wanted his restaurant to be here. Johnny's Pizzeria would fit right in with the other Italian restaurants – and the French, American, Brazilian, Japanese, Korean and Mozambique cuisine, as well as dishes from all across South East Asia.

I took out and read the *Eating Out* handbill I'd picked up from the airport limo stand and kept folded in my pocket:

> Among the most popular Macanese dishes are African chicken (grilled with piripiri peppers), tacho (a hearty stew of Chinese vegetables and different meats), galinha à portuguesa (chicken cooked in the oven together with potatoes, onions, egg and saffron).

There were more:

> minchi (minced beef with fried potatoes, soy, onions and a fried egg), linguado Macao (Macao sole fried and usually served with green salad) and porco balichao (Balichao's pork).

It all looked tremendously tasty and it wasn't a dream. Who Balichao was, I had no idea. I later learned that Balichao was not a person. It was the Macanese word for *belachan* in Malay, which I already knew from Singapore. Shrimp paste to everyone else. The possessive apostrophe in Balichao's Pork was merely an indication that it was translated from the Portuguese, which obeyed the rules of Latin grammar. The most popular dessert of course was the *pastéis de nata* (sweet egg tarts) with a caramelized top, lovingly known as a 'little piece of heaven'.

I'd expected sweet chili dips for my fries and afternoon dips for my thighs at the beach on Coloane Island. Maybe 50cc Vespas and a couple of temples. I had ideas for some new songs. My trusted companion, the wine-red Gibson Les Paul, came with me so I did not expect to be lonely.

At 23, I was too old to be naïve and too young to be retired to a gray-haired playground. I was enraged by Paolo's decision to move me here, and even more outraged that I'd been drunk when I agreed. Come to think of it, I wasn't drunk when I agreed. I was just desperate. A real drunk would have just passed out and agreed nothing. I just never thought I would be culturally cut off and alienated from everything and everyone I'd ever known. Well, to be fair, that would only be Dallas, but she was everyone to me. The real nightlife here, Paolo had neglected to tell me, was backstage at the casinos. There was little else to keep the place going. I should have put two and two together — what came with casinos? Topless dancing. And? Brothels, massage parlors and strip joints. Lewd imagery was everywhere. Posters and neon signs seemed larger than the buildings themselves. No wonder they called this place the Vegas of the East. I thought I was going to start anew, start clean. In my dreams, golden tiles of the temple spires glinted like the sinister grin of a Chinese demon.

McCow was becoming a bad beat. And that was me being positive. 'Ever the optimist?' A little voice in my head snorted. I'd have to give it a shot. After all, what else could I do? Go back to Chicago in winter and try fishing for the Christmas bonus packs from pockets of city scum? Didn't think to ask Paolo if he'd bought me a return ticket or a single. Was I here for two months or two years? I never asked questions. That was my problem in school, they said. I never even saw the ticket. There were all these handwritten, carbon paper red flaps in it, and I noticed he had stuffed it away in his jacket pocket. But a deal was a deal. It was still a far better deal than scoping. From Chicago's winter wallet wonderland to lobster and Semillon blanc. I'm getting way more Semillon than semitones. Hell, I'd never even seen lobster before in my life. It was so intricate it looked like a machine or an engine being taken apart, complete with gears and tubes. And then you eat it. I preferred the cultural, artistic, youthful scene and cared little for the sensation of sun and sea on my skin. I had what I called a third-degree tan, made more prominent by only wearing neon tees and white denim shorts. But would I really want to go back to my life of petty crime in the Windy City or remain here? I could go back to college to study music. And who would pay for it? I'd have to ask my mother because my daddy had zilch. He had drunk it all away. There were ways to 'work this thing', as the bankers Dallas and I taxed used to say about some idea or hiccup in their office. You make excitement for yourself. 'Only boring people get bored,' said Dallas. Only quitters quit. Maybe she was referring to Mom in an indirect way.

My mother had gone back to her birthplace of Singapore. She'd been disowned by my grandfather Ah Kong when she married but once she returned, like a prodigal daughter, she was re-owned, like she was a friggin' Mercedes Benz. When she was my age, she too was a rebel. But rebels grow up and grow old, like everyone else. She wrote to me about once a year, usually on my birthday. She couldn't do even that, now, because she didn't know I'd moved abroad. I thought back to the house that I grew up in, in Armenian Street, and its mosaic-tiled floor with a bleached cement smell. Today its smell was still as sharp as a broken mirror.

Three years ago, in the fall of '77, I was booed off stage. Nice. If Dallas hadn't worn military button epaulettes, I would have cried on her shoulder. She was always there to buy me a drink after I played. By then I was already 20. I say already, because my dream had partly come true: I was in a band. I still had to teach in the day and 'help' Dallas in her night-time enterprise, but I was in a real-life band.

I was playing in a disco-art-rock outfit called Mrs Dixon. My influences were the strong melodic riffs of Blondie, but my band mates preferred the flatness of Talking Heads. I thought we had a compromise by using pre-recorded percussion. Well, we had very few fans. Dallas was my biggest fan. She never failed to remind me that I was so talented it was heartbreaking for her to watch me perform to nincompoops. Though I could play any song from memory or by ear, I still needed to write that one hit. The world was waiting for me. But more often than not, Mrs Dixon were booed off (not by our very few fans, obviously). I was ever positive: a moment of optimism saved me a hundred days of sorrow.

Dallas supported me in my shows, and I her in our night-time enterprise. See, we were a two-broad act. I got bankers in the skid row area drunk and she took their money. This was easier than her doing it on her own. She needed a young recruit like me to get their full attention during filching. With full makeup and hair, I could pass for a 25-year-old. Dallas knew that the art of conversation might have let her down. 'You read. You listen t' music. You're into bands, movies, culture, travel.' Those were my skills apparently. They were the prerequisites to the art of seduction. She had these skills, too, but had lost her knack a few months ago when one of the artists she was posing for took a shine to her. She might even have believed he loved her 'cept for the fact that he was married and she didn't want to be second best. She'd get jealous. 'I'm vain,' she said, 'you gotta remember. Anyways, men in bars ain't dumb. They're just bored. That's why they drink, kid.' To them, there was nothing more interesting than a clever girl with full makeup and hair.

The most important thing was finding the right candidate. This was the hardest bit of the job. The rest of the evening would be plain sailing once the victim had been identified. You'd talk to a few guys at first. Get a feel for it. Get them chatting and distracted. Dallas was head of the selection process and with a discreet nod, which would simply mean looking down at her shoes for three counts, she'd signal we were on. If she looked at a chandelier or some ceiling feature for three counts, it meant 'this ain't the guy'.

Dallas would be a plainer version of herself, but not too plain, like a stylish aunt, a cousin or a sister, whiling away some time in a bar while waiting to be escorted to the theater or to a restaurant. She would be construed as the dull companion, the one who had to amuse herself, busy herself with slow actions of lighting a cigarette, applying lip gloss, crossing legs or rummaging in her handbag (slow because a magician always did things slow, it filled the time and was less distracting than a flurry of activity). A simple sweep of one leg over the other, rearranging of the skirt to accommodate the move, followed by a reversal of all that, could take up to a minute, for example. After some conversation, there would be talk of what next. Going for dinner had no positives 'cept for getting a free meal. If you weren't strapped for cash you could 'go for dinner'. During the conversation, Dallas would sometimes intercept and sometimes not, all the time listening in. She would administer the crushed tabs from a lipstick-like container and switch the drinks. It helped that we drank the same drink as the guys, however foul that might be. A quick eye signal to me, I'd know it was done and the countdown had begun. In 15 to 30 minutes, it would be time.

I would already have found out if they were married or not or who they lived with. Best was if they lived alone. Or you could go find a dark alley or courtyard, leave them in a hotel room where they would have their nap until the next day. 'You are my Cinderella, princess,' said Dallas. 'You got 30 minutes to get to the next spot while they're still awake or you'll have to find a way of moving a pumpkin.'

'OK, rules,' Dallas had said. 'We don't do this job lying down.' Dallas was the lookout while I was taking the guy down a dark alley or courtyard. 'When they wake up, they remember nothing, kid. Zilch!' That could be quite romantic. They would only remember the good things and the sparkly conversation. They wouldn't even know how they ended up wherever they were. Their memory got wiped soon as they drank the potion. Mostly I managed to totally avoid kissing anyone. Unfortunately, I remembered them the next day. I kinda knew this ain't a movie. It ain't the Disney fairytale Dallas'd like to think — Cinderella, Sleeping Beauty and so on. Only time I said to her I didn't want to be part of her enterprise ('cept that I'd already agreed to anything she asked when she took me in) she said I could move out and start again. *Quitter, I wish you well*, she'd said. She'd been kinda sad, yeah. And me, too. She'd given me money for my first month's rent.

I went back when the month was through. I roomed with a coupla regular girls who had regular jobs. I paid the bills and I kept teaching, but I never felt so bored. Dallas put food on the table, drinks in my throat and fun in my life. However reticent I felt about her enterprise, I had to put my hang-ups aside. A deal was a deal. Didn't need an attorney to tell me that. And, anyway, I guess I was looking for a home, and Dallas fit right.

From then on, she was my boss, my fence, my Fagin. 'After all, what else yer gonna do at night?' she demanded. 'Play Scrabble?' I got down to the business without thinking too much about it. The guys deserved it anyway. And I deserved to burn in hell.

I was spun the night Reagan got in. I remembered that I was here to do a 'job'. But what the hell was it? Paolo reminded me when we got to his amped-up, crumbling colonial villa in Coloane Island: I had the job of the piano-slayer.

He said, 'No good with drink equals: well-sooted to the jawb!'

I remembered now. Gimme a break, I thought. I hadn't eaten for three days that time! He had no idea. Dallas would be shrieking with laughter now. I ate like a Chinese person and drank like an Irish. *To the best of East and West*, she would clink her glass to mine.

'No, you'll be perfect, honey, cos I was looking for someone who was American but looked Asian, and not only that, you play the piano! Is that awesome or what?'

'Could you, like, not call me,' I swallowed, 'that word?' I was pretty damn polite all things considering. Only Dallas could call me kid, sweetheart, princess. 'Hon' was not even a word.

'What word?'

'You know. Hon. Honey.'

'That's cool, that's cool, sugar.'

Argh.

Someone who was American but looked Asian, he had said. Since childhood, I was the outsider from inside, looking out. In Asia, you can't question or leave your social standing, and I was considered modern and rebellious. The term mixed-race did not exist then. You were white or colored and I was not white, therefore I was colored.

Being a colored person, or rather, being reminded in Asia that I was a colored person, I wanted to work hard for my own money and I wasn't afraid of this, unlike my mom. She always wanted to be looked after. Marrying a white guy did not fulfil her expectations or requirements.

In retrospect, scoping was quite hard work. All that jive-talking. Though Dallas said it was easy, that was easy for her to say because she was not an immigrant. An immigrant didn't like speaking because the whole point was that you didn't want to stand out. Fact was you belonged nowhere, then you belonged somewhere, then you're glad to be just anywhere, now you ain't gonna wanna attract attention and unbelong and be nowhere again. On top of that you speak funny. The less you say, the better. Otherwise you're asking for trouble. The conversation always goes one way.

Auntie worked and saved like any other colored person. Unlike my mom, outside the palace gates would suit me fine. I couldn't 'live off' Paolo longer than I had to. I would be a bondmaid if I stayed in this position, and I wasn't sure I had the utter devotion and grit of Cantonese genes to see me through that kind of servitude and loyalty. When I got paid, I planned to pay him back the plane ticket, the Ray-Bans, the meals. I wrote it all out in a notebook. He just laughed and said I should be his accountant.

But I was aware that every day I was not earning money, I was spending his. And I knew that money didn't come from nowhere and, certainly, Paolo's wasn't mine in the first place. I had picked a very deep pocket. But I reminded myself this was a new start, decided that I would stay with him for free, now, but I was going to move out and get my own place like any normal employee. Otherwise it was bound to get suspish. Already he called me 'sugar', now I'd stopped him calling me 'hon'.

The days squeezed by real slow, like the end of a tube of toothpaste. Thursday. Day Three, I marked on my calendar. Jet lag caught up with me, or rather, I caught up with it. Decided to stay in. In my

Asian state of mind, I had been rushing around doing the sights because it was still like a vacay. And I actually did think I didn't have much time to do the sights so I'd better get them done, like they were a chore. But really, I was so not having a blast. I was like a spoilt child. Homesick and lonely. It might be because I hadn't started playing piano properly yet. It was the calm before the tropical thunderstorm. I didn't want to wish it or throw it away as my mother always bugged me about waste. ('Throwing away' was my mom's favorite Chinese expression: 'Look at you! You kept wanting it. Now you're just throwing it all away! Do you know what I just spent? OK, so what did I just spend?')

Everything had a value, especially this trip. Hence, the avoidance of waste. This house definitely had a high worth. I spent my third day exploring the ageing house interior, darkened by different polished hardwood surfaces and furniture. I felt like that woman who married some rich guy in *Rebecca*, which I read when I was in ninth grade. Although I wasn't married to Paolo, I already felt very bound and trapped in his home.

Paolo had arranged for some furniture to be shipped over ahead of us. When we arrived, I was speechless. He told me the price of the villa he'd bought in US dollars but it didn't sink in. What did a couple, two, three zeros mean to me? I just didn't want to deal with all that. He said it was a proper, solid investment. Property. He could always sell it when he needed to free up the money for something else. It was made for entertaining, and for having children in. Six bedrooms, a playroom, pool, parking for four cars. Filled with the atmosphere of the previous owners' nasty divorce.

The original owner-builder was a Portuguese trader. Subsequent owners had done various extensions and modifications but the main house still retained its character. In the Gothic colonial style, the green and white house was set on a large raised beachfront plot of land, surrounded by tiled verandahs and private lush tropical gardens. It was perfectly sited in what would be a prime location. There were only two other houses around us, and in fact they were probably half a mile away. It sat elegantly on a hill overlooking Praia de Hac Sa, with panoramic views over the South China Sea. The realtor had said to Paolo that the south was the most desirable and chic area on the island.

The dark wood-paneled dining area and adjoining living room were perfect for intimate dinners, or tropical island parties, secret agent style. The room had vaulted ceilings, chandeliers and large plain industrial-looking fans. In the middle of the room was the beautiful polished black Yamaha: a six-foot grand. There was no need to save space.

I lifted the keyboard lid and pressed two keys together, middle C and G above it, a perfect fifth interval. Almost immediately, I shut the lid. The sound was cold and modal, it was like a Gregorian chant. I sensed that someone else was in the room. I looked behind me. It was Auntie, which frightened me because the house itself was like a temple, so formal and quiet, and here she was just like a ghost.

'You… you here to play?'

'Yes?' I answered. It sounded more like I was asking the question myself.

She had a duster in her hand and a bucket of bottles of cleaning gunk in the other. She paused and scrutinized me.

'The others dint las long.'

'What others?'

'Girls. They come play piano. Now they gone. Two girls.'

'Where did they go?'

'They—' she started to answer with the characteristic Cantonese bark. She shrugged a little, cross, as if I offended her — but, how? She seemed to be suddenly aware that she was at work and practically skidded over to the windows, dusting the sills, ignoring my presence.

The servants knew when to disappear and did this best when they served you something. The instant the item was served, they were gone in a flash. The speed at which they disappeared was quite commendable. I couldn't say they were unpleasant or rude to me, they were simply ghosts, something you'd have to live with, like poor eyesight. Like fish sauce, I could get used to it. I left hairs in the shower every day just to make sure they cleaned it. I wanted to see those hairs gone when I returned to the washroom.

Two girls, she said. Who were they and what happened to them? I was intrigued. And of course, why did they leave? I had questions, and with Paolo, the dodge-meister, a direct approach never worked. The two girls were simply trashy piano players, in which case I doubted anything sinister had happened to them. I was not afraid of Paolo. Firstly, because I'd passed out in his apartment for six days (I was told). Nothing happened to me. I was fed. I slept. It was clean. Secondly, if he did anything to me, there would be no piano player. Don't shoot the piano player! Thirdly, I'd met guys. My instincts were sharp as my tongue. Paolo had enough amber in his eyes to light a small room. They were not dead and black. Sometimes that was all I could go by. I didn't have much choice when I woke up in that room in Morgan Park when he mentioned two other investors on board already, whom I met at the table on the night of November 4, whereas I was 'only' making an emotional investment in him. He said 'only' as though it was the least important. On the contrary, I was making a huge step believing in him and coming all this way. Before Macao, the financial gain from belladonna use was the height of my experience in foreign travel and cultural exploration. I trusted him, right? Turns out trust was trash.

The staff quarters, kitchen and laundry areas were not open to be viewed and I didn't wish to view them anyway. I was going around this whole house and it was wasted on me. I didn't know what I was looking at. Value and worth were not the same thing. I understood from Paolo that the fully equipped kitchen was more than sufficient to provide hotel standard catering, and so that was good enough for anybody.

I found the realtor's handbill on the marble half-moon occasional table in the entrance hall:

> *The terrace has a striking 75-yard infinity edge swimming pool and spacious sundecks, perfect for relaxing and enjoying the views and ambience of this magnificent property. The price. 2 Million USD (Offer invited).*

I played my Les Paul in my room for a few minutes but couldn't focus. I was playing all spaz. I headed for the pool. The odd sight of an inflatable raft in the shape of a pair of Salvador Dali red Mae

West lips intrigued me. Surely it wasn't Paolo's toy? He had too much self-conscious style. He would hate the lips. Sure he would. I called it The Kissers from that day. Perhaps it was the previous owners', when they'd enjoyed happier times.

The Kissers had a sense of mystery and fun. I was tempted to kiss it, in a cuddly way, not lie on it. A Wrigley Field drinks koozie sitting in Paolo's study on his desk made me nostalgic. The desk was heavy and old, European, though once again I had no idea how old or how European. It made me think of a poorly lit tanned gentleman with good manners.

I switched on the record player and looked through Paolo's collection. I hovered between Hiroshima's *Odori* and Jan Garbarek's *Eventyr*, but decided on Watanabe. Jazz fusion wasn't my bag, but 15 minutes of sax never killed anyone. No, ten. That was enough.

I sat in his antique swivel desk-chair until he returned from his meetings. The record was still spinning when I opened my eyes, and I hoped I hadn't worn out Paolo's stylus. He was very fussy about his stuff as they were all bourzhee things. Nothing he had was lame Walmart shit. Even his shoelaces (shoestrings, as I was now inclined to call them) were handmade leather fit for a president.

I was served dinner on the terrace. Auntie opened a bottle of chilled Australian Yarra Valley white, which she said one of Paolo's partners had given him. I watched the sun set over Macao's highest hill, Alto do Coloane.

Auntie said he left an envelope for me. It was bulging. I opened it and it was a typed note from Paolo saying here was 3,000 patacas to spend if I wanted to go into town. It was so crazy! That was like, at least 400 US dollars, right? I thought, 'Sure, thanks, man.' I didn't want to be given money again, but I had none and I couldn't pick his pocket when there was no one else around. Kinda obvious I'd be the only suspect. I wrote the amount down in my IOU notebook. I didn't ask him about The Kissers. It had gone from the pool when we had dinner. Someone must have put it away.

That night Paolo called from somewhere or other, probably the restaurant's temporary phone line, the property developer's or contractor's office, to say he was really busy. He was still aiming to open the restaurant on Saturday, November 15 to coincide with the summer vacation in Australia and New Zealand, when the hordes would arrive. The locals did not have the palate for Italian cuisine, he said; this restaurant was purely for the Western market, both expats and tourists.

I knew he was busy because the fax machine was screeching mental. A while ago, he had started phone-interviewing Italian chefs already working in Hong Kong and the three hired would have to be here tomorrow. Although the positions had been filled, new applicants' résumés were spewing out even at night.

I stepped outside the villa gates, wondering how many Singaporeans there were in Macao, not that I was Singaporean myself, but I was frighteningly close to my mother. After all this time, she still ordained anxiety in me, not that she was anxious at all about me. Hell no. I didn't have my dreams repeatedly squashed like hers. I thought about what she'd say if I didn't change my sheets once a week. Here, I would tell her, there was an entire race of servants living in the cracks of the wood in my pavilion. Pretty impressive. That would make her proud. Mom, I have servants.

Now that I had my mega-gilt cage to flap around in, it soothed me to recall the Chinatown pad that Dallas lived in above Happy Chèf, a tiny apartment that became microscopic after I moved in. There was a puzzling eyebrow above the 'e' in the word Chèf, as if that would make the takeout look like a fancy joint. There was a ginormous *Annie Hall* poster in the bathroom, which I thought was awesome not knowing anything about home decorating, but I knew I loved the movie and that if ever I had my own apartment, I'd have movie posters everywhere. Our Okinawan landlady thought we were nice girls, students. We could babysit for her anytime. We looked like good girls, she said.

We were. We paid our rent on time. Not only that, we were good time girls. We knew all the bars well — Joe's Bar, Drake, Indigo, Schaller's Pump on South Halsted. These were all the wrong joints for a girl like me. I was from Beverly. Then again, I wouldn't ever go to LeVee or anywhere on the South Side.

I was teaching a six-year-old boy, also from Beverly. Brick and limestone '20s manor, silk brocade triple-lined curtains, walnut-veneered Bechstein grand — the works. And only two blocks from Daddy and Sherylanne's apartment. After a few months, I noticed that the boy's dad was looking at me all spish. One day, he offered to pay me for a 'horizontal' lesson. What's the offer, I asked him, piqued. He said $300. Now, he wasn't a bad looker himself. Slim, tall, clean-shaven, graying hair, a dentist. Of course, it was way more than I'd make teaching per hour. But you know what? I said to him, 'I'll give you 15 lessons for that. You'll be breezing through Beethoven by April.' I mean, granted, baby Beethoven. Didn't say that out loud to him.

I didn't enjoy teaching music. Was all I could think of doing because my mom was a piano teacher. All the time I was daydreaming. Always thought I was going to be in a band again, be wowzers in the music industry, make records and plenty of mazuma, but Mrs Dixon wasn't an encouraging experience to go by. Since I'd left school, I'd lost focus. I wrote in a song once: I didn't want to be taught. I didn't want to get caught. I learned something every day and lost something every day.

I always knew I looked different. Being mixed-race made me stand out, especially since I grew up in Asia where it was rare to see a mixed-race person. Since I was a little girl, people would stop in the street, smile and wave at me, take photos of me or even hug me. My mother entered me for baby competitions and I won by virtue of cuteness. She was my modeling agent and I was on TV commercials for frozen peas before I was out of diapers.

Once the object of adoration and affection, however fleeting and superficial, I grew up in a glass bottle like a prized ornament, an illusion. When my mother left us, that bottle was shattered. Woke up, saw who I was and it was as clear as my heart of glass. I was just another immigrant in Chicago, just another bespectacled guitar-twanger with a home perm.

I stayed away from people and kids and I could not fit into my Catholic school that well because I was 14 when we moved from Singapore. The kids were way mean. School was hatesome but I made it through by keeping my trap shut. My friends were songs.

So, eventually, I didn't like guys that much. Well, maybe if they were attractive or friendly or kind. Kindness was a hard one to knock. But you couldn't be too damn sure. I was a victim once. A guy who seemed kind tried something funny with me on the way back one night and had me pinned. We learned from that experience. Insufficient dosage. In this line of work, it helped that Dallas had black belt kung fu skills from a school in Downtown. She had to learn it for self-protection. Dallas sent him away with a black eye. He'd have to explain that to his wife. He remained untaxed to this date as far as I know.

Paolo was an expat here. His status meant he would be able to get a table in any restaurant and a meeting with anyone. This wasn't new to me, I wasn't that impressed. See, I was once almost an expat.

I was born in '57 in Singapore General Hospital off Outram Road and my brother, Hei-an, three years later. We were raised in Armenian Street, where I grew up doing naughty things. Though I was born in Singapore, I was still American. You were what your passport said, capeesh? We moved back to the States in '71; my mother went back to Singapore in '72. I was 15. She knew no one and made no friends. Daddy wouldn't move back to Asia.

She took Hei-an with her — he was 12. She tore our family in two. A part of me, a terribly huge part, would like to see him again. Still carried his baby photo in my purse. He was the most ace-looking kid and he totally was digging what I played him on my father's Silvertone Solid State turntable, 'Ticket to Ride', 'I Need You', 'I Feel Fine' and other stuff. He always grooved like he knew how to. I showed him, sure. Still think of him as little, even though he would be 20 now.

After these eight years, I didn't think I'd ever hook up with my mother. It would be so warped. I received her letters, read them and threw them away. I felt very abandoned. But the reason she took Hei-an with her was (this is what she wrote in one of her letters a few years after she left) he wasn't very settled in his school and not really very good at anything, whereas I was an excellent student. My school was a top school, it was so hard to get in, I was top in math, music and English. All the time she couldn't have known that I wasn't fitting right in. That was her jive-talking, her guilt. I bet she was drunk when she wrote these letters. She was not as drunk as Daddy but she liked her cocktails and she liked champagne when there was mazuma going around and times were good with Daddy. And there was plenty of mazuma and good times to be had in the '50s. It was a golden age in Asia. Anyway, it was her fault for leaving, though not her fault for getting sick.

The expat type was almost Dallas's type. White, wealthy and privileged. She would be quite at home here and Macao would be broke by Dallas. Her ideal victims were white, married bankers. She would get them to like me so they'd buy us drinks. They liked me because I was more like a girlfriend, maybe a younger version of their wife. I was pretty, seemed quite smart (oh, I had different glasses for different outfits) and musically inclined (only one guitar at any one time, though). Hell, if we were in a piano bar, I would even play them a song or two. They were getting the geisha treatment without the geisha.

Sometimes, if we were lucky, their pockets had drugs too. We used what we wanted and after that we sold them. Dallas would actually laugh, for real, for she was happy as a child was happy with a shiny new toy. My math was not bad, Dallas used to say. Yeah, for that I had to thank my Chinese gangland ancestors. Was always volunteered to assist her with the 'accounts'. With the money, we did what we liked.

Dallas is how I amassed enough cash to pay for my wine-red Gibson Les Paul deluxe guitar and its silver padded bag. When I wasn't twanging it in my bed, legs crossed, Dallas and I indulged our pastimes. They included scissoring our fingers through the racks in record stores, seeing bands, movies (*Annie Hall*, *Star Wars*, *Taxi Driver*, *Godfather*... too many movies to name, we watched them over and over), a little coke, JD shots, television. We loved the safety and dark anonymity of the cinema but nothing beat staying in.

Sometimes Dallas had her dark days, when she had to stay in bed. She called them her all-day bedtime days. 'Y'know, kid, sometimes

I—' she would start. But she never finished. It was very upsetting for me to watch her on her all-day bedtime days. Sometimes, too, I brought her a sandwich and a drink. She appreciated it. I knew from hearing the way she chewed and swallowed in the semi-darkness. She knew that I would be there for her, with her, for when 'it' went away, whatever 'it' was. She had said to me she was a mom once. I never asked until she told me herself. Maybe a year later I found out she was still haunted by the memory of her daughter. I shuddered at the thought. I would check on her every couple of hours, sometimes sitting with her for a few minutes. There were piles of women's beauty and fashion magazines next to her bed. *Cosmopolitan, Ms., McCall's, Vogue*. I looked at the magazines once and was filled with sadness and horror that they were really old, from the early '70s or late '60s. I couldn't read them — they were way too weird. All these old-fashioned clothes, hair, makeup and articles. She stopped me from chucking them out. I guessed they were from 'that' time before 'it' happened. Before she started scoping, she said she worked behind an Estée Lauder makeup counter in Wieboldt's, she was married, she had a daughter. Then one day, her daughter died of pneumonia, aged only two, during a severe Chicago spring. Her husband left her after that. Dallas never told me the name of her daughter.

She feared the day that the pigs would come for us. Even watching TV at home seemed dangerous. And temporary. We were always waiting for the knock on the door.

I'd come to work in Asia just as my father had. It struck me that we now had this in common, when previously there'd been nothing except our love for records. He was a tools engineer brought out to Malaya to work in the Singapore shipyards in 1947. It was the year 135 Japanese war criminals were hanged after being convicted by a British War Crimes Court for committing atrocities during the Occupation. The '50s and '60s were the golden days of progress in Singapore and Malaya. He was attracted by the perks that wouldn't have been available to him in Chicago. Like him, I too was now enjoying the freedom and the sunshine of the Far East.

He met my mother, a music teacher, at a party on a ship. Parties were few and far between. It was both an exciting and depressing time in history. My mother had very high expectations of their relationship. No one knew why, but I guess it might have been because she thought in marrying a white man, she'd be made for life and would be living in a palace, forever.

Now that I was installed in a 'palace', she would be quite pleased with me, even if I hadn't met a prince or gone to a single party (on a ship or elsewhere).

My father's main fear was that his children wouldn't meet white people. Going to Singapore American School was a start. Membership at the Tanglin Club meant that his children would be playing tennis in white, with white. The expat world was a small one. Every little morsel of juicy news, usually relating to divorces, depression, garden parties, retrenchment and repatriation, probably in that order, was chewed up by earring-tweakers and stengah drinkers, that is, everyone and no one, regurgitated until the news was no longer desirable except to flies.

In that way he was Asian, or maybe he only became aware of whiteness on moving to Asia. In the States he was only a tools salesman, not that emigrating was a great step up, it's not like anyone else wanted the job he applied for. The general belief was that he was going to live in a swamp, but he didn't care. Just like I didn't care where I was going to so long as it was away, and a long way away.

Friday. It was still early when I set out this morning. Like my father, I was a little naïve and gung-ho. I'd only just gotten over my jet lag. Already I wanted to get out of this villa. I wanted to walk into town. I was free to go anywhere. I was an American woman, even if I looked like a local. Hypocrisy was a hard pill to swallow. All that scoping had taught me that. It was not for me. Sometimes it's easier to look like who you are, but sometimes who you are is an illusion in itself.

I stood at the timber porch outside our villa and waved to Thaew, who was polishing the wing mirror. I regretted having had a perm in Harlem Irving. It turned to candy floss in the humidity. I looked like an ancient, white magic witch doctor. Since I'd become aware of self, at about age seven, whenever I woke up and looked in the mirror I was constantly surprised by my Amerasian appearance. As I'd believed I was an American trapped inside a Chinese girl's body, I had been dyeing my hair since 1969 when blonde dye became available in Singapore on the open market, but only in one shade and only from Geylang, our red-light district. My hair was naturally curly, and perms altered my genetic hair structure but the dye broke the camel's back. You could say I had a concise afro now. Perhaps, perhaps, peroxide.

'Where you going, miss?' Thaew asked. I said I didn't want to be taken anywhere as it wasn't too hot and I was going to walk. He had no idea what I was saying. I had to simplify the content because I'd used too many words. 'No, not going,' I said. 'I walk,' shaking my head and making a marching gesture with my arms. The violent shake of my head and cartoonish arm-swinging cooled the perspiration on my neck. I felt like a rebel. Already.

Thaew waved back, nodding. He said, 'OK. But I still take you, miss,' and grinned. It was an innocent reply, one of duty — to Paolo, to my higher status, but it sounded monstrous somehow. He was nodding, yet he had defied me. I felt irritated by his strange reply. Paolo was already at the restaurant-to-be, where he was meeting the electrical contractor; it wasn't like he needed to know.

I stepped out of the villa gates and knew that, in a few minutes, Thaew would follow me, probably in second gear and about 50 yards behind. He would stop and start, in case I got tired and needed the lift he'd offered me in the first place.

I deliberately turned off onto a pedestrian path, through long grass and thick coconut groves. I regretted this decision immediately. I imagined rabid canine fangs, reptilian bites, mosquito stings and other nasties. When I looked around, I realized the path was full of other locals: women wearing pointy large farmer's hats sitting astride bicycles loaded with huge sheaths of straw, schoolchildren in pairs, old men shuffling with large shit-stained cages of chickens. I stuck out as a city-chica in this environment. It felt alien to me and I was pleasantly aloof. At the end of the path was another road where Thaew was waiting for me, grinning.

This must have been how my father felt, foolish and alien, as part of that dreadful expat community, though after he married my mother, his status diminished. The English could not and did not leave the snobbery of class division behind in England. Beneath the façade of the supposedly upper-class expats could be found a previously ostracized English second class, eager to feel superior.

While he wasn't English, my father fell into this category of second-class white expats, because there was no other category for white non-executive positions in government, banks and trading such as shipping companies. There were to be no more of the many benefits enjoyed by other expatriates, although one of these benefits was free, first-class travel back to wherever home really was (the States, Canada, Australia, England), and my father continued to be eligible for this. Unfortunately, as locals my mother and us children weren't granted this privilege and would emerge from second-class travel to meet him at our destination.

Now, as I got into the gold Mercedes, stared at by the schoolchildren and elderly Chinese ladies, I could plainly see that I was no longer a second-class passenger. The locals all waved to me as though I was royalty getting into my bejeweled glass coach.

'Now I take you,' Thaew said.

'Where?'

'You tell me where.'

I thought about it. 'Take me where there's nightlife, but please, where there's music, not girls.'

'They go together,' he said.

'OK. Just take me there then.'

We went to Largo do Senado, the main square. I wasn't a tourist and I resisted all tacky souvenirs — after all, I had lived in Asia and it wasn't like I had never seen an elephant whittled from a coconut husk. In the light of day, the seedy establishments looked like bashed wedding cakes that had lost their icing. That was why Macao was more charming by night, when the romance of old-fashioned lamplight bathed the Portuguese-style buildings in a flattering aura.

I was hungry for real music. I ached to hear trumpets stab a second verse, or the *wah wah* guitar starting a groove for the bass intro. It was the love of my life and the life I love. I had played a record yesterday but it wasn't the same as listening to music played live. How could it be? I'd heard no real music for two weeks now. I was empty, and no amount of Chinese food or massage was going to replace music.

I wondered what it was Paolo saw in me. I was just a regular girl in stretch Wrangler jeans and a striped top. Chicago was crawling with replicas, complete with the red glasses I favored. Now here I was, returned to Asia, to a backwater, an even smaller place than Singapore, where the tallest building was a nine-story brothel called Hotel Central. My world had shrunk so much, my eyeballs were now bigger than coconuts.

It was impossible for my brother and I to meet white people, part of the unspoken cultural alienation. We were stengahs, a drink popularized by Somerset Maugham, part water, part whiskey. It was a Malay word meaning 'half'. Ironically, it was my mother's, not my father's, profession that elevated us from mere locals to second-class expats. At least she wasn't a prostitute, which was the common assumption, her being so pretty. Well, I thought so, anyway. I adored her. I remembered that I wanted to be her, a full and not a half-Chinese woman. Her killer cheongsams were bias cut to flatter her statuesque figure. Even after bearing two children she fit into them. She had only two dresses, which she mended meticulously. My mother continued to give piano lessons after she left me. Her work was the reason Hei-an and I were musically inclined from a young age. Music and teaching were my only way of connecting with her now.

The word 'expatriate' means 'out of fatherland', a reject, expelled, sent away. The short form 'expat' sounds like spit hitting a spittoon. Our home was a rented shophouse in Armenian Street at the foot of Fort Canning Hill, where the British troops were garrisoned. We did have the luxury of a Cantonese *amah-cheh*. There was little or no home entertaining and we seldom went out, except for a walk in the evenings up the hill or to see a movie at the Capitol movie theater. My childhood now seemed dully idyllic: a golden retriever named Venus, swimming pool at the 'Y', tennis lessons on Saturday in white ankle socks, 'just hanging' at the Cathay on Friday afternoons.

My father decided we had to meet white people. Enough of rich white people in Singapore, but white people of all class. Regular white people in a regular school. It was the start of all the trouble.

Coloane was an islet full of pine trees, eucalyptus woods and farming land. We drove past dusty pink 1930s apartment blocks, in front of which carpets of red chili peppers were laid out to dry in the sun. In the distance were green hills and flat green vegetable farms parted by winding hilly paths. A lone cyclist wearing a conical straw hat meandered along the path. Egrets rose from shallow rivers. In the tin huts of makeshift factories adjacent to the sea-salt farms, anchovies and sea creatures were dried to make sauces.

'See? Too far to walk,' said Thaew. 'Want go shopping?'

Yeah, why not. I kept telling myself that I was really very lucky. It was the second time I got a job without even trying. I was saved from my utterly half-ass life.

There were scruffy-looking backpackers sniffing fruit at the Red Market, or Hung Kai Si, stalls, and fresh-eyed fish displayed like jewelry in baskets on the floor on beds of ice shards. It was Macao's main 'wet market'. It stank. It was in a 1930s colonial red-brick building; no tourists, just locals, fresh seafood, meat and green groceries. Little stalls were huddled close, the tastes and smells woven in and around the market. I decided to try a few sorts of Cantonese street specialties and other exotic snacks. Everywhere the signs were in Chinese. I could not read them. They may as well be diagrams scribbled in code. Technically my mother tongue is Cantonese which was spoken to me by my *amah-cheh*. Gradually, however, I was decultured from growing up both in Asia and Chicago in American schools. My mother did not teach me any Chinese though she spoke it at home with her own mother. It was as if my mother was invisible except at home. When she left, she had not left me the gift of language and culture. She was whitewashing. There was no future in being a stengah. She wanted us as a family to blend in with white people due to the stigma associated with being mixed, a sense of shame.

Language and culture — they were like your toothpaste and toothbrush, what you were using daily, your current routine, a part of you. You did not use your previous set of toothpaste and toothbrush, you only had a set at a time. In the '50s, no one had the sense to think maybe you could have a spare or duplicate set. It was actually believed that learning more than one language or culture impeded one's mental ability and confused one's identity. In fact it was the opposite: my own confusion and mental impediment were caused by NOT learning my own language and culture. This was made clear to me only when I was in adulthood and was asked 'Where are you from?' and man, I was asked that a lot when I was scoping. I couldn't figure out why that question freaked me out so much. At the historic 'Three Lamps District', on Rotunda de Carlos da Maia, I got a feeling of the city's day-to-day life in its most unpretentious form. It was totally untouristy and cool in an uncool way. No casinos, bar girls, or money changers. The roundabout and its offshoots were packed with small shops, boutiques and street vendors that specialized in inexpensive clothes. At one stall, I bought an oversized T-shirt with my 'allowance'. It was nothing special, just something to sleep in. At another, I bought an entire outfit: loose silk top, jeans, big earrings, blue shoes — remembering that I had nothing.

Part of my wanting to make this trip was for my own sake, my identity, my need for a new toothpaste and toothbrush. This was what I was born to do. After all I was living in the American culture already, my 'fourth'. I was not Irish, Chinese or Singaporean. I was all of them. Now I was experiencing my 'fifth', the Macanese. Plus I wanted to see if I could do what I was born to do — move country, reinvent and renew myself. Just like my ancestors on both sides, the Irish and the Chinese. What I was doing was so rah-rah, so easy compared with the poverty and hardship that my ancestors endured. It's like slash and burn but with more dignity and less global destruction.

There was one moped per man, woman, child and animal in Macao, driving recklessly about. Somehow, we got back to Coloane alive, making for Johnny's, where Thaew opened the car door for me. The protruding awning in Italian 'tricolore' stripes welcomed us in. I could see Paolo inside gesticulating at the electricians, in his Neapolitan manner. Yesterday the plumbers and today the electricians. Hopefully, tomorrow it would be me.

The restaurant was still enveloped in construction hoarding panels, in which was cut an access door. The hoarding had once been painted white but was now covered in advertising posters. Paolo didn't have these removed so long as they didn't cover his own screen-printed sign: Italian Restaurant Opening Soon. His logo had been designed by a graphic designer, and it was a neon rabbit in outline filled in with the three Italian colors. People looking at the posters would also look at his sign, which was undoubtedly larger than any of the other little paste-ups.

Most of the ads, like the signs, were in Chinese, so I couldn't read them but those that stood out were in English. It meant I could actually read them. There were ads for land for sale in English, with phone numbers. A sign that caught my eye was:

Green Parrot Bar
Rua de Negociantes 45
Live music and DJ every night except Mondays
Fridays playing the best and newest disco, funk
featuring DJ Ben Mizrai from New York

'What day is it, Thaew?' I asked, aware that he was reading over my shoulder. Of course, had I thought about it, I knew what day it was, but my impatience, disorientation and tail-end jet lag made me ask rather than think.

His gigantic fake mirror Ray-Bans reflected two of me. My hair was a total mess and I was ashamed that I'd let myself go since arriving in a hot climate.

'Friday,' he said. Yes. November 14.

Something in me clunked like a key in a heavy lock that suddenly turned with ease. 'You wan go?' he asked. Of course I did, but I didn't answer him because it felt like he was asking me to go with him, though I knew that of course he wasn't. 'OK, I take you home now,' he said. I noticed that it was already almost six o'clock in the evening.

Everyone in Macao, including Thaew, was there to get rich. And by any means possible. Macao was to Asia what Costa del Sol was to Spain. The low cost and high standard of living here made it possible for Paolo's business to flourish and for him to expand into other areas, such as property.

Paolo had another apartment in Chicago's Morgan Park, which he was renting out, besides the one with the gilt furniture in which I had stayed for six days after collapsing in a heap the night Reagan got in, now also rented out.

Paolo was already at home. He was getting dressed all smart. Suit and all. No ciao, no hey there. He launched straightaway into talking about Johnny's. He said the restaurant was only a stepping stone and his heart was set on buying up land banks and building fancy resorts. 'It would be an incredible opportunity for us,' he said.

When he said 'us', I asked him what I would be doing. He smiled.

I understood that I was fully provided for. There was nothing for me to do but to play music to customers. But I didn't just want to play music. I wasn't sure now this was the right job if it was just playing music. It was normal, wasn't it, to feel a sandpapery scrape of desperation in my head? Everybody had doubts when it was a new job, especially one where you had to get on a plane to do it, as far from home as you could get. I was pleased on the one hand that I didn't have to sing for my supper but I wasn't ready for listening to Billy Joel in Paolo's restaurant while I crunched on thin crusts in the kitchen during my breaks.

Paolo made a sympathetic sound. If I wasn't too brain-dead, he said, I could get a day job. I could teach music. 'And you can write more songs,' he said. He was right. I wanted to create something too. To make new music. There was a sense that some kind of new movement in music was coming, a craze, a fever, an excess, though I hadn't yet fully understood what it would be. There was no question that one of his rooms could be kitted out with equipment that I could order from the States or from England. I would write and record music. But what for? Who for? Not for the first time I felt I was in exile, an outsider, an islander, someone excluded from some mass thing.

'One thing at a time,' Paolo said. 'Write the songs first. Without the artist there is no art, and without the art there is no artist.'

Yeah, whatever. I thought I'd believe him anyway, just to end the conversation. Most artists would be more than happy with that deal.

I just hadn't expected homesickness to hit like a blast of hot, humid air, or that adults would suffer from it. I hoped it would come and go like seasickness, and that it would disappear. It made me realize that I called Chicago home. I missed Dallas, but I missed Chicago for the vibrant night life and the stimulation it gave to my songwriting.

'We are opening tomorrow, Li-an.'

It was the first time he had called me by my name since my arrival. It felt good to hear it, yet kinda awful. I still felt like a Madison.

'Have I started yet?' I thought I had not. But now seemed a good time to check if I had started the contract, not the job. They were two different things.

'Officially, nup. But in theory, yup.'

I was right. I had started the contract but not the job. 'I can have a night off?'

'When?'

'Tonight?'

'No. Why dja need a night off? You ain't been working all week.'

'You weren't open yet.'

'Why dja need a night off so soon?'

'I want to go to the Green Parrot.'

'Why?'

'I just want to go out. On my own.'

'Well. That just ain't happening tonight cos we are having a working dinner with the three partners and their wives. Dja forget? I told you about it. They can't wait to meet you.'

'OK.'

'Li-an, listen. I'm sorry. You started when you got on the plane. Dja read your contract?'

'OK, no sweat.' Uh-huh.

'You can go another time. What's the rush?'

'I can't wait to listen to real music. I can't listen to the records in your house.'

Paolo sighed and made a fake sympathy Robert de Niro face and fluttering gay hands. 'Oh well, poor you!' he said sarcastically. 'I am sorry. You been here a week. What's got into ya?'

'How about next Saturday?'

'How can that be possible? I told you we are opening tomorrow night. The 15th. It's the big night! The Saturday after that, the 22nd, I will be up to my eyeballs. You can't leave me on my own on our first weekend trading. How about Monday night, like it says in the contract? That's your official night off.'

'There is no live music on Monday. There are only bands on Fridays and Saturdays followed by a DJ.'

'What? You gotta job to do here, signorina. Remember?'

'You said it was a flexible thing. That I could talk about the hours.'

'Oh jeez. You can have any night off you want after the first week, is that fair?'

I said nothing. He liked my piano-playing, didn't he? I was Kool-Aiding. I knew I was being a jerk. This was only my second job. In my first, my boss Dallas said to me that working should feel like not working.

'Now get your ass into that dress I got made for you,' said the pimp-dog. 'We ain't got all day.'

I smiled.

I got into the dress he got made for me. It was as inoffensive as a backless plunging V-front dress could be. I slipped on black patent stilettos. I regretted that I didn't have a pedicure beforehand.

I was standing outside Fernando's restaurant, overlooking the beach. Thaew had left me here and gone to sit with other drivers in the back room, which was also the restaurant staff room. He would wait there until we were finished. He'd be given the same meal as all the other drivers who were waiting for their masters and mistresses.

On the streets, neon lights glittered and blinked from the bars and restaurants and likely brothels. I felt the pounding bass from bars. It felt strange yet familiar to hear electronic music. I wanted to dance so badly yet I didn't want to dance in a sleazy bar. I wanted to be in the world-class Red All Club, the Manumission of Macao. I hadn't picked up my guitar since I arrived and I only played that Gregorian two-note chord on the grand piano. I looked hard on the streets, and across the street, for my villains and heroes, for I was thinking of a little riff to write a new song. My eyes ached from the flashing colored lights.

Paolo was at the entrance to Fernando's already, just finishing a conversation on the restaurant's telephone. He hung up and gave me a big smile.

'I need to ask you about something.' I picked a moment when no one else was listening and I was looking like a million watts in my dress.

'What?' he said, and when he turned to look at me under the starlight, he was so distracted he looked dizzy. 'Oh, lookatcha! You are a doll.'

Mmm. I tried not to barf at his comment. 'Auntie said two girls came before me. They're now gone.'

'She told you that? I mean, sure,' he shrugged. 'The first one was pretty but only knew about ten choons. In the audition, she played one of those and got the job. The second one played beautifully, but couldn't sing a damn note to save her life. And she weren't no looker. Nobody's gonna wanna listena croakin' from a frog.'

'So why did you hire the second one?'

'She was somebody's niece's second cousin. I had to. Y'know? We're Eyetalyuns.'

'I thought you said this was a new restaurant.'

'Do you know anything about business, doll? We've been through many owners, different names, locations. Hell, even a few houses before this villa. But just two piano players. You are the one, trust me. Now can we just get to our table? Damn!'

So, no pressure, then. I was the one. I'd better not screw up.

We heard an aria over the sound system as we entered. It was a beautiful spot, and wonderful to hear the classical singing. I hadn't opened my mouth to sing once since I arrived. I'd become self-conscious that the servants were listening and it pained me that my first audience were my servants.

I sat down with him at a round table. The partners and their spouses were already there. First I met Liu Hak and his wife, Theresa, who were Hong Kong Chinese. Then I shook hands with Alexander and Gillian Richardson, who were Australian (well, they said they were from Australia but Alex's accent was British and, to be specific, probably Cockney, which was similar to Down Under). Knew my accents, watched enough movies. I had met Alex before. It was the night Reagan got in, the same night I met Paolo. The third couple were called Peter and Olivia Wong.

I couldn't help sneaking a quick take on what the women were wearing. The Chinese wives were expensively but conservatively dressed. Olivia Wong was in a Thai-silk blazer and tailored silk trousers, a tiny diamanté brooch in the shape of a crocodile on her lapel. Theresa Liu was in a loose leopard-print dress with a wide gladiator-style belt, over black trousers, no brooch. Gillian was short for an Australian; she was probably smaller than I was. She was in a gold-braided navy blazer with such killer shoulder pads they looked like she wore her bra on her shoulders. But I liked her drainpipe jeans under that blazer.

It felt quite formal already. I couldn't imagine how long this would all take. The introductions seemed to take about ten minutes, judging by the number of songs they took (barely audible but I heard three songs by Carole King, including 'It's Too Late' and 'Jazzman'). The earlier aria tape had probably run out.

My mind soon wandered. These guys were Paolo's fellow businessmen, so they all dabbled in property and now his restaurant. Alex was Paolo's lawyer and had known him before pizzas were invented. Olivia was the only woman who was also running a business, a florist shop. She and her husband Peter had two children, both girls, aged two and four. Gillian was doing marketing and PR for one of the realty developers and she was quick to hand out her card to me, which I gave a cursory glance at and tossed into my sequined clutch. She said she was pregnant, though god only knew why she was sharing this info with me. I wasn't too enthusiastic. I think I said, 'Oh.' The others chinked glasses and congratulated her. I followed suit, in order not to offend her. I thought I'd have liked to be someone like Gillian but without such a boring job. I'd be great at PR with my background, I tittered to myself.

Paolo gave Gillian a special look, straight in her eyes. It was a sweet look. I could see he was genuinely thrilled for her.

As far as I could work out, Theresa Liu helped keep books for her husband's company while looking after their son, who was a year and a half.

'Oh, they are such a handful at that age,' said Olivia, shaking her head and throwing it back to let out a silent scream. She poured white wine down her throat to emphasize her point.

The women all talked about children. Gillian had a Wonder Woman perm I didn't trust. I expected them to dwell on the subject of children for the whole evening, but they turned swiftly to moaning about or praising their help.

'Oh, mine doesn't. Mine washes out the bin before putting the new bin liner in...'

'Oh, yours is good. Mine doesn't know what a bin is.'

Hysterical laughter ensued. Mine. They talked as though they owned these people who were scrubbing their pans and underpants. Was I about to become like them? After all, Paolo's house was creaking with servants. I disliked the person I was becoming. Gillian refused wine but Olivia poured a tiny amount for herself.

The men talked figures and dates and the development on the coast. The men moaned about or praised the government and their policies. It seemed the state of domestic service was a microcosm of the country's politics at large.

Conversation soon petered out, just as my eyes momentarily rested on Peter Wong. I laughed aloud.

'What's so funny?' he asked.

'Nothing.'

'Come on! Must be something. Share the joke. You've been quiet all night.'

'I'm... just... so happy to be here. I'm speechless.'

Paolo laughed. 'She is. Wait 'til you hear her play "Stella by Starlight". I tell ya! I ain't goin' nowhere when she starts tickling those ivories! Li-an, welcome to Johnny's, McCow.'

He hugged me. I heard glasses clink and we drank to it, even Gillian on the juice.

Sunday morning I woke up late. The sun was already boiling my feet into a potent soup. I turned off the air-conditioner and was relieved not to hear its dreadful hum. A bird was calling outside. It sounded so strange and so close, as though it was calling me.

It had gone rather well, if a little anticlimactic, at the opening last night. The restaurant looked beautiful, just like a wedding. Flowers decorated every balcony. Little glass lanterns sat on each table and as I had never been to Italy I would say it looked like a traditional little Italian gem in Chicago. Nothing glitzy, just simple wooden furniture, chic black and white checkerboard marble floor, red neon outlining the bar, black grand piano, white tablecloths, the scent of jasmine and orange blossom and of course, Chicago-style pizzas. It was the unique feature of this restaurant. My job was probably the easiest job in the world. I had to play three sets with two breaks. Each set had around 15 songs. In the morning I had a quick warm-up so that I would not get tired out or bored by the evening. I wrote out a set list so I wouldn't run out of songs. Each night I would have a different set list and rotate around each of those through the week. Journalists, photographers and food reviewers arrived. Those people I met at Fernando's arrived. For a first night it wasn't very busy, but that was understandable as it was early days yet. Paolo was still getting a feel for the place and the palate of the tourists and expats. During my second break I had pizza for my dinner. Guess I'd be eating a lot of pizzas, pastas and salads, like a proper Italian girl.

I dressed quickly in denim cutoffs and flip-flops, placing my red plastic sunglasses strategically on my head. Thaew was not around. Was Sunday his day off? It was OK. I hailed a cab and went into town myself. I was probably ripped off when the driver agreed too quickly on my offer price. *Better skills next time*, I thought. I might as well learn to be a local the hard way. I wanted to see a different Macao. I'd had enough 'business' talk.

I went back to Rotunda de Carlos da Maia and whiled away my time at a trinkets stall. I bought a chunky plastic bangle, later noticing it was 3 for 2. When I went back, the lady was kind enough to agree to the offer post-deal. I chose one in each color.

Then I found a stall selling cassette tapes. They were a mix of pirated versions and originals but it was hard to tell which was which. I browsed and committed to buying XTC's *Black Sea* and Joy Division's *Closer*. Again, I thought perhaps I'd paid too much. I wished I had a local friend to consult, but there was no one. The only Cantonese I'd come into contact with was Thaew and those two broads from Friday night I had dinner with, the partners' wives. If I told them I went to the market and bought tapes they would probably think I was insane. Or they would shake their heads and tell me I'd paid the equivalent of a month's salary. I couldn't face telling them what I'd done, yet I'd done something I enjoyed so much: being alone and shopping.

I thought I'd get something for Paolo, a small gift. I wanted to like him. I really did. We seemed to get along just fine, in small doses. I bought him a large painting, so cute I couldn't resist it. It was of a blue elephant hiding in a bamboo grove of gold. I wouldn't give it to Paolo yet. Perhaps it would be my little secret and I could whip it out as a standby gift if I forgot his birthday. I had no juice in dates and things. I was poor at history, biology, geography. Come to think of it, I was bad at most things except for math, art and music. If I was on the verge of losing my job and being the third girl banished, I could whip it out too. Ta-da. The painting was rolled up and slotted into a cardboard tube with plastic lids at both ends.

I walked into a little traditional Macanese café and sat at a table near the entrance. I leafed through the advertisements of things to do and stopped at the Green Parrot Bar's handbill.

'Hey, you should go to that.'

I looked up. He was tall, in his early twenties, all made of wire and rags. It was a guy with dark curly Giorgio Moroder hair, a flat white cap and corduroy jeans (in this heat?) and a graffiti-covered oversized shirt that looked like it had bird shit all over it. His forehead was red from the heat. He took off his Wayfarer sunglasses.

'And who're you?' I said, a little suspicious. He looked a little like a cartoon character, though I couldn't think which one.

'I'm the DJ who'll be playing there.' He was spittin' real fast, with a Harlem accent.

'No shit.'

'Ben Mizrai,' he held out his hand. 'From New York.'

'I'm Li-an Donohue. From Chicago.'

'That's cool. You're into music, I see.'

'Er, yeah. I guess. I'm a musician,' I never thought I'd put it like that again, but if there was any time to do so, now was it. 'I got a gig here too!'

'No kidding.'

'Yeah. At Johnny's. You should come down sometime. It's a new pizza joint. We just opened last night. I played. It's proper Chicago pizzas.'

'Man, I miss that.'

'Well, come on down.'

'OK. I will. What do you play?'

'I play keys. And guitar. But at Johnny's I play an awesome grand piano. Just, you know, standards, show tunes and shit like that.'

'Mind if I sit down?'

I gestured to the empty seat across from me. He pulled out the bamboo stool and sat.

'What do you play?'

'I play guitar, keys. Anything and everything badly.' He gave me his first smile. His teeth were stained from too much amphetamine, which indicated a level of debauchery that intrigued me. His golden tan made his teeth less stained-looking.

I didn't laugh. 'No, I mean, what kind of stuff are you playing?'

'Ah, a mixture of funk, soul, disco.' His long eyelashes were about the only thing funky about him. In fact, it was his lashes and green eyes that were illustrated on the handbill. I looked at the handbill again. He rattled off some bands I recognized. Clinton, Voyage, Chic. The usual suspicionados.

'Well, this is a small place, you know.'

'What d'ya mean?'

'Well, there's not many people who are musicians.'

'No,' I agreed.

'Thigh?'

'Say what?'

'You Thai?' he said, sounding weird. Thigh? Or breast?

'Oh. No. No.' I gave him the polite smile, the stay-out-of-my-Kool-Aid grin. I told him the same thing I had to tell everyone who asked. I didn't ask him whether he was Jewish. Of course he was. 'What's the scene here like? I mean going out, staying in and so on…?' I drifted off and used a hand wave as a vague gesture to see if he knew what I was saying. He did.

'Waaaaay lame. Foot-tappers come here from all over Australia and New Zealand, but mostly from the rest of Asia, for the casinos. I don't know what a New Yorker like me's doing here but I'm doing OK. There's like a couple of discos for the local and Hong Kong day-trippers, you know, a younger crowd. How about you?'

'How about me?'

'You got a band?'

'Nope. Not anymore.'

'Playing any of your own shit?'

'No way. Are you kidding? This is Asia, right? Only covers and standards. You writing your own stuff?'

'No,' he said, shaking his head. 'I just—, I can't—, I'm not…'

I was nodding like I understood, though I couldn't really see what he was trying to say.

'Why don't you—'

'I'm just DJing for the bugsy,' he cut in. 'Quick cha-ching.' He rubbed his fingers together in case I didn't know what cash was. Bugsy, Bugs Bunny, money.

'You need the money?'

He laughed. 'I just do, don't you?' he said, although I didn't ask him why. 'It goes fast.'

Yeah, well, tell me about it, I thought. I nodded.

'You playing tonight?' he asked.

' Yes. But Monday's my night off. Tomorrow. My first night off.'

'You wanna hook up?'

'Yeah. Why not?'

Ben was staying at the oldest hotel around, the Bela Vista, on Penha Hill. He said it was the Fawlty Towers of the Far East, built in 1870 and now totally run down. The analogy was lost on me. Clearly, he was more cosmopolitan than I imagined myself to be.

I just didn't even think of asking for his number. It seemed so lame and corny. And I didn't know if there was a number for where I was staying. It wasn't a date, though agreement on time and place. Equaled. Date.

We were to meet at the Bela Vista, at eight.

He seemed to have arrived in his fall/winter collection and not replaced it. The heat and the sun had cooked his Greenwich Market reject shmutters and he could pass as being hip. Dallas would say he was one phat bun, don't touch him, he's mine... that kinda thing. I missed Dallas, missed her looking out for me all the time.

'If one of us can't make it, we wait half an hour before giving up.'

After that we parted ways. He got up, saying, 'Dammit.' He had to go and see somebody about something. 'Slater.'

I got the price of the cab journey home down to half what it cost me coming into town. On the trip back, I used my teeth to open the cellophane on the tapes. I examined them. They looked original enough to me. Holding them in my hand made me feel close to Chicago again. I could already hear the music running through my fingertips and feel my heart getting excited as I remembered the clubs and bars. I ran my fingers over the holes with the tiny teeth in them and checked that the tape was fitting tightly and wound to the end. I couldn't wait to get back and play them.

I kicked off my shoes in Paolo's study and I stuck the tapes into the player. *Oh.* I sighed as I listened to *Closer*. I sat in his chair, eyes closed of course, though I couldn't help noticing with slight irritation that Auntie had brought me a drink and placed it on a coaster on Paolo's desk. Why could she not leave me alone for at least a few minutes? I just wanted to listen to the music, undisturbed. And I wasn't thirsty.

I looked at the gold Seiko chiming desk clock in front of me. It was after 2pm. I hadn't had anything to eat all day. Auntie seemed to read my mind, leaping into view. Was she in the room all along?

'*Siu-cheh*, Sir been ringing and ringing. He say, "Where you?" I say I don' know.' She called me 小姐 or Siu-cheh, which meant Miss.

'That's OK. I will call him.'

'*Siu-cheh*, if you wan' lunch, I fix now.'

I stared at her. Threw my hands in the air. She knew everything.

'What you wan' eat?'

'Anything.'

'Straight'way,' she bowed.

She hesitated before leaving. 'I ask round. What happen dose girls before you.'

'And? What happened to them?'

'They still here. Dancing. In casino. They never go home to America. Macao is place you don' leave.'

I pictured the girl Paolo called the frog kicking her green legs in a tutu on some casino's stage.

'You must be careful, *Siu-cheh,*' she whispered.

I was thinking about why Auntie said that Macao was a place you couldn't leave, but she was already gone. No, she said they didn't leave, not that they couldn't or didn't want to. She probably couldn't explain herself very well.

I called Paolo to ask him why he was looking for me. He wasn't at the restaurant, so I left a message.

Five minutes later, he called back. 'It's Monday tomorrow,' he said. 'That's all I was gonna ask you. You gonna take your night off?'

'Yes, I think so.'

'OK, good. Just wanna make sure. The deal was that after the first week you can change it and you can have any night off except Friday and Saturday.'

'Yeah, I know the deal.'

'Is that cool?'

'Sure.'

'Can you make sure you stick to the deal. Dja like it here?'

'I love it, Paolo. So far, it really has been wonderful.' It hadn't, but things were looking up now that I'd met Ben Mizrai. I felt something between my ribs flutter a little.

'I enjoyed going out on my own today, too,' I said. 'I think I needed to do that to enjoy the place properly.' I had explored every corner of Macao, even the red-light districts, because I like to find the soul of a place.

'Promise me you'll be careful.'

'I'm careful. I'll see ya later,' I said. Two people had said the word 'careful' in the space of 15 minutes. Plus me makes three. Must be the buzzword around here.

'OK. I've got a few meetings now with the local authority and some lawyers, but I'll be back as soon as I can.'

'OK, bye.'

I hung up and put my feet back up again. I had jasmine rice, peppers and fried monkfish with a coriander sauce for lunch. I played guitar all afternoon. I wrote down melody lines and chord changes. I wanted to be happy here, but I struggled to imagine just playing the piano and living in a gilt cage called the pavilion. I was used to a little danger, darker nights, a deeper shade of lipstick, a faster pace. I might go crazy here. I wanted to play to young people. Where were the young people?

I went for a swim in the pool. I found The Kissers again. I geeked up when I saw them. I lay there floating on them for about half an hour, until it started to get cold. The weather was changing, I could feel it. Evening came on suddenly and it was time to get ready to go out to do my job. After tonight, I would get my one night off! I wrote another set list of three sets with 15 songs each, making it 45 in total. That night I had such a fantastic audience. It was an incredible feeling. It cheered me up. They asked for more. They whooped. They were old, young, tourists, locals. I could get used to being popular. They liked the swing tunes more than the ballads.

During the breaks, I started to plan what I would do the next day. I decided I would start looking for a place of my own to stay as soon as possible, and at the end of the month, I wanted to be able to pay Paolo back for rent, expenses and so on.

On Monday, that was what I did. I got the local papers and circled ads that looked promising. I made a few calls, left messages. Dallas used to say, 'What else are you going to do at night? Play Scrabble?' Scrabble didn't seem so likely, now. It was time for my date!

To get me in the mood, I played my new XTC tape quite loudly in the Toshiba tape deck in my room while getting dressed. I always liked to play loud music before going out. I put on my neon pink origami kimono top, leggings and bohcoo d'eyeliner. I was so excited about going out for the first time here, it made me want to go out and buy new clothes soon. My head hurt and my neck veins pulsed when I thought about Ben. *I am reformed now*, I said to Dallas silently.

I could even be considered a minor star in this town after playing only two gigs. I was performing again. I was somebody. I didn't want to find a pocket to pinch. That was for kids. I had been at it since I was 12 but now I was way too ancient to be kidding myself.

Evening came and I went. No one would know that it was a Monday. Every night the city was packed.

The Bela Vista was a delightfully eccentric colonial Portuguese mansion. There was a strong sense that Bogart, Bacall or Hemingway could be here. While waiting for Ben, I read the leaflets in the lobby. Apparently, the hotel building, with its characteristic shady terraces and arches, was constructed around 1870, possibly by a wealthy trader. Masonry from the 17th-century Bom Parto Fort may have been used in the foundations. William Clarke, a young British sea captain, bought it and with his wife, Catherine Hannack, opened the Hotel Boa Vista. There was indeed a 'good view', looking out over the Praia Grande.

I thought it was a little divey, even for my taste. Ben appeared in his fall/winter collection. He said, 'You should have seen it 10 years ago.' It had now been amped up to be more quaint and tourist-friendly. 'C'mon! I'll show you my Macao,' he grinned, like a talk-show host. He'd done something to his teeth, they were less stained. We walked up to the Ritz for drinks, then went downhill using the Calçada do Bom Parto, passing a children's playground and some very old houses, and we strolled along Rua da Praia Grande, admiring some incredible old mansions.

'Someday, one of these'll be mine!' Ben fantasized. 'This is where I'd live, with the view of the sea and the junks, sampans and schooners all beautifully lit.'

'Really? You would?' I said.

'I mean, wouldn't you?'

'No, no, I wouldn't. Or rather, I don't know,' I said. 'I don't know if I'd like to stay here forever.' I looked at all the mansions and boats and I pictured how these riches were gained — by money-grabbing landowners, colonialists, thugs.

'Oh, you will. Once you've been bitten by the Asian bug.'

'I already have. I'm from here,' I explained, more to myself than to him, 'from Asia.'

'Where's home to you?'

'It's where I put my hairspray down.'

He smiled a while. So what if the chilly breeze was ruining my hair and makeup. We turned to admire the view again.

'This whole place looks just like the old days, except that we weren't there,' I said.

It was all kinda ace, being with Ben, staring at the view. Until I had a terrible feeling that Paolo was going to go all green and freak out. But then I thought, why should he? I was not his boo. Still, I couldn't quite shake the worry.

Ben must have noticed something. 'Li-an, let's go,' he said. 'Man, that's a pretty name!'

'Oh!' I said, surprised and speechless. For a long time I'd been happier as Madison, but now someone liked me for me.

We went up the narrow cobbled Travessa do Padre Narciso toward Rua Central. We passed the Dom Pedro V Theatre from 1858, the oldest European theater in China. We saw the imposing old cathedral of San Agostinho, in front of which was a wave-patterned mosaic square and green lamplights. It was like what I imagined Chinatown in Europe would be like. Everything was old, and weird and wonderful. Once we arrived at the grand square of Largo do Senado, we stopped for a bite to eat. We decided on the Macanese version of tapas, petiscos, so the new kid in town (that was me) could try it. Finding the right place was fun. I felt totally relaxed and at ease with Ben, who was ugly. Ugly hot.

There were several charming little bars here, where you could sit and just soak up the baroque ambience. There were also sports bars, which were a little rough. Sweaty bodies bumped against each other in thumping clubs. Somebody in an open-air bar turned the conversation to Reaganomics, and the exchange got heated. We went past Molly Malone's, an Irish pub serving Guinness by the pint and cranking out live tunes, fiddle and all. Televised Australian football matches attracted boisterous crowds from Down Under in such large numbers, it was a wonder there weren't any kangaroos. Long-haired, leather-clad men swapped stories in bars done up in orange and black — the colors of Halloween and Harleys. In every bar, we stayed for a drink.

We spotted an unnamed, unmarked, kinda traditional place down an alleyway, a cute old European bar with lace everything — curtains, tablecloths, aprons. Whenever I was in a lane or alleyway, I still had the occasional unpleasant scoping memories, which I swatted away like flies.

'OK, this is where we should eat!' he said. 'So how did you end up here?'

He seemed to read my mind and I had to think quickly. Which of course was what I seemed to have to do a lot of these days.

'Well, Ben, I was playing piano in a bar one night a few weeks ago,' I said, 'and this guy Paolo, he's some business kinda guy, heard me. And he offered me a job here.'

I discreetly cut out the more poetic details — like when I was spun and out-of-whack and lay like some zombie in a gilt apartment for a week.

'Why'dja take it? You been here before?'

I took a quick look at the menu, but Ben knew what to order like he was a local. We went for the *Galinha à Portuguesa* (chicken cooked in the oven together with potatoes, onions, egg and saffron) in petiscos-sized servings and had a couple of bottles of Vinho Verde between us. It was a dream to be eating and to be eating out on a normal, social occasion. He had no idea. I really had had enough of the cycle of scoping and starving. I never wanted to see a man's wallet again in my life.

'No, well. I wanted to… to leave Chicago.'

'Why?'

I groaned. 'Oh, you know? For a change?' I said.

He nodded.

'How about you? Why did you end up in Macao?'

He sighed. 'It's a long story. I was in med school at Columbia in New York.'

'Huh! Wow. That's pretty impressive, right?' He might be ugly hot but now he was smart too.

'Yup. But then I dropped out due to spending too much time in clubs, DJing, you know. I mean, I just really love music. I live and breathe it. I'm kinda obsessed with it. Someone I knew said there were all these new clubs in Hong Kong. Try having a break from college. Make a few bucks. They pay good there. Y'know? They really need and want DJs from abroad. And maybe I'd go back to med school after. Maybe I will. It ain't over for me yet.'

'But why Macao and not Hong Kong?'

'The casinos.'

'Casinos?'

'The money is here, Li-an. This is where they have money to spend on you, on themselves. If you got it in ya, you're gonna make plenty of the good stuff. It's cheap to live here. Even the garbage men go to the casinos.'

Meeting Ben had completely changed my view of Macao. He seemed to have ambition and I could feel it rubbing off on me.

'Well, maybe this beat ain't that bad after all,' I said. It was now seeming much, much better.

'No. It's cool. You're gonna get to play stuff, your own music if you wanna, nobody to dictate what's next, what's hot, what's not. You're gonna eat and drink and smoke some good shit and you're gonna do it cheaply. If you want art or some high-class shit, you can still hop over to Hong Kong, Singapore.'

A day ago I wanted to leave but now I just couldn't. Auntie was right. How had she known?

'Sure there will be bad days when the club's not full,' he said. 'You're, like, playing to five people and they're already way spun. But that's to be expected, right?'

'Right,' I said.

'You'll do great,' he said. 'You'll love it here and you won't wanna leave. I mean, where can you get Europe in Asia? OK, maybe Shanghai or Hanoi.'

These cities sounded so thrilling. I had never been to them.

The next night was Tuesday so I played again at Johnny's. From then it was buzzing every night. All these silver-haired diners with their bifocals were humming and even singing along. My music transported them to a time far, far away and they were young again. It was like a dream. I was floating all week. Ben and I didn't contact each other. It seemed natural and real that we would see each other again. I played and sang all these schmaltzy show 'choons' and actually meant them. I sang 'At Last' like I was Etta James in 1960. I felt doused with romanticism and Paolo was so pleased with the music, with me, with everything. At last!

Monday came around again. My day off. My Ben day. I had been looking forward to it all week. Ben called and left a note at the restaurant. Paolo didn't see it, one of the waiters handed it to me. Ben asked me to meet him at Café Opera at 8pm. If I couldn't go, he just asked me to ring the Bela Vista to let him know. If I could go, then he'd see me there.

By ten past eight he hadn't turned up. I was dying. I felt like an ice cream sundae no one was eating. I didn't go to pieces, just slowly melted away in all my finery. Surely it was the longest half-hour of my life. By the time it got to half-eight, my nails were down to the quick and I was glad I hadn't got myself a manicure. What a goddam waste that would have been. Just when I thought things were looking up in this town for me, they'd slipped into bummage.

Everything I looked at, which a moment ago had seemed raw, now was fooey. I was seeing things as they really were, and down at the skinny it sure was familiarly repulsive. Macao had a few spots where you'll almost forget you're not at home, wherever home might be. I had already forgotten what my mother looked like; I thought about her only in the theoretical sense, like what she used to say, what she used to cook on Fridays, her loud laughter. Her favorite piano pieces. I inherited my skill from her, we both played by ear. Yet her face was a blank. I had forgotten Dallas's favorite smell — I knew it was cedar wood air freshener over smoky dashboard, but I could no longer actually call it to my senses. All the important things were vanishing from me.

Ben came to Johnny's on Tuesday night, wearing a red shirt. Despite heavy makeup, I was sure I looked barely alive, having suffered a first-degree stood-uppance.

'Look! Look! Li-an, I can explain—'

'I'm listening,' I said, without looking at him.

'OK, you see, I was supposed to meet you at eight but I had to stand in for someone and having to do a radio DJ job at RTHK in Hong Kong, OK?' he said.

'Uh-huh,' I mumbled.

'Please look at me. Please. I had to do the sound engineering for some show for a sound engineer dude who never showed up. He's a friend. He somehow got caught up, blah blah. He said sorry about a bazillion times.'

'OK.'

'I am also saying sorry to you to the factor of a bazillion. Li-an, please.'

'OK! I said OK! Like, already?' If I could hear myself, I would be shaking my head. No, wait, I was shaking my head. There was really nothing more to add. I knew he was sorry, and these things happened and like some twisted Taoist idiom: you can't say he wasn't here when he was now here, wasn't he?

'So to make it up to you,' he said, 'as I am not DJing, I'll stay all night and listen to you play the piano and sing, what dja think of that? Please, I would love to. I told ya, I'm obsessed with music. You can't turn away someone obsessed with music, your number one fan.'

OK, I thought, *so what did he want to hear?* Cos I couldn't do Abba and stuff. By strict orders, only show tunes. This was an American bar after all. He pulled up a barstool. The piano had a curved custom bar top around it for sitting around. He put his elbows on the bar top and rested his chin in his hands in a way that said I could sing whatever song, and he'd love it.

I played and sang 'Long Ago and Far Away'. I was getting good at this; I might even be considered a professional musician pretty soon.

'You did a real nice job there!' he applauded. 'Walking bassline, syncopated sevenths, hell yeah.'

'Really?'

'Really! I mean, I could almost have been back in New York City.'

He high-fived me. I felt very encouraged. He seemed genuinely interested. This was odd because I was used to being booed off stage when I was in Mrs Dixon. I had come to expect it now.

The pimp-dog came out from his office at about 9.30pm to greet some VIP diners, businessmen from Hong Kong, all with the surname Wong. Paolo sat and drank with them for a few minutes, always aware when to offer to open them another bottle. Milk had to flow before cash could grow, as Chicago musicians I used to jam with often advised.

'Hey, Paolo,' I called out. 'Come meet my friend.'

'Hey, s'up,' Paolo said, cos he was trying to act 'cool' but he only ended up sounding assful.

'This is Ben.'

'Hey, how're ya doin'? Great to meet another American,' said Ben, extending his hand.

'From New York, right?' said Paolo. 'We don't serve pastrami here.' He laughed at his own lame joke, since Ben and I (Ben and I! — already I thought of us as a like-minded team) didn't laugh, and didn't even think it was a joke.

'Aw, no way,' Ben joked back, 'I was really looking forward to a pastrami on rye sandwich with cheese, mustard, onions. Oh, New York! New York!'

'And pickle,' I added with a dash of deadpanning.

'And pickle,' he agreed.

OK, I think we were playing it up. We might be on Broadway. It was theatrical, a little indirect flirting on my part and on Ben's. I got the impression Paolo was tense, maybe even nervous, though he was grinning at our stage play. But from the way his fingers gripped his wine glass so tightly his knuckles were white, he was clearly unhappy. What exactly was his problem?

I fully expected Paolo to give me the third degree after work, when Ben was safely out of sight, but Ben didn't seem intent on leaving.

'Let's do "My Funny Valentine",' he'd said and we were straight in.

'Let's do "Cheek to Cheek",' I'd said and he'd shrugged and we'd harmonized as smoothly as butter on toast, in the middle eight.

'Keep playing the "Great American Songbook". My mom loves it.'

'Oh yeah? She is a musician too?' I said.

'Actually, both my parents are musical. She's from Detroit. She's a pediatrician and she was also a jazz singer. My dad's from Harlem and he's an orthopedic surgeon and a trumpet player.'

So, Ben's family were not only smart and rich, they were also musical. Uber-talented, these Jews. Ben and I sang song after song, like birds. It was all so easy. We both knew all the words. Old songs, new songs. All the show tunes. The hits and the bombs.

Ben was buying his drinks, as well as sitting at the curve of the piano, so he wasn't in my way. Many customers, including the Wongs, came over and paid us — and not just compliments. Sure, I saw them put something in the cognac glass on the piano lid. At the end of the evening, it was the heaviest cognac glass I ever picked up, and it was bread, not milk.

'You've got an interesting voice,' he said. 'Sounds like a mixture between Debbie Harry and Natalie Wood. Maybe we can work with that.'

'Work with it?'

'Yeah, sure. Maybe we can make a record together. So I can listen to you every day.'

Sure seemed like a compliment if I ever heard one!

Ben had a lovely Chet Baker voice, tender and moving. When I wasn't closing my eyes better to listen to him, I could see the pimp-dog was watching like Bela Lugosi from the wings (or should I say the Wongs), his widow's peak rising in displeasure. But, oh, how quickly and easily Ben slipped into thirds and sixths, backing my vocals, hitting reverse order chromatic harmonies. After 'We Belong Together' and before 'Cuddle Up a Little Closer', I knew he knew his tritones, which I scarfed down like cupcakes.

'That was from that movie,' I said.

'Oh yes, I know,' he nodded, sipping his drink. 'I know exactly which one.'

'It was— um— I can't think… I think it's—'

'It's *On Moonlight Bay*. Doris Day. Gordon MacRae. 1951.'

'Yes!' I said. 'I can't believe it, you know it?'

'Well, I don't know-know it. I know the song.'

'What about "We Belong Together"?' I grabbed my water and took a big gulp, head back.

'Jerome Kern. Thirties. Exact year? Can't say. *No lo sé.*'

'1932,' I said, knowing well that it was from the obscure musical *Music in the Air* by Jerome Kern and Oscar Hammerstein. 'And I ain't suing you for not getting it!'

'You were testing me? Go ahead and call my lawyer. I got nothing and you're getting all of it!'

We got into talking about Doris Day after that, but I was aware that I was supposed to be working, so I carried on playing. No solos now, I didn't want to waste time playing 32 bars of fiddly honky-tonky, key-changing wipeout when I had a backing vocalist to hand.

It was midnight when Paolo said to call it a night. My job was done. No more music. I saw Ben off outside the restaurant.

'Ben? Um. See ya?'

'I had fun, Li-an. I never thought I'd have so much fun just with a girl and an acoustic piano,' he laughed. 'And I didn't even get any pizza,' he said.

'No, you didn't. You want some now? I could get a takeout.' I was only offering because I felt I ought to. Realistically, the kitchen was already shut. I hoped he would say no.

'Nah! But it was the most fun I've had in a grip.' I thought he would kiss me. I'd forgotten what it was like. Dallas hated it. The only kiss anybody was getting was 'a smack in the skull cave', she said. The possibility of being kissed was so much more petrifying than the act of it. You have to have quite a nerve to invade a personal space bubble and make that kind of contact. I was feeling kinda reticent to initiate anything, in case I actually sucked at it.

'Catch ya later!' He tossed his head back and laughed, jumping onto his bike, a Chinese-made Victory — 'the trusty black-winged beast,' as he called it.

I went home in the Benz and Paolo stayed on late, to close up and count his millions. 'See ya tomorrow morning,' he said to me, thereby also saying he didn't want to know about Ben. All my fears had been unfounded. He made no attempt to kiss me. I thought of the big red inflatable Kissers in the pool. Maybe I'd kiss them instead.

It was so dark at midnight you couldn't see the sea. The stars looked like they were suspended in permanent ink. I shut my eyes and remembered that a night ago I melted away in agony at being stood up and now we sang in perfect harmony.

I felt I hadn't heard music until now. XTC was hatesome. What was I doing all this time? What on earth was I thinking, buying those goddam tapes? None of it made sense to me now. My heart was singing, and the melody sure sounded loud and clear. I was in love. Or I felt I should be if I was not.

I thought about how I'd braved it and called out to Paolo asking if Ben could have a job doing my BVs, Paolo shaking his head from the bar where he sat doing the tabs, not looking up, not turning around, not even deigning to reply to my outrageous request. I'd rubbed his nose in it and he ain't down with that. A tiny part of me said that I was gonna screw up. Whatever. You only sign, seal and deliver once, right?

I didn't see Ben for a while after that. That was cool by me. He'd put something in me that had more lasting power than a couple of Bacardi and cokes. The songs we sang together fizzed around me for a few days like a warm spell. Every muscle in me ached with tenderness and I glowed like a worm. I replayed and re-sang the songs alone during my working hours in the restaurant, imagining Ben's thirds and sixths harmonies in my head. After three days and five hours, the worm began to lose its glow. I could no longer bear not hearing his voice again, never mind not seeing him.

I thought it was gross that I went to his hotel but, hey, I was a modern girl, right? I didn't have his number, after all. Forget Natalie Wood. Why couldn't I be Debbie Harry? What century was I living in? Who was I kidding. I hated that I was chasing him. Anyway. On Saturday morning, I went to Thaew to ask him to drive me over to the Bela. He said he couldn't. Before I could ask him why, Paolo had appeared in the hall with his golfing equipment.

'Hey, I was just waiting for you to wake up. Dja fancy a round?'

'Of golf?'

'Ya-ya.' He was nervous, I could tell, but I didn't want to think why. I couldn't understand his jitters. Jesus, anyway, I wasn't, like, fifty. Why would I want to play friggin' golf?

'No, I'll take a rain check, thanks.' I paused. 'You know, about my visa?'

'Your *visa*?' He pronounced the word incredulously, as though I had just said caviar.

'Right. Do I need to do a visa run?'

'What? Doll, didja read your contract like I said?'

'Well, do I need to do a visa run?'

'What is this "visa run"? Where didja hear dose damned words from? Over my dead body! We are not some Russian *émigré* fugitives. You are good to stay as long as you're staying for good. Damn! Where're you going?' he asked.

'Out,' I said. I wanted to say I was going to see Ben, but Paolo was already talking at me.

'Li-an.' Paolo started to gesticulate in that mad southern European way he did when he couldn't think of how to say something. 'Dja ever think how I'm feeling 'bout cha?'

I couldn't really reply. I sighed and shook my head. What to say? This was one jive I'd rather not be talkin'.

'I'll see ya round,' I said. I had my own hate-ons about 'older' men. Main reason being I was felt up by some nastafied landlord in our house in Armenian Street when my daddy was late with the rent. I felt so violated I made up my mind that I'd be a smart-ass and do the feeling up next time. And it was gonna be someone my age or younger. I assumed being felt up was not part of my job description. There was something oppressive about being with a person who you knew disapproved of you and loved you at the same time.

I thought I heard the pimp-dog throw down a golf club. Thaew started the engine. I figured he was going to load up the car so I made myself scarce. I would hail down a tricycle trishaw when one came along. If you waited long enough, one always came along. This wasn't Chicago, after all.

After about ten years, a trishaw came along. During the ride to town, I thought perhaps I should quit my job as piano player. After all, there was now an explicit conflict of interest, which affected my ability to do the job well. You could say it was sexual harassment. Hmm, yeah, that was what I would say. Poor Paolo though, he didn't mean to be such a veg.

Older men deserved it, whatever it was that they deserved. Why was my dad late with the rent? It wasn't like he was strapped. He was an engineer! He was working or drinking hard and it was often both. He often disappeared for a day. Sometimes he caught up with his Zs at the office, other times, who knew where he crashed?

Anyway, I didn't fancy myself as a piano player of these dumb-ass 'sho-choons' for the rest of my life. I could have a real career in music if I joined forces with Ben. After epileptic uphill pedaling by the trishaw rider, whom I swore was half-blind, and what felt like another ten years later, the trishaw arrived at the Bela Vista. I wanted to catch Ben before he went out for the day, and at the same time I didn't want him to think that I was somewhat stalking him. Oh God, no! I couldn't possibly let him think that I was a saddo.

My imagination ran for it. We could pen some totally funky new shit. We'd record it very cheaply in a local studio that he knew at Las Docas, the docklands area. We could have a worldwide hit! How awesome would that be! I would sing and Ben could play guitar. He had all the record industry connections already from his DJing. I would tell him all that today.

I asked for Ben at reception and was relieved when he was in. He came downstairs to meet me. 'Hey! Wotcha doin' here?'

I rolled my eyes, shook my head and sighed. I was looking as pleased as a puppy. I could find nothing to say, puppies don't say nothing.

'You wanna grab a coffee?' he said.

Thank heavens for that.

We went to the Café Opera — where he never showed up — and had the Macanese Crispy Bun for breakfast. It was a freshly baked golden bun, split in the middle and topped with a slice of butter and some coconut jam. We had strong *nai cha*, milk tea, drinking from thick enamel cups, and I told him my plans. Ben thought I shouldn't quit my job.

An ant bite of disappointment showed in my face. 'Why?' I asked.

He laughed. 'Because you don't have a record deal yet. So where's the money coming from? Stick with Mr Pizza.'

I drank my tea in silence; in my mind, the plans for recording a hit were still stewing. Wasn't disco still totally new here? There could be a tight little market for electronic music. I kept my excitement simmering under my heavily made-up surface.

'Besides, I don't think I could commit to that.'

'Why not? It would be fun.'

'Li-an, I got a job to do tomorrow. That's why I haven't been in touch. I have to travel to Singapore.'

'Why? Are you DJing there?'

'Yup.' The way he said 'yup' was like a ventriloquist's detachable jaw and… not… too… convincing. He elaborated when I repeated the word 'yup' to him, like I was a dummy. 'OK, OK, it's a delivery job. Courier service. But I may not be back.'

'Whadja mean?' I asked.

'Well… I… if it goes kaplonk, I wouldn't be able to come back.'

'I don't get it.'

'It's strictly work. I have to keep schtoom. Besides, my three months' tourist visa is up and I have to do a visa run to get another three months. When your three months is up, I mean, you are on the tourist visa, right? We can go away together somewhere and do your visa run.'

I pretended to look at my watch but realized as I was doing it that I wasn't wearing a watch. 'I gotta shoot,' I said. 'Sorry.'

The temptation of being allowed on a visa-runner with him was too great for the capacity of my puny little mind. He was one bad, bad kitty! Why did I have to meet him? My head pulsed with pain. Ben had made me feel so awesome but for me to find out that he might not be back? It really kicked my head in. He'd talked me out of quitting the piano-playing job. And just like that, I was no one again. I'd got to a point where I was soaring with excitement for this new city and had gotten over my loneliness, but now it was just like when I first arrived.

I put my key in the door and thought I heard someone in Paolo's study.

'Hey, thought you were gonna play golf?' I was almost happy to see him, even though I couldn't wait to get out of his sight only that morning.

'Dja know what? My golf buddy pulled out. So I stayed in instead.'

'Whatcha doing?'

'I'm listening to Spyro Gyra.'

'OK.'

'How 'boutchu?'

'How 'bout me what?'

'Whatcha do?'

'Went to town and had tea.'

'With Ben.'

'With Ben.' I paused. 'Now I'm back.'

'Wanna have lunch out? Catch a movie?'

'Sure.' I was so beat by the time I came back, I was fired up for anything. Even a trip to the stinking Inner Harbor with its rotten drains would have smelled like ice cream waffles. 'Sounds good to me.' He said just the right thing at the right time, just like what Dallas would have done for me after a bad night.

'Come 'ere. Whatdja wanna eat?'

'Not pizza.' I said, feeling a lot more cheered up. 'Just kidding. Anything will do.'

'Listen,' he said, 'about Ben.'

'About Ben,' I parroted.

'Yup.'

I waited for it.

'Ain't workin'.'

Uh oh. Screwed up.

'I don't want him in my joint. What you do outside work is your tin can, but don't bring him back.'

'You didn't like us singing those—'

Paolo chuckled, a little sadly I thought. They didn't make guys like Paolo anymore. He was still stuck in his Rodgers and Hammerstein *pristino condicionado* vinyls and I had my Kool & The Gang tapes. We were like oddly matched housemates.

Ben had said he might not be back, and I didn't want to get hurt because, yeah, I was afraid. I didn't want to howl like some friggin' widow. I spent the next few days with my mixtapes again, swimming with The Kissers (before the weather got too cold), just hanging with the pimp-dog when he was around, avoiding golf trips with him, learning Cantonese with Auntie, going to Café Opera, and all that kinda shit. I needed to know when I was getting paid. It reminded me to check my contract like he said. Seemed like a good time. When I was in my room I dragged out the bag I came with from the closet. The contract was typewritten and not exactly a thin document. It was at least an inch thick. I started when I got on the plane. The date was Monday, 10 November 1980. Working hours were from 6pm to midnight, every day except for Monday. If I had to work any other hours, such as in the daytime, it would be considered overtime, pro rata. There would be moderate cash spending money to cover the first days, from Monday to Saturday November 15 when I started actual playing. Accommodation was covered as long as I lived in the pavilion apartment. If I moved out, I'd have to pay rent. It would not be covered. All meals were covered, as long as they were at home or at work. A driver was covered for any trips for work or just getting around. However, if I was to eat out or to take cabs or public transport, this was not covered and not reimbursable. Two weeks' vacation may be taken but not in the first six months and only during off season, which was October or March. That meant the earliest time I could vacay was October. Nearly a year away. One trip back home was covered. I would be paid into an account in my name, 2,000 US dollars. That wowed me! That was way more decent than what I'd been scoping. I stopped reading.

I started to get used to things around here. I started to think that, hey, maybe Ben being the total turkey and my only friend, that somehow he was unlucky and he had gotten caught. Maybe I was not to see him again. But I was wrong.

Ben got back from his 'courier' job in Singapore. I guessed that it had gone well. He came by my pavilion but I was out. I didn't go back to see him, only cos I wasn't sure, myself, if I should. He could leave again. And would he make it back the next time? I carried on at Johnny's, playing and singing the songs that Paolo loved, knowing full well the songs would get me nowhere and I didn't even like them, especially without Ben on BVs.

I didn't even mind the pimp-dog having his occasional arm around me. He was a friend, too. And it was kinda cultural for him, but I knew I was weak to the max. This was my first job without Dallas and it was hard. There were lines to draw and lines not to cross. But those lines were unclear. They were gray scribbles, or they were invisible. I needed rules. And Dallas had been my walking rulebook. I was just a confused kid again, told myself it was OK to be mixed-up if you were mixed-race. I had chattering monkeys in my head all the time. Dallas would say, 'Yeah, you're totally bananas.'

Ben knew that Tuesday night was not a busy night at Johnny's, so he chose a random Tuesday to turn up, and during my break too. Paolo gave him a 'da fuck chu doin' here' look from way over at the bar, but it was too late; Ben had sat down and ordered a drink. I thought perhaps Paolo would throw him out. He was a green saddo but he didn't want no showdown, not in his joint, anyway. Think what that would do to your clientele.

'So, you lived,' I said to Ben.

'You know what? We'll do the album.'

'What album?'

'You wanted to record an album. We'll do it.'

I didn't believe him. 'Didn't you say you couldn't commit to it because you're too busy shoveling somebody's shit?'

'I didn't say that. Anyway, I been thinking, it's a good idea.'

'Whatcha doing here anyways? I thought you were dead.'

'I'm not dead. It was just business, OK? That cat still owes me big, but I got most of the moolah. I came back to see you.'

'Why?'

'Cos we're gonna do it. You, me. You write the songs. I help you record it and play it at the club. We got record companies coming in all the time, man.'

'You mean it?'

'Li-an, I always mean it. I never lied to you before.'

'Anyway, my break's up now. I gotta get back.'

'Wanna sing?'

'No, Ben, no singing now. Schtoom. Paolo don't wantcha here.'

'Ask him.'

I made a face. I went over to Paolo's office and asked him. He looked over and there were some customers from the last time Ben was here, already chatting with him, all friendly. They... loved... him. They knew his voice. They wanted him again. They wanted me. They had already crowded around the piano and were shaking his hand. So Paolo sighed and nodded gravely.

Ouch, the irony! All those godawful songs that Paolo loved. We were doing 30, 40, maybe even 50 songs that night. Jerome Kern, Rodgers and Hart, Kurt Weill, the whole shebang. All my feelings of isolation and awkwardness, the emotions of being excluded pretty much my whole life, uncertainties of growing up in different cultures — they dissolved like aspirin in a whiskey glass. First time in my life I was popular. Here, tonight, I was admired, observed, even adored — by Ben, Paolo, all these people. The place was full and it seated seventy-five. Never had I been noticed at a party, I was always the observer and not the observed. They listened to me and gazed at me as though they had never seen or heard anything like this in Macao before.

They probably hadn't. I was sure I could hear Paolo slamming the dishes or the glasses, fuming, adoring, whatever. It was cheesing him off big time that Ben was here. What could I do? I ignored these disturbing thoughts, because I was wanting so badly to concentrate on my own pleasure.

It surprised me, constantly, how many songs Ben knew. I believed him — that he never lied to me. Liars had bad memories and Ben's was good as Goldie Hawn. I played beautifully. I sang better than I ever did. I had forgotten the chills that Ben's voice sent down my spine, like I was a fluted glass. I ached to hear his soft and sweet Chet Baker voice. And the tips poured in again from appreciative customers.

This time, before he left, he said we should meet on Monday, my next day off, to talk about putting my songs down at the studio. When I was working, I had to get to the restaurant by 6pm, all fresh-faced like a kitten. I knew studio time was exhausting. We could only do it on my day off because we needed a minimum of ten hours clear. I asked him how much it would cost and he said he'd take care of it. He knew I wanted to clear my debts with Paolo and that I was looking to move out. In the meantime, Ben said I had to practice back home on my guitar or piano and get my songs ready. We were looking to record six tracks. I was so excited it was like I was a child again on my first trip to the zoo, when my parents were still together. When I got back to my pavilion, I was light-headed from the endorphins. I stayed up 'til dawn practicing on my guitar quietly and refining my old tunes. Some of them were written in the apartment above the Happy Chèf, bringing back tears and some way decent memories.

All week I tried to avoid Paolo, but it was no good. I explained to him what Ben and I would be doing at the studio but it was like explaining to an uncle I was planning to let down his tires. No way did he get it. He tried his dang best not to be mean and discouraging, but in general he seemed all eaten up and spazzed. He just about kept his cool but his gritted teeth told me, 'Don't bring him back to my joint,' without actually saying it. He couldn't even utter Ben's name.

'Fact is, I'd like to move out as soon as I can,' I said.

That news really cut him up. With difficulty he gasped, 'Anyways, you got every day, all day spare to go hunt down an apartment. You've been here nearly a month. You're getting paid very soon, hon.'

As long as I lived under capitalism, I expected to have my life influenced by the demands of moneyed people. I tried to pay Paolo back the spending money that he'd loaned me when I first got here, but he didn't accept it. Though, I thought, he was pleased that I offered. It showed a grain of integrity in me.

'You know, actually, you can't move out, Li-an.' He spoke with such intense calmness that I had to stop myself from the usual Li-an-type shrugging, 'Oh yeah? Says who?' rebuttal.

'Gawd, I would lose my mind,' he whispered. 'Course, at no point could he look at me.

When Monday came, I was ready to lay down my tracks. Didn't think I'd ever woken up so early and so easily before. I wanted to tell Dallas, it was like my new life had begun at last. She'd been my biggest fan for so long. I met Ben at Las Docas, where the 32-track studio was, and he said we had all day, probably time to record two to three songs, leaving the rest for another day. I said that was cool.

We went through the sound checks first, which took a good two hours. I tuned up my wine-red Gibson Les Paul. There was no drummer, which I was glad about, but there was a Roland TR808 drum machine we could use. Actually, it was a new thing and this was the only studio in Macao that had it. I was steering away from the live sound anyway. In terms of equipment, there was a Minimoog, and an old Korg with some nice synth sounds; I played around with a few chords and solo lines.

The plan was to record all the tracks for each song first, and the vocals another day. I told Ben I wanted to be completely involved in the production and he said that was OK. It was one o'clock in the afternoon before we laid down the keys and the guide vocals using a click track for lack of a beat. Ben said we could really do with a real piano, recorded live. 'All these synth sounds,' he said, 'I'm just not sure.' I said we could do it at Paolo's. There was a heartbreaking work of art there: a polished, perfect and unused grand piano. So it was agreed we'd do guide keyboard lines as well. Some would be replaced with the real piano, when Ben brought some DATs and his 8-track. Another project for another day. The digital audiotapes were cute little things that fitted into your pocket like a cigarette lighter.

Ben said the guide vocals were only rough, to be replaced with the proper vocals at the next session. (Session — I was using band speak!) Ben picked up his Epiphone and played some riffs he thought would suit the sound. Here we disagreed a little. It was inevitable. Sometimes he gave in to me and at other times he stood his ground. It was hard to find my sound, the feel for the music. I played my own Les Paul on the tracks and Ben added his decorative or atmospheric sounds with his Epiphone. It was all new to me. I had never had this opportunity before; they did say that once your songs were recorded they were no longer yours.

At the end of the afternoon, we'd done the basic tracks and now came the fun stuff: we messed around with the drum machine and some synth textures to complete the sound. This was the most important bit.

Then, when I thought we were excellently swinging, Ben said to call it a day. Leave while the party was hot. It sure gets ugly after you get ugly. It was close to 8pm, and we were both pooped and pleased. We headed out into the busy, narrow Rua da Felicidade, a red-light area turned neon-light district, where we ordered four Tigers straightaway because two sure wasn't enough. We ate clay pot seafood at a 23-hour roadside kiosk. Well, it was more of a shack. And then we took in the view of the calm water, glittering in the bay.

After two beers we gave random gross titles to the songs and joked about, imagining if they got released. We were in peals of hysterics, but the spell was broken when Ben said, 'Yo, give us a bone.' I looked at the empty packet. We'd used up all his smokes, so I got up to get some. I noticed that his were contraband stuff from Thailand. 'No, let me get them,' he said.

Smoking was mandatory in Macao — a person must smoke at least one pack of cigarettes a day — so it wasn't hard to find a tobacco stand. He looked all serious when he came back; threw a packet of Double Happiness on the table.

'I got these,' he said.

'That's cool. You know, Ben, about the courier job you're doing?'

'Can we lay off that? Another time.' He waved around him and scratched his ear. 'Place is amped and all that, man.' I looked around at the crowded open-air stalls, where people were eating and drinking, and I felt dumb. I didn't think I'd offended him, because he smiled and put his right hand on my face. He let it sit for a second and slip to my neck. The night was so humid and it was a little windy. I felt sticky and his hand didn't actually slip that well to my neck, more like skidded to my collarbone. I felt chilled and something tingled inside. He looked at me all unreal and tough.

Briefly, his mouth met mine. I stopped him and pulled away, all my modesty flaring up when I least expected it, like a belch. I suddenly felt embarrassed and self-conscious. I didn't usually, back in Chicago (I wouldn't have been able to hit on guys and take their money if I was a shy bunny). A girl comes to Asia and Asia comes out in the girl.

'Let's be outta here,' he said. He had a firm dry grip when he held my hand. I was disoriented by the rush of chemicals to my brain, the powerful taste of the Siamese contrabands in Ben's mouth. We were knocking glasses over, stools, all witnessed by the mild-mannered and quizzical Asians around us. The white, newly divorced middle-aged ladies who'd stepped away from their slot machines temporarily didn't bat much of their kohl-lined lids. I found myself in Room 603 at the Bela Vista smoking a joint and rolling another on the white cane coffee table.

If I hadn't wanted him so much, you can bet I would have gotten my size 10 ass straight home with my tan-colored UnderStatements firmly in place (yes, I practiced girth control). They weren't my actual skin coloring, they were no one's color, they weren't the color of any tanning lotion, ointment or application known to mankind in all of history. They were the color of a Mexican sofa that had been left in the sun for too long.

I had about three minutes to decide if I'd do it, but within two and a half, my Uncle Sams were peeled right off like I was being reupholstered, spilling my fat layers out like over-stuffing. It killed me to think I was wobbling in front of Ben Mizrai, but I never said I was a Jacuzzi salesgirl cum part-time model. I just thought, firstly, I was bored, and secondly, man, I hadn't gotten any round midnights for four hundred years. He wasn't my customer — I wasn't nipping this guy's breadbox, right? The Mary J was hitting the spot. It was all the more fantastic considering he'd risked his life to get it in this room. 'You're one bad kitty,' I whispered to myself in Dallas's voice.

To me, the creative process was an aphrodisiac to the max. A man whom I was being creative with was someone I could get fired up about. Even his kiss was creative, hitting the spot in more places than one. It was no coincidence that Ben and I were rebels. We'd left our own community's expectations and aspirations — to be doctors, lawyers, accountants, basically white-collared money-makers — and taken the long and wind-up road. We had been left to our own vices.

When I worked with Dallas, we were flimflamming con artists. Yes: artists. Ben helped me discover my artistic nature, the whole reason I was born. I was a world-class musician who just happened to be marooned on a Far Eastern island now, lying low, while Dallas was rattling her cage. I wasn't wrong to take her advice and leave town. I thought of her every morning when I received my cup of *nai cha* made by Auntie. What time was it in Chicago and what was Dallas doing right then? Did they let her have her 'happy things', as she liked to call them — high class Estée Lauder makeup and McCall's magazines?

Ben had an adorable smell that, years later, I discovered was Halston Z-14. Lying beside him, I inhaled his lavender scent, the smell of sleep, and something hot and tangy, a mixture of sweat and pepper. My pert Asian nose told me to trust all things sweet and spicy. My large American eyes told me to shut them tight, and go before it got too late, but I fell asleep entangled with Ben. I was pooped. A hard day's night and all that. It wasn't like Paolo was my dad or anything, but it bugged me because it sure felt that way.

When I got back to the pavilion, it was already one in the afternoon on Tuesday. My head was spinning. I needed Auntie to put some grub in my mouth quickly after my 24 hours with Ben. Paolo was in his office, listening to the BBC World Service.

'Never guess. John Lennon's dead. Two hours ago. Shot by…'

I lost my appetite. I checked the flip-card calendar on Paolo's desk. On Monday, December 8, 1980, my one day off in the week, at 11.48pm New York time, which was 11.48am on Tuesday 9th here, the world lost the greatest songwriter ever. Part of me died, too.

With the passing of Lennon, an era ended. I would always remember what I was doing and where I was on that day. It was the saddest day, that of the assassination of my songwriting hero. My throat dried up like a piece of paper in the oven and I felt my knees weaken.

I collapsed in the armchair and listened with Paolo. John Lennon died from five gunshot wounds made by some loony called Mark Chapman. It was a warm December day in New York. John and Yoko had just released their joint album, *Double Fantasy*. The radio DJ in Macao played some songs, 'Nowhere Man', 'You've Got to Hide Your Love Away', 'Starting Over' and, of course, 'Imagine', which drove me to tears. I was sobbing like some busted drainpipe.

Paolo put his arms around me but I was inconsolable.

'Hey, it's not that bad, it's not like you knew the fella?' He was perplexed. I put my head on his shoulder. I could only attribute my emotional outburst to my state of mind. Paolo didn't know what to do. 'See ya later. I gotta run through the accounts before tonight. You wanna Jim Beam or anything?' I laughed through my tears and shook my head. We were so many worlds apart, I might as well be an alien with a wet face to him. He was just someone I ended up living with, performing for, eating out of his hand.

After John Lennon's death, it took at least a week for me to truly believe it. I kept replaying what I'd heard on the news, and at one point even convinced myself you couldn't always believe everything you heard. John Lennon was alive, he had to be. I felt bereaved and betrayed. And get this: I couldn't face Ben for a week, which was saying something. It was partly my vanity. Didn't want Ben to see the state of my nest de rat hair or my puffy eyes. I read the classifieds, shortlisting the apartments I would look at, but I couldn't really focus. There was a pain in my side that would not go away. The radio and the shops (and the radio in the shops) wouldn't stop playing Lennon's music, especially 'Woman', which just killed me every time I heard it. Sure, I was jealous of Yoko. 'Woman' was written for her. I hated it and loved it at the same time, if you know what that means. If a great musician's life was a short one, I was determined I needed to get my album out there as soon as I could. Once my demo was produced, cut and finished, I would make my entrance and present my art to the record industry honchos that Ben knew.

When I next met Ben at the recording studio, I was ready to belt my heart out and write over the guide vocals. As before, I played the guitar parts and Ben filled in where he thought it would warm up the sound. In the mornings I would make myself get up early and go to the studio to work on the production and the arrangements. This was the fun bit, and I didn't want to leave it to Ben. Besides, he would get it all wrong — they were my songs.

On a Monday when I knew Paolo would be out on the courses, we rigged up mics on the grand piano in Paolo's villa to record the piano parts. I left it all to Ben, who knew what he was doing.

Every night became a Jekyll and Hyde situation for me. Ben's spiel wailed inside my head like a siren. I couldn't bear to play the show tunes that Paolo loved and knew so well. Yet I did, because I was doing my job and I kept telling myself it was a job I wouldn't do forever. Most people were out back, sweating over their giant cleavers and mopping filth from the floor in buckets the size of trash cans (maybe they were trash cans?) so I knew I should count myself lucky to have been out front where the hard work wasn't. I sat at the piano and I sang. The hardest part of my job was putting life into my voice. My mind started to wander every time I sang. I was seasick from singing about sailing on a moonlight bay…

''S the matter with ya, kid?' The pimp-dog came over to me at break time. I lit up and blew a grand chimney of smoke from my nostrils.

'OK if I just chill on my break?' I snapped like a gator on acid. He made a face and gestured like some Italian cab driver, which I took to mean 'You want out?' I knew that even if my voice was in tune, my heart wasn't hitting the notes and my dukes were banging out bad honky-tonk changes.

Night after night I got worse at my one and only gig in town. Winter had come and with it the festive season. I was in a sweat and failing fast.

'Kid, you can't quit and you most definitely ain't movin' out.' Paolo ticked me off at the slightest opportunity while he was totting up his moolah every night. My tips were dropping and so were my jaws. I felt that, indeed, I had sold myself into slavery.

I looked forward to Christmas and New Year, because there was no other escape from my dictator. I was burning out. I couldn't move out because I now realized I wasn't paid enough. I thought 2,000 US dollars was a lot until I found out I'd have less than 1,000 left if I moved out. The rents here were sky high. All I was thinking of was my demo, which was now finished. I handed about 20 tapes to Ben for his recording bigwigs. The rest, another 20, I was going to send out myself by airmail to random labels in the USA. Might as well have put them in a 7-Up bottle and thrown them into the South China Sea. I didn't know if I would ever hear from anybody, let alone anybody who'd be interested. Ben was my best bet.

Johnny's (uh-oh, there's the reminder again) was busy with all the Christmas parties. Every night there was an office party of some description, as if John Lennon hadn't just died. No one cared and no one remembered. They were having too much fun. I must be the only person in this town who thought about him.

We were making thirty to fifty thousand patacas. 'And that's per night,' said Paolo. The local joke was that if the cash desks and the phones were ringing louder than your wife's voice, you knew you were cruising. Businesses were expanding and new bars and restaurants were springing up. More money was spent on fresh neon than new hospitals.

The cast of the musical *Oliver!* and their hangers-on were coming for their Christmas party. They were touring Asia and playing at the Sands casino. I had another blow up with Paolo. He made me learn the entire score so that I could play it to them when they came. My point was: they'd been rehearsing the same songs for yankee doodle years so why would they want to hear them played back acoustically by someone else? 'Trust me,' Paolo said, 'You don't know shit about business. You get paid to play back what they are paid to play.'

I was a half-alive live recording machine. Paolo's monkey. I'd been taught tricks. What they were performing in a five-star resort, I was spewing back at them, two-star motel style. Of course, Paolo won and he was right, they lapped up every note. It was the highest form of compliment.

And you know the hardest bit was trying to rearrange the score, to segue every final chord sequence to the next song so that it was a seamless medley. I had to use every artifice I knew, four bar turnarounds, eight bar turnarounds, with modulation to higher keys and tempo change for that uplifting effect, four bar pedal on stationary bass. All the time, I was using my brain for something, so I managed to stay on top of what I did best — music was still music. It was forever, not just for one gig. I could adapt any musical into a continuous piano solo now.

In the daytime I carried on writing songs, lying by the pool, or searching for an apartment. I got nowhere. Actually, I couldn't afford anything that wasn't like Ben's dive at the Bela Vista. Either that or where casino workers roomed together way out in the Iao Hon district full of gritty, drab concrete apartment blocks, dripping with stained pipes and draped with electrical cables and bird shit, devoid of any colonial charm or casino city-glamor. I could bet on it that they could never afford to bet and if they chose to, it would be an early death. Blackjack tables started with a minimum spend of a hundred US dollars. The house always won. After them, the government and after them the sharks. The rich–poor gap was huge and the government totally corrupt. Typical third world problems. I'd seen Iao Hon for myself the two times Thaew took me there, to view a couple of apartments in the walk-up buildings. Ben himself came with me on one of these jaunts to what he fondly called 'El Dorado'. Mine were first world problems: what music should I listen to today? What time should I wake up and am I drinking too much coffee? I needed some perspective.

'You've looked at maybe four apartments now,' Ben said in the ride on the way back after a viewing with the realtor. 'A nice girl can't live in those places. Trust me.'

'I want my own place,' I said.

'Why? You got your own place! We were trying to save money for this deal. You're living in a palace, like, with a pool?' Ben said. 'These guys?' he shook his head. 'They ran away from their rural poverty-stricken dead-end lives in China. They paid smugglers to hide them in the hold of a ship for the overnight boat ride. And here they are working 12-hour shifts in casinos without ever tasting food from a restaurant, like ever. And you? You're living the dream!'

Not sure whose dream. It wasn't mine. Maybe it was his.

Johnny's had gotten so busy that after Sunday, December 14 there was no more opportunity to write music, lie by the pool or search for an apartment. I was working all day, with a break for lunch and a break to go home and get changed, and then I was working all night. I never saw Auntie, who had been so kind to warn me about getting stuck here, and who didn't say, 'Be careful of working too hard'. I would have scrammed if I could. In the day, I found myself doing all the stuff people who work in restaurants do. Short of serving, I was ordering, doing accounting, doing meetings, organizing deliveries. It was the craziest job to be doing: two jobs for the price of one. How was I supposed to have any time to look for an apartment and move out? I was getting overtime, that was the good news. I might even be getting great at restaurant management, I thought. But how about the bad news?

Paolo ensnared and enslaved me. There were no good times. There were just rushed meals standing up, greasy hair, greasy paws on the piano, leering drunks who put zilch in my whiskey glass. It was the P.I.T.S.

I asked Paolo for a raise, but he fobbed me off. He said we'd discuss it after the New Year. We wouldn't have the chance or the energy to have a Christmas party at the restaurant, said Paolo. We were going to have a New Year's party instead, and it would be at home, because New Year's Day was not a big deal here. It was just a holiday. I could invite anybody I wanted but I only knew Ben and Paolo's other partners, who were strictly his associates rather than mine.

I hadn't been here long enough but I was burning out. The fire was gone. Only ice was glowing blue in my heart.

Ben came to my pavilion three days before Christmas Day.

'Geez, this place is cooking!' His eyes gleamed like Burmese jade. 'Mazel tov! I got the A&R guy from RCA calling me back. They're hot for you.'

'Wow. I'm listening.'

'How much does he make per night?' He always referred to Paolo as 'he'. I said nothing, I shook my head absent-mindedly and shrugged.

'How much are you getting paid?' he asked me. 'I mean, I've seen the light! The size of his pad, and yours.' His eyes shot around the room like a wet kitten.

I told him the truth, 2,000 US dollars a month.

'No! No! No! Tell me it's not true!' He started shaking his head *adagio*, upped the pace to *moderato* and then to *presto*. 'You're getting ripped off!' He screamed like some train in a tunnel. And I believe he was gesticulating, too. *Agitato con brio*. 'It's not like you love what you're doing. You'd be better off selling used Mercedes Benzs to the Germans and Japanese. At least you'd be on a commission.'

I couldn't think what he meant. I was getting myself straightened out, right? How was I being ripped off?

'Think about it. You're the star. You're the nightly feature. None of that Chicago deep pan shtick compares to a real person performing real stuff. Without you, what is his joint? No, tell me *what* is his *joint*? Kaputz. It's just another fake Italian beestro relying on hicks and tourists who don't know where to spend their money. What does the alrightnik do all day? Add up his money, cos as you know, he's got way too much of the good stuff!'

I didn't like the way he said 'way', which was more like a horse whinnying.

'Hear what I'm saying, right. You're still young. Now is the time. Don't waste it patshkeing around in a factory. Cos that's what it is. You're never gonna skitter up another story being a hepcat. Ten years from now, are you gonna be sitting there on that stool sipping your jitterjuice and thinking, boy that was fun?'

'Whoa, whoa! Ben? Will you just cool it? I thought you enjoyed coming in and singing.'

'That's just for muggin' round. Was coming along for a ride — you were in the driver's seat.'

'A ride? But they're Jewish songs! From musicals! All the songs you and your ancestors write, sing and love! They're Broadway hits—'

'Whaddya kiddin' me? I look like a schmuck to you? Why do you think I left?'

'What should I do?'

'Mensch shall not live by pizza alone. You gonna need a lot more juice for your sound machine a.k.a career. You should milk as much liquid out of him as you can now, while you can — which you can. After that you may call it quits.'

'I thought the record companies put out the money for me to re-record?'

'Li-an. Listena me. Now this A&R guy from RCA who's hot for you. Dan Shapiro.'

'Yeah-yeah. Dan Shapiro,' I listened so hard my eyes bulged. I sensed there was to be more name-dropping to follow.

'He's a former sound man at CBGB, right? Now. He's a good guy. He really digs your shit. Problem is the guys he's working with. Former editor of *Bomp!* fanzine, Greg Chupowski? Anyway, he's not so keen on the electropop sound.'

'How do you mean?'

'Well, he's more a rock 'n' roller. You are too, how I say this, advanced for him? Too ahead of your time? I tell ya, the stuff you are doing is gonna be huge. It's totally new.'

'OK, how about this Dan Shapiro guy?'

'He's young, right? He's same as you and me, so he knows what's hip. He knows the scene. He's one of us, right? Not some fat old turd in a hat. He digs what we dig. No one will be messing round with the creative process. If we sign with RCA, we're really signing with him. He's on our side.'

'But?'

'But Greg is controlling the gelt belt. Artist and Repertoire agents cannot write contracts. What Dan can do, and is ready to do, is give you a letter of intent, or deal memo, which loosely states some terms, basically saying you will sign with the label once a contract has been agreed on.'

'When will that be?'

'Oh!' He gasped like he had been stabbed. 'Could be minutes. Could be years. Spooky thing is that this memo ain't just a harmless little piece of notepaper. Once you sign it you are under legal obligation to conclude a deal with the label, in this case RCA. If RCA gives you a contract that you don't want to sign, you're screwed. There are thousands of bands willing to sign the exact same contract, so the label is in a strong negotiating position. These letters never have any terms of expiration, so the band remain bound by the deal memo until a contract is signed, no matter how long that takes. You can't sign to another label and you can't release your own material if the agreement is terminated, which never happens.'

'Gosh, Ben, you know your shit. Thank you so much for—'

He waved the thanks away dismissively. 'Once you've signed the memo, you'll either eventually sign a contract that suits the label—'

'Or?'

'There is no or. You'll have to get a lawyer to get out of the agreement, and who's going to pay for that?'

'So we don't want to do that? We don't want to accept Dan's memo?'

'Not yet,' he said.

'What about other labels?'

'Li-an. RCA is as big a deal as you're gonna get. The bigger the advance the better the deal, because you may never be able to pay it back. Now the problem is we need to negotiate with Dan because he'd said he would need money to back us up. Then Greg, the ex-lowbrow rag schmeditor, will take you up and the risks are lower for him, since he is not so fizzy about pop.'

'Sounds way spish, Ben. Not sure I'm digging it.'

'Well, fine. Suit yourself. The record industry is full of hopes, dreams, deals, people like you. No way are we in a strong position. The most important thing for you, at this point, being actually not even in New York, is to get a deal memo for your songs to be released on RCA. Capeesh?'

'How much are we talking about?'

'Oh. About 30,000 US dollars? Not a lot, you understand. We should only accept Dan's memo when we've negotiated him down, to maybe twenty. Fifteen should do it. So let's just say 15,000 US dollars. To release a top hit, it would cost you at least a hundred thousand bucks. We just need enough to back up Dan because he believes in you. You will get it back, you know that, right?'

Didn't sound too convincing to me. I was done with picking Chicago's pockets and now somebody in some studio in New York was trying to pick mine. I sighed. 'Well, you don't know that, and I don't have that kind of money, Ben,' I despaired. 'Not even fifteen. Not when I was in Chicago; not as a piano player now. Are there no other labels? What about the independents? That's more my scale. Y'know?'

'Li-*an*! I told ya before. You don't have any following. It's not like you'd been playing in clubs in New York or even in Chicago or Timbuktu for that matter in the last five years. As you say, you're only a piano player in a pizza joint. Who's heard of you? Do you think the indies are gonna have the budget to promote you? You'd want a major label so you can have some security you know, get some good equipment, tour in a proper tour bus… Nothing fancy, just a little reward for all the hard work. Oh and, yours truly would love to be a manager.'

'You would?'

'I know all the right people. I wanna have my cut too! Sure, it's only 15 percent, but the bigger the deal, the bigger my cut.'

'What makes you think I'd want you to manage? We haven't even talked about the deal yet.'

'We have to talk about this now, there won't be another time. I helped you to record your demo, didn't I? Studio fees? How much do you think that cost? I didn't mind, because I know you're a gem, and it would be worth it. Neways, it's only money.' Ben's eyes looked sad. 'You're gonna be a big star. I don't want to be left behind while you're touring.'

I put my arms around him and he kissed me. 'I love you,' he whispered. He *what*? I groaned from the electromagnetism that spread out before me. I felt an unbearably strong connection with him and could hear his heart pounding. My head hurt from all this business of doing the business. One day I was drugging men, and now I was releasing my own music. A lot had happened in a month. Chic happens, as Dallas would have said with a shrug.

'Big break time,' said Ben, shaking his head like he was sorry to see me soar. He gently dabbed his eyes.

In some deepest recess in my heart, I wanted to find other labels, including the independents. But there was no way for me to do this.

Well, there was a library here but it was full of dusty leather books like the *History of the States of Malaya from 1880 to 1957*. I was relying on Ben totally. I really should go back to the States, if only to do my research and to taste the different A&R cheeses.

Christmas Day was our busiest day, preparing family lunches and all you can eat deals. Paolo was already out playing golf with his mates. Although he didn't have to explain himself, he did. He absolutely had to, he said, they were Eyetalyuns, capito. And he also never had a day off, unlike me, so Christmas Day he was playing golf and only for a couple hours. Much as he made me sick, I gave Paolo the elephant painting in the cardboard tube. It was like saying 'screw you'. After the New Year, I was out of this beat. I needed to chase up all those leads that Ben had given me. I'd really had enough of this quits-pits, now. Paolo was so delighted with the painting he got it framed and hung up in his study straightaway.

Ben came round to the pavilion on Boxing Day. I gave him an alarm clock, as he often said he could not wake up, thereby totally ignoring all Chinese tradition that you should never give a clock as a gift because it was a reminder that the recipient's days were ticking away. Ben was his usual adorably disorganized self, apologizing for not getting me anything big. 'Just a little something,' he said, 'open it.' I gasped, tears filling my eyes, when I opened the small box he'd given me. It was a bottle of Yves St Laurent's Opium, the most beautiful thing, and I'd never been given anything before, let alone something luxurious.

He said he would like to take me out to lunch anywhere I liked.

'Anywhere?' I said. 'How 'bout New York?'

'Don't think I've heard of that bar.'

'Ben. You know what I mean.' I looked at him, all serious.

'Yes,' he sighed, 'but not without the money. I got Dan Shapiro down to fifteen grand plus deal memo.' He pulled a smoke from his new pack and lit up.

'Pardon my ignorance, but don't record labels have tons of money?' I asked in all sincerity. 'Aren't they living in LA in 85-bedroom mansions?'

'Yeah. Hotels.'

'Ben, I don't get it.'

'Forget the indies. Look at all the records you can buy here on the shelves. Are they indies?'

'No.'

'Exactly. You're not going to get any distribution, promotion and marketing.'

He seemed to know the score, so who was I to protest? 'But where am I gonna get this money from?'

'Pimp-dog.'

'Paolo? No, jeez, I can't.'

'What? He used, chewed you up and spat you out. Don't be a schmuck. He makes fifty gees a night. He's not gonna notice. It's nothing to him.'

I stared at Ben. Sure, I could ask pimp-dog for a loan, but to steal from Paolo? I couldn't. That was one pocket I could not pick.

Ben read my mind. 'Beautiful, listen. If you asked for a loan from him, how are you going to explain getting on the first plane to New York? You can't get a loan from a bank because you make peanuts.' Me monkey. Me eat peanuts. Me wear brass button suit. And all for nothing.

I couldn't think through the concepts that Ben was putting in my head. True, I wouldn't get the Pope's blessing even if he gave me this so-called loan. Besides, Paolo might never see that money again. And he might like the look of me but he didn't love me.

Or did he? I didn't want to test the theory.

'Li-an, know what he said to me the second time I came round to the restaurant and sang with you?'

'What?'

'He asked me to get out of his restaurant, out of your life and his life. When I said "No", he said he found you first. I said you loved me, not him. He said you're his. First come. First served.'

That was slightly flattering and creepy, all at the same time. It was what I was afraid of, that Paolo loved me.

'Even said you asked for his help that night,' Ben added as a final sprinkle of moondust.

'Yeah, well, I was spun. I didn't need his help.'

'I couldn't bear hearing this shit. He asked me to leave and never show my face again.'

Ben allowed me a generous minute to think about what he said.

'How do I know all this is true? That Paolo said any of this?'

'Li-an. Firstly, because I love you, and you know that. And secondly, the name Dallas. Now how would I know about this shiksa if I didn't hear it from Paolo and how would Paolo know this very same name if you didn't mention it to him when you were drunk the night Reagan got in?'

'Wait, wait, wait,' I stopped him. 'Ben, why would he mention Dallas to you?'

'I said to him, you brought her here and she was miserable. He said, "I didn't bring her here. Dallas brought her here. Someone called Dallas asked her to Get Out of Town. She wanted to come with me!"' Ben pounded his chest, ha, as though Paolo would have done something like that. '"No, she didn't," I said. "I have to save her from you!" Then we had a… a somewhat childish fight — all for you, Beautiful!'

I pictured the bust-up. I pictured them shrugging, ripping collars and shoving like boys in a playground next to a graffitied wall. *I saved her. No you didn't, I saved her. No, I saved her. No, no, you didn't, I saved her.*

'What does he want from me?' I said.

'I think you know.'

'And you? What do you want from me, Ben?'

'For you to be happy and successful, in love and in music.' He held my hands and kissed me on the forehead like he was an esteemed sadhu, blessing me. I expected to be covered in holy colored ash. I didn't know where to look. I couldn't look at Ben, not after all he'd said. So I looked at my dukes, the key to my future and the culprits keeping me stuck entertaining punters at Johnny's.

'Convinced? No?' said Ben at last, exhaling a very long stream of Marlboro fumes. 'Do you or do you not—'

'Want to be a pop star?' I finished his six-million-dollar question. ''Course I do, Ben.' I looked at him with pleading eyes.

'I love you, Li-an.' He looked me straight in the eye. 'The alrightnik deserves no sympathy. He's got no heart and he wouldn't hesitate doing something nasty to you if he had to. After all, he blamed your journey here on Dallas.'

Dallas. I wished she could be here to make me laugh. I missed her, and right now would have done anything to be in cold, wet, windy Chicago, sitting behind a wire screen and touching her hand in MCC downtown.

'If you can't get the money, then I'll have to help you.'

'How?'

'Soup job.' He stubbed out and reached for another from the pack. 'Make it look like a burglary.'

'Whaddya mean, "it"?'

He rubbed his eyes with one hand, shaking his head slowly. 'We get into the safe and if there's not much in there, top up with stuff, like antiques.'

'We?'

'Yes, we. This is your music career. You're good at this. Think of it as going back on one more job.'

'That's not what I want. That's all behind me.'

'Just, listen. This party you mentioned.'

'The New Year's Eve Masquerade Party?'

'Perfecto. Everyone's in disguise, right?'

Given that I knew the combination, the safe would need to be blown up to make it look like a regular robbery and not an inside job. It wouldn't cause Paolo any grief if it was a regular robbery cos he'd get it all back on insurance and everybody'd be skippin'. Ben persuaded me this was good for everybody. I would have to distract Paolo for a few hours and stop him going back into the house. This was to enable Ben to bust the safe and scope the rest of the house for valuables. First, he told me, he had to fold a piece of cellophane into the space between the safe door and frame. Next he would knead a cup and funnel shape out of soap around the cellophane. Soap because it was malleable and would prevent the nitroglycerin from leaking out of the funnel. Once the soap was in place, the cellophane was removed, leaving a channel in the soap cup for the nitroglycerin to pass through. Then he would place the blasting cap and the wires connected to the battery igniter in the cup. Lastly, the 'soup' was poured in. About one ounce was enough to remove a safe door. The wires then had to connect to the battery terminals, which would set off the blasting cap. The blasting cap then ignited the 'soup'.

'OK, but Ben, how do you know what's valuable?' I asked. I imagined him in his own disguise: a Zorro mask, a striped tight T-shirt, a torch, carrying a sack full of strings of pearls and silver candlesticks just like a cartoon burglar.

'I can take random things someone might find valuable. You can case the joint and give me the tip-off.'

After meeting with Ben, I felt furious with Paolo, furious with myself for not seeing how much he'd used me, how powerless I'd made myself. Paolo was a snake all along. I wowed him with all those damned tunes that he loved. That busted me.

The feeling of despondency grew into rage. It was the morning of New Year's Eve. Paolo was out already doing some shopping for the night's party. I played the six-digit combination, the almost-tune of 'On Green Dolphin Street', and opened the safe. There was cash and a pile of documents. The sight of Ali Baba's cave quickened my pulse. I didn't count it, but there were so many bundles of cash I estimated probably 100 to 150 gees, easy. All the takings from the Christmas week not yet in the bank. Maybe a quarter mill? And I only needed fifteen to fuel my music career. Maybe another ten for my music video... I'd return it to Paolo as soon as I became an internationally successful artiste, if the insurance guys didn't pay him first. They were notoriously tight when handing payouts back to claimants.

I knew all along that Paolo had used the safe for his files and so on. After all, there were two shelves. I was surprised he didn't keep his vintage whiskey in there too. Hell, I didn't feel like or need a drink now, anyway. There were enough uppers here to keep my spirits high.

I looked through the documents. My heart raced. I kept looking over my shoulder in case Auntie was hovering like a ghost beyond the door. It irked me that I was worried she'd appear, so I locked the safe and took the entire stack of papers with me to the bathroom, concealed in the *Macao Post Daily* that Paolo had read and left on his desk.

In the bathroom I locked the doors and began some 'light' reading. I discovered that the restaurant was in my name, both the premises and the business. This house, the outhouses, the grounds, even the contents, the furniture and fittings, were all in my name. What else? What else? That was way more than enough to start with, but there were some share certificates. I wished I knew more, or could ask a lawyer to help me understand what was in front of me. Yet I saw my name so clearly on these documents.

My heart leaped and banged like a souped-up drum kit. But I wanted none of it. Ben and I were only after the cash. I needed to get back to New York for my recording deal. Fifteen grand meant a deal memo. QED. I never realized Paolo actually loved me. But he must — to have given me all this. The revelation was enough to make me feel quite faint and cold. My hands dripped with perspiration and I wiped them dry with toilet paper before handling the papers again. I put them back in the clever 'folder' made of Saturday's papers. I unlocked the bathroom door, replaced the documents where I'd found them and locked the safe.

With my newfound knowledge, I strode about the house like a *tai-tai*, a mistress. No longer was I an employee lodging in Paolo's mansion. I was a millionaire. Oh yes. How drunk I felt just then, how high and dizzy. Who'd have thought: from a delinquent to a duchess. 'Dallas, you won't believe what I'm going to tell you,' I said aloud.

The pool terrace and the main hall had been decorated with lanterns and fairy lights. As ambassador for the Chicago deep pan pizza, I was going to wear a fishnet body stocking over black underwear for my costume as Roxie Hart from the Chicago cabaret show, with matching satin eye mask. I got my outfit from a sleazy establishment on a back lane off Travessa da Dorna. 'With those pins, honey…' Paolo began to say, but didn't finish. He was very excited about my outfit, naturally, and he wanted to keep going on the same theme. He went as Billy Flynn, my 'lawyer'. Nothing could be further from the truth.

The pimp-dog looked the part in his white sharkskin suit and slicked-back hair. Actually, he already was Billy Flynn even before he got into costume. He was just going as himself. He had that old-fashioned look about him, a prohibition era mystery. He was in high spirits and singing to himself, or perhaps to me, at the top of his voice while he adjusted his tie about how he would be giving them the razzle-dazzle.

I kept my cool and my animosity to myself, giving away nothing. Before the party guests arrived, Paolo presented me with a gift. I felt extremely reticent to accept it, knowing well I was going to let in Ben in two hours. Paolo misread my expression and said it was not for Christmas since that was already old news. It was in a tiny carrier bag from Yaohan, a department store I knew didn't exist here. It was taped up at the top, but I didn't want to open it. I was a little confused. I launched him a look that said I hoped he wasn't doing it because he knew I was with Ben. 'What's it for?'

'Just a small thing. One of the partners just came back from Singapore and brought it with him. Aren't ya goin' to open it?'

I unpeeled the tape to avoid tearing the bag, an immigrant habit I had inherited from my mom who had grown up very poor. All packaging should be reused until it could not be. I folded the bag into its original shape before I even attended to the gift. 'No kidding,' I couldn't help crying out. It was a boxed Sony Walkman, with headphones in a metal arc. I opened the cardboard box and fitted the little round swimming-pool-blue sponges around the headphone pieces. I wore them straightaway, though I had not plugged it into the socket yet. I had never had any gift so cool before. The Walkman was only launched in Japan the year before and they were not cheap. 'It totally rules. Thank you,' I said.

After that the cat got my tongue. Two members of the male gender had given me gifts, which had never happened to me before. Sure, Dallas gave me everything else plus the odd smoke and glug of Southern Comfort. She sure ain't male. If she was male, I was a dancing raccoon. My father gave me nothing. Well, nothing except Sherylanne, who in turn gave me icy cold glares. I sighed and shook my head, not knowing what to say to him. An assful sense of guilt overwhelmed me, knowing the heist taking place tonight. He hugged me and I resisted him at first. When I remembered what Ben said, I softened. I reminded myself that he was only using me for his business. I needed him to suspect nothing. Were we not a pard-o-vit? After tonight, we would be on our way to the airport. Noo Yoik! Noo Yoik!

I was reeking of Halston Z-14. Ben's. That should be the warning for the betrayal to come, but Paolo was oblivious. He was a straight-talker. Subtleties like looks and smells were lost on him. If a Chihuahua bit his toe, he wouldn't know.

'Thank you,' I repeated. I hardened my heart slowly, but it wasn't easy. It was quicker to break ice than to freeze water. For a long time, perhaps more than a minute, we each were in our own world. Then I pulled away and sat down on a pool chaise longue. I started filling the Walkman with the two AA batteries. I felt so deprived of my American life that I didn't want to waste any time. I had to switch it on and put my headphones on, even for a minute. The wires got caught in my fishnet body stocking and I felt silly. I was a child again. A cheat. 'You haven't got a tape, have ya?'

'Oh no, that's not on the house.' He laughed his Billy Flynn laugh. 'I'll go find one.'

I went back to my pavilion, but I didn't really. I gave him that impression, but in fact I went to the safe as per the plan.

I opened the safe in Paolo's study in the basement. I knew the number by heart, and even in the dark I got it right — I heard the whirr of success. All the time I checked over my shoulder. My heart raced and I feared most of all Paolo discovering me in the act. Then I certainly would be on the plane tomorrow. From red-handed to empty-handed to handcuffed even.

I heard a sound from outside the room. It could be Auntie rustling around for a plastic bag. The interruption meant I did not peep into the safe. I didn't want to raise suspicion. I had already checked this morning. I could not remove the money myself that morning because there were too many hours between then and the party, and if Paolo had gone to the safe in those hours, he would have discovered the money was gone. It needed to be as late as possible, as in, during the so-called burglary. Also in the safe was my passport, which I had removed and kept under my pillow for quickness and ease of getting away.

I went back to the party that was about to begin. I slipped away two hours later, and slightly drunk, to open the gate to an entire busload of 18th-century Straits courtesans, a few Sir Francis Lights, Sir Stamford Raffles, Chinese triad mobsters, such as Kapitan this and Admiral that, a couple of Yul Brynners from *The King and I* with their Annas in crinolines, and a few Sultans. All with their own masks. In the last group, I imagined Ben, but of course I said nothing to him all night. I trusted him to do the job he was contracted to do.

1981

Rifle Range

At dawn, I awoke to the sound of a siren blare. What time was it? It was New Year's Day. My clock had been knocked off my bedside table. The roosters were crowing. I could hear the daybreak shriek of gulls. I remembered the party up to the point where the guests were still swarming. Was relieved to see I was in my own bed in the pavilion, alone. I thought, where was Ben?

Outside my window I saw the alternating flashes of blue light. I went outside and there were several guests still around. They had taken off their masks though, and other accessories if they had been wearing them, like hats, turbans and ties. It was like seeing them in the Universal Studios trailer park after shooting a scene. Except they were all looking horrified.

'Where were you?' said one of them, a Sir Stamford Raffles or maybe a random Jane Austen hero type. Hell, I didn't know a Raffles if I ever saw one. An ambulance was parked in the sweeping driveway.

'Uh... asleep?'

I looked down and found I was wearing a big old T-shirt over my fishnets.

Raffles had taken off his long-tailed coat, leaving just the frilly shirt and those knee-length boots. He had put his coat over a body on a stretcher. I strained my eyes to look at who the body was, but in the deepest chamber of my heart I knew it was Paolo. Call it a hunch.

Paolo was being loaded into the ambulance. 'What happened?' I said.

'No one knows,' said a Yul Brynner. 'Paolo's had an accident in the pool. He fell in.'

These were regulars at Johnny's. My heart was racing in desperation. I was gripped with fear and of course the terror of ignorance. What was actually happening? There was a sense of panic, a lot of weeping, voices I had not heard before.

'Oh man, I had no idea. Will he be OK?' I stammered. I was beginning to wake up fully but my head was throbbing.

'We don't know, but you'd better go with him to the hospital.'

'Well, I–'

I was thinking of Ben. What about this flight we were going to catch today? I had my bag all packed. I was to meet him at 9am, before anyone knew that I had escaped.

'Don't worry about your clothes,' Yul Brynner said, misunderstanding my look of despair. 'What's your name? OK, Li-an. Go and grab some jeans now. The ambulance will wait for you. Hurry.'

I was no one to these guests, regulars, whoever they were. They had seen me playing night after night yet they did not know who I was, what my name was. Yul Brynner talked to me like I was a child on an errand. Well, he was right not to trust me.

As Paolo was wheeled into ER at Hospital Conde São Januário, morning had arrived. The sun beat down on his forehead, and he looked reasonably calm, like he was asleep. There was blood on the crown of his head where he still imagined he had a lot of hair. It had dried now and been cleaned up by the paramedics. He must have hit his head on the pool edge or bottom. He must have been a lot drunker than I had ever seen him.

I felt worse by the minute, the combination of sleep shortage and alcoholic indulgences, no breakfast, no coffee, T-shirt over jeans over fishnet (which really should have been put over my head). I was in a mess and could hardly ask for a wheelchair. I found it an Everest task walking the length of the brightly lit corridors without wanting to keel over.

Suddenly a forest of orange row seats came into view and I collapsed onto the first one. A few minutes later someone handed me the obligatory polystyrene cup of brown liquid that was supposedly coffee, while Paolo disappeared through double doors. I waited until I fell asleep and the remaining brown liquid spilt onto my jeans…

When I opened my eyes, the waiting room clock said it was 10.23am. Ben! I had overslept. The plane! My flight! Oh God, I said, please God, no. My worst fear came into view: that Ben had taken the money and the plane that morning. He would already be on his way to the airport now, while my passport and packed bags lay safely like children in the pavilion. Why had I been so stupid? I couldn't believe what had just happened. I wanted to trust Ben to be still at the hotel waiting and I was not expecting to be duped. Not if he found all the money, which in my count was easily a quarter mill. Wait, I told myself, I had not been duped yet. Ben would be at the hotel waiting. Of course he would. He would have no idea what had happened to Paolo.

An Indian doctor, or maybe a surgeon, in green scrubs came out to see me, bearing a large brown envelope.

'Li-an?'

'Yes?'

He introduced himself. He had a strong Australian accent and it was slightly surreal. 'You're a friend or a reladeef?'

'A... an employee,' I decided I wasn't a friend since I was about to steal from him. 'I work for Paolo at the restaurant.'

'Right. He's not... He's in critical condition. We really need to speak to his reladeefs or family. Do you know where they are?'

'No.'

'He's got head injuries, which are minor. We've already treated them. What I am concerned with is the cause of the head injuries. He's been bitten by a snike on his left wrist—'

'A snake?'

'We've sent off his blood to the lab for testing. But we believe it's a *Bungarus candidus*, a Chinese krait. Nocturnal bites causing neurotoxic signs without local necrosis are typical of krait bites. Did anyone see?'

'I don't know.' I didn't understand most of what he said except for krait boites and did anyone see. He made it sound like some kind of crunchy TV snack.

I shook my head to say no, even though I had actually said I don't know. I thought of the guests and they all said they didn't see Paolo fall in until they discovered him floating on The Kissers.

'He's very lucky to be alive. He would have drowned if not for the inflatable pool object that he fell onto.'

Inflatable pool object sounded like a UFO, unidentified floating object. How romantic I had been to name it The Kissers, when in fact it was a life buoy for the pimp-dog.

'Now it doesn't matter. We've transferred him to the emergency unit. His breathing hasn't improved, and he's come in very late after the bite. Six hours. Much too late. He was conscious for about half an hour a few minutes ago—'

'Can I see him now?'

'No. He's very weak. He's on a mechanical ventilator because he can't breathe, his blood pressure is high at one eighty over a hundred, his pulse is a hundred and he is suffering ptosis in both eyes.'

'What dya mean?'

'His eyelid muscles are paralyzed, making them droop.'

Like, man! why didn't he just say: Eyelids. Droop.

'When he was still conscious, he responded to the questions. He said no one saw him have the bite or the fall. He went into his office to get a bottle of whiskey on the safe at about 9pm. He wasn't sure of the time. He felt a sharp scratch, which escalated to severe pain in his left side, and he thought he was having a heart attack. He staggered out and fell into the pool. They thought he had fallen onto the inflatable bed and was asleep.'

I nodded and clamped my lips. I'd have been one of those who thought he was asleep, because he was no party animal unless it was work. For his restaurant he could stay awake as long as it took. But for everything else, including me and my music, he had no patience and got easily bored.

'We've given him three vials of antivenom…'

I was beginning to panic. I was hyperventilating at that point. I just heard this Australian voice droning on, peppered with more medical terms. But what would happen to Paolo? The restaurant? The partners would just sell it, wouldn't they? Ben and I were in limbo now. Would we go back to the States, with the money from the safe? That sounded lame. I kept thinking that I could not leave Paolo here if he was so sick now. You did not leave a fellow immigrant who was in trouble. You were supposed to look out for each other. That was the unwritten code.

I couldn't believe what had happened to him. It could have happened to me too. It was supposed to be a straight heist. It was not thought through. There was no Plan B. Would they fly him back to the States for intensive rehabilitation? He still could die, couldn't he?

There were too many questions and I was sure the doctor (was it Dr Raj? I couldn't remember what he said) would not be interested in the details, just the patient's condition and the bills.

My hands froze. A familiar buzzing started in my fingertips. I really needed to get hold of Ben then and there, because he might still totally rip me off. What if he did? No, it was not possible, voices said to me, the Greek chorus of Li-an's head. I felt a sense that I was falling and falling and had not landed yet, like those dreams where you can't wake up. Paolo had had an accident. It seemed so incredible and coincidental that it was the night of our plan. I simply could not think what was happening to both of them. Dallas said I could think quickly. I was good like that. But I couldn't. I was at a complete loss. Possibly I was numb from shock. And my legs had lost sensation too. I was dragging them round like a couple of dead sharks. I had to trust Ben to come back to me, and that Paolo would be OK. What could have happened to the safe seemed too trivial now, like an ancient exotic folktale you once heard but could not relate to.

'What? I am sorry, I wasn't listening.'

'Yes, I understand this is all very distressing for you. There's a lot to take in.'

'What did you say?'

The last thing I heard him say was that I should call back at around 3pm. 'I said don't get your hopes up. He may or may not make it.'

There seemed to be too many may or may nots for my liking. 'You said three o'clock this afternoon?'

'Yes. As I said to you, he's under strict observation while we give him the antivenom management at the appropriate intervals. He is very sick now, Li-an, but he may get worse.'

'Can I go now? I just need to pop home to get a few things.'

'Yes, of course. You must be very tired. We will call you. What's the number?' He clicked a pen that he withdrew from his scrubs pocket. He scribbled it on his pad and repeated it to me.

I gave him the main phone number at the house. If I didn't answer it, Auntie would. I was hoping I would not even be there when he rang. I wanted to get back, pick up my things, get to Ben and tell him what had happened to Paolo.

I called a taxi from the hospital reception. Every minute waiting for the taxi, nursing the thought that Ben had Paolo's money and was himself on a plane, left one more nerve in me paralyzed. Every bead of sweat on my forehead was cold as a can of Coke.

When I got to Ben's hotel room, I didn't know if I should be relieved or utterly pissed.

'Where were you?' he said. 'What took you so long?'

'Oh Ben, thank God you're here.' I think I was gripping him like the claws of some demolition vehicle. Sweat was pouring through my hair like I'd been in a downpour. How could he not understand what I'd been through? 'Do you know what I've been through? I've been at the hospital all this time,' I gasped, crying with fear. 'Paolo could die. He was bitten by a snake, Ben, can you believe that?'

'Well, where's the dough, hon? Huh?'

'Whachamean? Don't you have it?'

Ben was quiet.

'What's wrong?' I asked.

He sighed. 'You know. I—'

'You're not telling me everything,' I shrieked. 'What's happened?'

'Not what has happened,' he said slowly. 'It's what happened.'

'Ben. What. Has. Happened. Tell me what is going on or I'll scream.'

'Li-an, I knew about the… those documents before. I knew he had given you everything. So I brought in the snake—'

'You brought in the snake?' Oh, OK. This news had better get better. 'Where did you get it from?'

'Chinatown, like everything else—'

I shook my head violently to lose the image of Ben in a San Ma Lo traditional Chinese medicine shop coiling a snake into a frilly basket like it's some kind of fancy pastry before casually sauntering off in the direction of the bus stop. It was as crazy as Ben was. I put my hands on my sweat-drenched temples.

'What are ya — nuts? You were supposed to just take the money from the safe, not kill him! It was supposed to be a soup job?' I reminded him. 'Quiet little boom? Inaudible in a party with music and people? And I was supposed to escape with you to New York? To get out of my contract with Paolo?'

'Geez, Li-an. There was nothing in the safe but those damn papers. Listen to me Li-an, Li-an, you're getting hysterical. I'm doing this for you. For us. For Chrissakes, I was on LSD. I sure didn't think he was going to make it. Paid 350 US dollars for that damn wriggler. Howzat for a gamble.'

'When — how did you know that he gave everything to me?'

'It was a conversation I overheard.'

'What?' I said, barely audibly. I felt dazed, not sure if I heard right. I thought only I knew, when I read the contents of the safe documents. It seemed he knew it too. 'When?'

'Weeks ago. Yeah. You were too busy on the piano. I was outside the restaurant window one night when the dog was having a conversation with his lawyer. They didn't see me. What was his name... um...'

'Oh, cut it out.' It was greed. Once he found out about my assets, he became dissatisfied with the cash in the safe. And now it seemed there was no cash in the safe. So not only had we got nothing, we'd got somebody very sick.

'Yeah. I swear, Li-an. I knew that you hated him.'

'Oh! Not that much!' I looked disgusted. 'Maybe not at all! I wouldn't kill him. I just want to leave this place and my contract quickly and with money.'

'Well, so do I, princess. You need to get down from your palace walls and see for yourself if you can earn this sort of money in a lifetime.'

'Why didn't you tell me all this before? That you knew about his will and that you were going to kill him?'

'You wouldn't agree to it.'

'You're right,' I whispered, shaking my head. 'I can't believe you did that. I would never — I would never have agreed! You... you... you tried to kill him! And for nothing.'

'Oh puhleez. So sue me.'

I just stared at him. On the one hand I was glad Ben hadn't run away, but I was perplexed. I swore all the cash was there when I looked two days ago. The only person who went into the study was Auntie, who cleaned it. But she would not know the combination.

'We got nothing out of it,' I yelled. I hammered my fists into his chest.

'Shut up,' he screamed, 'do you want the entire hotel to hear you? You sound insane.'

'You're the one who's insane,' I screamed. 'We gotta go find Auntie. She's the only one who goes into Paolo's study.'

He seemed to have read my mind. 'We got no proof! She's not capable of it and she would not have. What's her motive? Neways, she would have done it long ago if she wanted to.'

'Yes… yes,' I wasn't thinking straight. 'Fair point. I need a shower.'

'Go for it. We got nothing to rush for now. We ain't got a dime. And now the old man is in the krankenhaus.'

'Oh, geez.' I sighed as I grabbed a clean towel from his rail. I drenched myself in hot water for about forty years. I nearly fell asleep standing.

'Well,' he said, when I got out. 'Are you paying his medical bills? What's gonna happen?'

'It don't matter, honey. They'll still treat him whether or not the bills are paid. They can't and won't let him die!'

'Yeah, well, don't look at me like that. You gonna hang around till he buys it?'

'Ben, I'm still thinking about it.'

'Well, I'm outta here.'

'When?'

'Now. I'm finished with this place. I gotta buddy with an apartment in Harlem—'

'No! You can't leave.' He was calling my bluff. He had to be. If he loved me as he said he did, he'd stay. I couldn't let him leave me, after all this, for the same reason that I could not leave Paolo. What would I do without Ben? Just stay here and carry on? I was ready to start my life as a professional musician with Ben. When I first saw him, I felt a deep sense of belonging to him and I still felt it. I loved him for bringing music, love and the love of music back into my life. We connected on so many levels and not just recently. It was like I had met him before, many times over, from the '20s and beyond. We were related through music. We only needed to hear the opening riff of a song to remember where we each had been at the time. We had just started our discovery of the depth of our music obsession. I was doing it for Dallas as much as for me. There were too many reasons. And not enough dough.

'How? No gelt. Not a shine. You don't even have a plane ticket and I can't loan you 5,000 dollars for your trip. We're not going to get your record made.'

My heart sank as I thought of the glossy black piece of plastic 12 inches in diameter disappearing from view before my Warhol glasses. That was the plate I had been living for, that I would be eating out of, the circle of my life that the Chinese called 'the singing plate'. What would I do on this island now? I wanted the money to get to New York with Ben. How I was annoyed with myself for coming out here, yet without it, I would never have met Ben. But now things had changed. I could not leave. I was torn. Could the promise of a deal memo take priority over one very sick dog, boss, friend?

'I don't need five thousand for the trip. I've got two and a little more, about two hundred. Two thousand two US. I've been working, remember?' The two hundred was what was left of my cash allowance from Paolo when I first got here. 'Oh yeah? Where is it?' He bared his teeth like a monkey.

'In the bank,' I said quietly. 'Don't leave me,' I pleaded.

'Can you go and take out your money? Can you even do that? It's Thursday.'

'Yes, course.' I squeaked. 'But it's not open today. It's New Year's Day, remember?' My eyes were filling up with tears. I clenched my jaws. His dark eyes were dark. He was still my Ben. I wanted to put my arms around him. He edged away.

'I just — I just feel I wasted my time, all my time, all this time. We got nothing out of it. Nada. Zilch,' he mumbled.

'What about me?' I cried.

'What about you? You went to a party. Big deal.'

'What about this morning? I spent the last four hours in the hospital. You've been asleep all this time.'

'That ain't nothing to do with me.'

I gasped. 'You tried to kill him!' I shook my head and licked my lips. I was stating the obvious but he needed to hear it and truthfully I didn't know how to sugarcoat what he needed to hear. I needed to sleep. I left and slammed the door. I kept my fingers crossed. I did not want him to leave me and go back to New York. I know I said it to myself more than once, but that was because saying it helped me feel less scared and even convinced me to believe that he would never do that. Apart from anything, we had only good times. He was still my buddy. I had only pretty decent memories of our short time together. We had only each other now.

If he stuck with me, then it proved he loved me too. I was used to confrontations. Daddy and Mom were forever having 'bad patches'. They never patched over the patches. On the plus side, my fears that Ben cleared out the safe had been allayed. If he already got everything, we would not still be here. He would be thinking the same: if I had taken everything, we would not be here too. I would be on the plane to New York with him, ready to make my mark in the music world. Actually, there was no plus side. It was now a fantasy.

When I got back to the house, I did not go to sleep straightaway. It was almost noon. I picked up my Les Paul but only dud chords came to me. Schmaltzy singalong major-minor yuck chords. I lost my groove long ago. Paolo was not going to be home for a long time. I could not help going back to the safe just to make sure that Ben wasn't an idiot and didn't make a mistake. What a freaking joke it would be if everything was still in there! I doubted it. Somehow.

I staggered up the stairs, out the door and to my pavilion. If I didn't collapse in my own bed, I sure would collapse right here in the marble-lined hall. The chandeliers dazzled my eyes even though they were not switched on. The cut crystals caught the sunlight and I could not bear looking at anything a second longer. The white light was the last thing I saw.

When I awoke, it was night. I was back in my bed. For a dreaded moment I thought I was in the yellow mock-Versailles room with Paolo attending to me and emptying my handbag, using its torn lining as a tissue to wipe his nose. But no. Today's most dreaded person was in front of me. Auntie. 'Oh goo,' she grunted in her husky voice from smoking all those packs of Double Happiness, 'I thor you weck up now. I bring soup. You drink.'

Before I could protest, she had already lifted my head and inserted the rim of the blue Chinese porcelain soup spoon into my mouth.

'What happened to me, Auntie?'

'You faint in hall. You sick. They already call about the Lo-ban.'

老闆 Lo-ban was boss, and that was Paolo. 'What did they say?' I asked, assuming that 'they' was the hospital.

'They say no good. He not weck up.'

'Oh,' I uttered. I sipped some more soup. It was strong, tasting of ginseng and another terribly bitter herb, which was more like the crusts from engine oil than an herb. I also swallowed some goji berries. The fact that she was here made me think she did not take the money during the hour between my opening the safe and Ben appearing at the safe. If she had taken everything, she would not be here right now. Why would she work again her 14-hour days if she was already rich with Paolo's cash? She seemed to have read my thoughts. 'Last night, have burglary. They cut through safe. I make report. Now police must take statement from him when he come back.' She nodded sagely, because we knew no one gave a damn here about reporting anything — the government and the cops were more bent than the crooks.

I already knew that if Paolo did not ever wake up, then I would inherit everything, the property, the business, the robbed cash (albeit via insurance payout), even Auntie and Thaew the driver. I would be able to produce my album and live quite well. 'Course, thinking about it again made me sick with fear. I knew that I knew nothing and problem was everybody knew that too.

'Drink!' instructed Auntie.

My breathing quickened. The diesel ginseng root stench of the soup dug into my nostrils.

I finished it directly from the bowl. Auntie took it away on the tray.

I looked at the Sony Walkman and felt like a brat who had tired of Christmases. The gift had lost its excitement and I needed another gift to open. Knowing that he loved me made me even sadder. I held the Walkman without being able to look at it, and tears came to my eyes. Was sorry the same as love? Or a kind of love. Yes. A sickness. Why else would a man give a woman something, everything? Why else would I hold an empty Walkman and weep, with no tape playing.

I also froze at what Ben would think about Paolo being in love with me, that Paolo loved me. Someone did. That was enough for me, and I was prepared to take my winnings and move on.

It was an unpleasant thought. Well, for Ben at least.

At 3pm, I crawled from my bed and tiptoed into the hall to use the phone. I lowered my voice in case Auntie could hear me from the kitchen where I could hear her washing up my bowl. Dr Raj said that Paolo was in the ICU, in a coma. He thought that because of the delay in getting Paolo to the hospital, the prognosis was poor. Two hours before, Paolo was already stuporous. What did that mean? The man was hatesome. Could he not speak regular?

'Paolo showed no response to stimuli, his pupils were fixed and dilated at five mill and he had full ptosis.'

I had to think back what that word meant again.

'His eyelids are fully drooping,' he said, sensing my silence as ignorance. The Paolo I knew rarely sat in his chair for more than ten minutes. He moved with haste and efficiency in the house and in the restaurant. Even when he sat, I could see his mind pulsing with ideas and thoughts, his fingers twitching with the excitement of a new discovery. He constantly worked, for thinking was equivalent to working. He never listened to a record to the end. It was hard to imagine him now lying down, his darkened brain only flickering slivers of light, his body cold, stationary and his eyelids hooded as a serpent.

'There's a very slim chance that he'll make it,' said Dr Raj, 'but don't hold your breath.' They were doing their best, they could not guarantee anything, our doctors are the best on the island, and all the other clichés they must be reeling off every minute there was a tragedy in the hospital.

'God bless America!' I think was what Ben said later, when I repeated the doctor's remark to him: it would take a miracle for Paolo to survive such a snake bite. It would only be another couple of days, that was what the doctor said. That meant that Ben's plan had worked. It seemed morbid and wrong, as though he had already gone. Yet again, tears started to form but I blinked them away. I didn't wish this on Paolo.

That night I did not feel like celebrating, something in me went cold. But at Ben's insistence we were out. Cheer up, he said to me. Amazing what you could put yourself through with a brave face, tears dusted away with your Cover Girl powder compact. It was still New Year's Day, and what a long day it had been. First we went to the Stardust Casino, then Circus Circus, then the Ruby Luck Luck and a couple of dives in the Inner Harbor area where tattoo-less souls would not get in. Luckily, we were subversive types who met the entry requirements. We turned onto Rua de Felicidade, a dying red-light district. Neon was reflected on the carved red lacquer turn-of-the-century facades, and split bamboo sun blinds filtered electric light and noise of merriment inside. I wore my sequined beret with the cute little black and white hat ribbon trims cut with V notches. We walked hand in hand in light and easy steps like children, yet my heart felt heavy as an anchor. Tinny Chinese radio jazz from the 1930s floated over the roar of laughter and a slap bass funky beat from a basement somewhere. The streets were more alive than we were, I thought. We bought a deck of Luckies each. We passed more shops selling dried salted fish, kiosks vending Macanese biscuits and open brazier barbecue stalls cooking squares of beef and pork.

We came across a hole-in-the-wall barber shop. As if it wasn't cramped enough, there was still enough room for a Chinese fortune-teller's child-sized desk, over which he hunched like a parrot. Ben demurred when I urged him to go in. I went in and sat down on the child-sized stool and bravely held out my palms. I looked back at Ben, who chose to stay outside. He leaned against one of those red lacquer carved columns as though he himself was a puffing dragon.

'Put them away, I read faces and cards only,' said the man, who wore a black satin skullcap, in Cantonese. 'Happy New Year! I see a man who loves you. Very lucky... I see illness. Possibly death. I see flight. Lots of money...'

We got into the Sol bar and managed to scribble out on the backs of receipts some sketchy ideas for new songs we'd record at the studio the moment we could. In the back of our minds, sure, we knew that Paolo hadn't actually bagged it yet, but the consultant gave me a strong impression that that was the case. I restrained myself. I needed all my strength and to be totally well the next day. This waiting around in limbo was hatesome. Also, me knowing that the money indeed was missing and that Paolo had been robbed not by me, Ben or Auntie, but someone else. It created a deep-throated stress for me all evening. There were many unknowns — the robber's identity and Paolo's survival.

From Auntie, I learned that the place had been crawling with pigs as soon as she'd reported it, all that time I was in hospital with Paolo. Fingerprinting, interviewing, recording. They got the guest list and investigated them all. They were tracking every move, every bank account. Ironically, I was glad they checked my bank account. Naturally I had not been the recipient of large sums. Our alibis were good to go. I was at the party and it was confirmed by more than one guest, and Ben was not even invited. He did not exist.

I got to the bank the next day, a Friday. Ben frog-marched me and made me withdraw eleven hundred dollars, which he insisted he really needed for some sound equipment failure. Now I had no idea what it cost, but presumably a lot because this was a small place and it was likely to get repaired in Hong Kong, so there were the transport charges and so on. Still, it seemed a lot. Ben said he had not been paid and he would get it back to me by the end of the week, which was the following Friday. It did not seem that bad and I did not want to quarrel about money the way my parents did every night. I did not want to turn into my mom or my dad. I told myself that I was not them, and if Ben said he would give it back, he would give it back.

Saturday night. January 3. I had been avoiding the restaurant. I had no idea if it was to be opened or not, or if the staff were turning up. I asked Thaew to drive to the restaurant and gave him a roll of Scotch Tape to hang on to. I opened up just one shutter and went inside the dark interior. I hoped to call the chefs. They were the engines behind the pizza-making but they only spoke Italian. I had to communicate with them quickly. I found their phone numbers in a notebook behind the cash desk. I tore a sheet from it and scrawled a messy note, 'Shut Until Monday January 5 1981.' As an afterthought, I wrote 'Happy New Year to all our customers' in the space that was left on the piece of paper and taped the note to the door. I didn't want to be there on Monday, but I had to be back. I felt responsible for the opening hours even if Paolo never walked through its doors again.

Two days passed and Paolo was not dead yet. I never went to see him all weekend, but I waited patiently for news. The hospital finally rang on Sunday morning and said he had remained on a mechanical ventilator since my last phone conversation with Dr Raj. Paolo was still in critical condition. 'You mean he's alive?' I asked.

'Yes, you won't believe what we've been through. He's alive.'

Dr Raj asked if I was ever thinking of coming back to see Paolo. It was more like an exclamation. He sounded peeved, like a schoolteacher demanding me to claim my report card. Of course I cared. I needed to know what would happen to Paolo in due time because since Ben's crazy scheme, I had been in nowheresville. What had been a stable and unpleasant situation before had now become simply unpleasant.

I went back to the hospital later that day to see Dr Raj and get the full story. After all, what had I to do? Ben was AWOL. He was not calling me back now that he had my eleven hundred. I reluctantly agreed I would see Dr Raj at about 2pm, which gave me enough time to have lunch prepared by Auntie and drag my mortal self to the Hospital Conde São Januário.

Dr Raj said that 30 hours after the bite, which was early on Friday morning, Paolo was responding to verbal commands and his motor power was Grade 1. He had hypotonia, weaknesses in his neck, jaw and respiratory muscles, numbness in all extremities.

They kept administering more antivenom, and after 32 vials his motor power improved to Grade 4. His eyelids opened two days after the bite but his speech was slurred. Dr Raj would not wean Paolo off the mechanical ventilator yet because he was suffering respiratory paralysis.

'Now, I wanted to discuss with you the medical bills.' Uh oh. I knew he was coming to this sooner or later. Man!

'Do you know that the antivenom treatment costs 1,800 US dollars a vial? This is very expensive treatment. Paolo is an important man, we cannot do this for just anyone who comes through these doors.'

'You only save rich guys' lives?'

Dr Raj didn't answer. 'People who can and will pay. Some village boy whose parents have only 10 dollars would not even come here. They know there is no hope. Sadly, this is the way, not being crude. I have not seen Paolo's insurance documents. That is why I got you to sign the document when he was first admitted. Do you remember?'

'Vaguely.'

'His hospitalization in ICU alone costs 1,300 US dollars a night. This is not accounting for the consultants' fees.'

'You can't stop treating him. Don't worry about… the bills. But can I see them?'

'We can't stop treating him. Correct. This is a top hospital, Li-an. This is not a sprained ankle he's suffering. Are we not keeping him alive?'

Aloive. A noight. Accanding fah the cansultans' face. I paused to take in what he said. It was true, were they not keeping him alive? At this point, I was confused. I could not imagine what size of bill they were talking about. This wasn't a new turntable or new boots. This was going to be in figures I had never seen or understood — well, not from my previous line of work, anyway. 'Um, OK. Let's have a look at the bill.'

'Come into the cashier's office. I believe the accountant has printed off an invoice for breaking down the costs.'

I sighed.

'You'd better believe it,' he said.

Summary of Patient Services:
Pharmacy 54,341.25

Laboratory Services 13,286.00
Intermediate Care Room 13,343.00
Intensive Care Room 9,882.00
Emergency Care Services 4,386.00
Therapy Services 1,875.00
Radiology 858.00
Special Services 328.00
Total charges: MOP$ 98,299.25

'You might like to check it,' said Dr Raj. He grabbed a calculator from the accountant's desk and punched in some figures. He showed me the digital display of the equivalent in US dollars. It was USD$ 14,757.

'What am I checking?' I said, like how would I know what I was checking and it most definitely ain't math. The machine had added it up. I'd like to check if the decimal point was in the wrong place or if I had fainted yet. I noticed that he didn't answer. He just looked at me. I looked back down at the sheet. What were special services? I wondered. Didn't matter, it was the smallest amount. Probably the use of towels at the rate of MOP$90 a towel or something crazy like that. I didn't quite have a heart attack but my world closed in and I had to sit down. Bang! Bang! 98,000 potatoes. Would the restaurant pay? How could I pay? Where were Paolo's insurance documents? Did he even have health insurance? Even if he did, I would have to pay first and claim later. I didn't know how to do any of this. The most paperwork I had ever done was after I'd cuffed a car back in '73 and had to fill out something for its new false rego in a Vermont junkyard where a sleaze and his dog watched every inch of me with bloodshot eyes. I believed one of them had a paw on my ass before I jumped in and floored the gas.

There was no gas to floor now. I was trapped in a corner where I had to pay the bill. Not a good gamble from 350 US dollars' worth of cold reptilian blood, Ben. If I could put my ivory-tickling Herculean flippers and real nails on his neck right now, I'd wring it.

Before I could say 'beef pepperoni sausage', I was back at work from Tuesday, January 6th as instructed by my own pretty cool scrawled note. I had managed not only to call the chefs since the incident, but to spit the three most important words in Italian and it ain't I

Love You, but close. It was domani lavoro, OK? (Tomorrow, I work, OK?). It was really important that I got some Italian up to scratch because work was the only way I could earn the money for Paolo's bills, until he came out dead or alive. And earning is the only way you earn, geddit? Dallas used to say. Before you earn, learn, and after you learn, earn. That was one of my mom's wisdomisms. Did anyone even understand it? It was total B.S., just like they said poor Paolo would not make it, then would, then would not, and now he was both dead and alive, a brain-dead zombie with fried lungs.

Every night after that, the place sank to a low without Paolo. Regulars came in asking for him. The whole vibe had gone. He was the soul of the party. They did not come to see me — I who had banged out choon after choon every night, singing 'til I was hoarse about trips to the moon on gossamer wings. Did they come for the pie-dust then, or did they come for Paolo? There was just a big empty moon crater that he'd left. But I'd better get used to it, since he might never be back and now the whole damn establishment was in my name.

Ben… no sign of him. He literally wrestled the wad from my flippers with his sweaty palms and disappeared. Had he gone to Hong Kong to sort out this equipment problem? Or somewhere else? I called the Green Parrot, and he was not DJing there but maybe in Hong Kong which he sometimes did. They knew as much as I did. In fact, they didn't need him for the time being. They'd got a live soul band in. It was really drawing in the crowds.

That did it. I was fuming. He never mentioned this. I stopped calling. He was not returning my calls and I'd already left so many messages at the Bela Vista they must be sick of me. To take my mind off it, I spent every morning combing the entire estate looking for the money robbed from the safe. I went through the house, the pavilions, the outhouses, the stables, the gardens. I could not get access to Auntie's quarters until I got her to run an errand, but there was nothing in her cupboard except what she came with as a young girl. It was quite sad, some old photos, a jade bangle, an ivory comb, some letters I could not read as they were in Chinese, and a sandalwood fan.

The money was obviously not around anymore, quite likely as far away from me as I could imagine. The robber had fled. I don't know why I thought it was still in the vicinity. It was a feeling that I followed. I just thought I could still smell it nearby. Possibly because of what the fortune teller said.

I spent every lunchtime at the hospital during the stipulated visiting hours. I needed to make sure for myself what was happening to Paolo in this weirded-out space between death and life. I needed to know what to do with his shit that he left to me, with Ben, and all that. It was too much. I couldn't think straight, let alone sing and play musical-sounding harmonious notes in sequence. My brain was pizza. Splat.

At lunchtime, I was reading the *Macao Post Daily* aloud to Paolo. Seemed like a peaceful respite for both of us. After that I got back to the restaurant for the repetitive and gargantuan task of being on the phone. There were orders to be made, basil, parsley, rocket, Chiantis, Valpolicellas, Proseccos, arborio vialone rice (there were always two risotto dishes for the bored and/or fussy diners or for those who came to a pizza restaurant to not eat pizza), sea bass, veal, pepperoni, salami, tuna, Parma ham, radicchio, it was ceaseless. It was a shopping list for 75 people, not a family of four. God, how much did all these people consume? There was only an hour left by the time I had finished paying bills and placing orders and receiving deliveries. I was using the takings to pay the medical bills and the creditors. We owed so much to so many. I had to duck home, change into a swan, come back and start croaking without a care in the world the songs of Paolo's youth.

How my knowledge of Italian had flowered, from adagio, allegro and pianissimo to ristretto, macchiato and prontissimo! If I could not go to the Mediterranean, then it must come to me. It was almost enjoyable, except that the fine line had been crossed and it was not enjoyable. The irony was that Paolo was in darkness and I was in all-seeing fluorescent strip lighting. I was up to my ocular spheres in work, his work… for no one cared about his business but me. The partners and their wives did not come back at all. I didn't need them. Once they put money into Paolo, now they had forgotten about him. Was he not punished enough? The robbery achieved nothing. I had to keep him alive as well as my dreams of making music. Ambition looked me in the eye. It danced before me and teased me before it disappeared to torment other souls. If anyone cared to believe it, I would call myself a feminist.

After the guests left, I had to total up the evening's takings, so I sat there with my glass of obligatory white splasher and Paolo's accounting Casio calculator, working out every last pataca until the stalks of my eyes very nearly touched the white tablecloth and the last employee had dumped his black apron in the laundry bin. I said good night. They assumed that I was in charge from now, and I assumed the same. Everything happened so suddenly and on the square, I did not even know how to shut the place for two weeks while Paolo got his brain and body back. But then that was a long shot, so it seemed crazier and easier to keep going the only way I knew how. Endlessly.

The week vaporized. I thought little or nothing of Ben. I cursed him for a second before I went to bed each night, like some kind of prayer. I was exhausted and collapsed into sleep at half-past two in the morning, cupped by the benevolence of darkness. Paolo was a zombie. He'd turned me into one too. Must be contagious. I thought to myself: I don't think I've ever worked so hard in my life. Correction: I don't think I've ever worked in my life. On Fridays in the late afternoon, everyone had to be paid. So there was that to go through, clock cards and overtimes and so on.

The Macao Policia found nada. No one's account got fat and no one was buying property or a one-way ticket to Rio. No one was arrested, so someone must have been paid off. That was usually how things were solved here. Drove me insane thinking where and when the money in the safe went AWOL. I replayed the events of New Year's Eve minute by minute and could not forgive myself for not checking a second time that it was still there in the safe.

One night, a shadow appeared like the Grim Reaper on my pristine mandatory white-clothed table where I now lived. It was a Tuesday night, January 13. I looked up and it was Trouble. My heart liquefied. Ben. He kept his word and it was all that mattered. His shirt was ripped but hurriedly sewn up. He had a shiner and what looked like blood crusts on his nostrils. His eye was red as a traffic light. 'What happened to you?' I jumped up and threw my arms around his neck. Hell, he stank of sweat and for some reason diesel, as though he had traveled for miles and miles, but I liked sweat and diesel. I covered him in kisses. 'Who did this to you?' I said.

He simply shook his head sadly. He had lost weight and looked ill. I would have forgiven him even if he didn't have the money that he owed me. It seemed like a bazillion years ago when we went out hand in hand to the Docks, me in my black sequined beret. Now I had no makeup, and my hair was as unwashed as cash tied up in an odd-sized bundle.

'I am so sorry,' he said, 'here's your money. Sorry I made you take it out. Thank you. You saved me. Everything is OK now.'

I was glad that I trusted him to return the money and he did. I quickly put it back under the cash desk where I would retrieve it later and put it in my purse since it was my personal fat that he squeezed, not Paolo's or the restaurant's. My ignorance seemed to have ripened. That much of business I knew now.

'What is OK? The DJ equipment you got repaired? Did you get in a fight?' I spoke in a hurry, like I knew time was short.

He shook his head. He was so fatigued he could not speak. I got him a glass of San Pellegrino water. 'Sit down,' I said. 'Get you something to eat? I just need to do the wages first.'

He sat down without answering any of the questions. Once he had his special pepperoni, which I knew was his favorite, we started talking. I wanted some time with him before the evening guests arrived. I told Ben that I could not believe that Paolo was doing all this before. [Note: He didn't have to sing and play the piano and juggle. My hands were fuller than his, to be fair to me.] After a week, I knew I didn't want to play or sing a single note again. I could not do all this. In fact, I told him this when I went to the hospital on Saturday, whether or not he could hear me.

Ben was not really listening, I could tell.

'The truth is… what happened was…'

'Just say it. Don't try to make it sound nice.'

'OK, I won't. I owe money to these assholes. I got into a gambling debt pretty quickly about three months back. I really got into it. It was anything. Blackjack, baccarat, roulette. I just kept going, thinking I was going to make it big.'

'Why? Ben? Why did you do that?'

'Because I really, really, really, really love it.'

I shook my head. I couldn't find anything to say for a minute. My daddy loved his bottle and nothing could come between them.

'So how much is it?' I said.

'We… we're talking close… nearly… eighty thousand patacas,' he whispered.

I gasped inaudibly. Oh Jesus! I divided it quickly in my mind. It was 12,000 Uncle Sams. I wasn't the only one in trouble now.

'And I can't pay it back except by gambling more and paying a thousand at a time. They come and bang me out every now and then.'

I looked at the kitchen clock through the swing doors. 'I gotta go, Ben. I have to go back, have a shower, get changed and make myself beautiful. I'm still working, remember?'

'You are so beautiful. You don't need to do a thing to yourself.' He stroked my cheek. We kissed a long time and I felt that ripple of current again. When we finally stopped, I rolled my eyes. 'Come with me. I need to tell you what's happened.' He followed like a puppy dog and rode pillion on Paolo's Vespa. 'It sure feels good to be back, Li-an. I love you.' He was almost in tears and so was I. I'd been in agony for a week. Every inch of me hurt. My head was throbbing as I put on my helmet. When we got back to my pavilion, we wept and we made love. It felt like we had known each other a long time, yes, since the 1920s, since Prohibition, wartime, postwar, the Sixties and now. How else did he know all the songs that I knew? We met before, I was convinced. We had lived many lives together before this and destiny brought us together again. I was crazy to be crazy about him. But I missed him big time and I missed his voice, his smell, his Greenwich Market reject shmutters, everything about him. He was chocolate to the chocoholic. I popped to the kitchen and asked Auntie to fix us a ginseng tea each. We really needed it. She pursed her lips and would not look at me. It must be because I brought Ben back to the Lo-ban's house but she could not say this much. The Cantonese were more loyal than a pet German shepherd.

I had a shower and told Ben over steaming hot tea everything that had happened — the treatment, the planetary medical bills, the galactic amount of work I'd been doing at the restaurant, the black hole of the missing money, which still had to be recovered.

It all seemed like a fantasy, yet it was real. 'Tell me, you didn't want the money originally for your debt. Tell me, it was for recording my album in New York.'

'Of course, Li-an. I would never lie to you. That was your money. You earned it. I have my own problems, but they are mine, nothing to do with you.'

We embraced.

'Ben. You need to pay them back somehow.'

'Think I don't know that? They'd kill me,' he said. 'They know where I am, who I am. When I went to Singapore on that trip, I made a lot of money. I was helping a dude move gold out of Macao.'

'You smuggled it? Where were you this week?'

'Hong Kong. I never lied to you. I was carrying the DJ equipment.'

'But that's not all, Ben. You never tell me everything. Inside the DJ equipment?'

'Opium. Pure Chinese white. On its way to the west.'

'Ben. You're so bad news it ain't funny.'

He sounded so proud of his activities that I began to fear for his safety. He was getting sure of himself. That came before a fall, I wrote once in a song. We only laughed cos we walked tall.

'You're going to work with me this week. I need your help myself. I am up to my eyeballs. Can you tell me that you'll work with me in the restaurant?'

'What? Why would I do that?!'

'Is DJing enough? I can't... just give you the money right now. I need it too.' He looked like he was saying 'great, I'll do it' but pulled himself together with a brave face. There was a brief moment when he was working out what I was thinking and I was working out what he was thinking. He only slightly demurred because he was feeling rough. I wanted him to help me out because I wanted to see him and the only way I could see him was if he was in the restaurant since it was where I spent all my waking hours. By agreeing, I knew he wanted to be with me too. He didn't look too bad after I cleaned him up. We sighed simultaneously.

'Li-an, you're paying his bills. Why? Why don't you just leave and go back home?'

I hesitated. What Auntie first said came back to me. Macao was a place you couldn't leave. 'It's not a done thing.'

'What's not done?'

'I've got nothing, remember? There was nothing in the safe. All I have is Paolo's house and garden and he's not dead. How could I go back to New York for my recording deal?'

'You got the demo tape.'

'Ben. I did not come here to make a demo tape. I could have made one back in Chicago. I came here to stop living the life I was living and to make something of myself here. I've done nothing but got some guy in hospital. And he's coming out of hospital cos every day he's there costs us a grand easy. Fangs for that.'

He winced at the word 'us', acting all innocent and goody-goody. 'So what are you going to do?'

'He's not getting any therapy. No more treatment. He's going to vegetate at home until I get this place hopping again. The partners may not even find out about it. Auntie and I will look after him.'

Ben stared at me as if I said I was going to the moon and back with my pet giraffe.

'Look!' I despaired. 'I've got expenses, right? Who's paying for all this?'

Just retelling Ben the short, short story of it made my blood boil. Both these guys had me trapped here. I could not leave because of their debts, which were in effect mine. Now I totally got what they mean when they say 'all ribbed up'. I did not want to stay here but I had to. Everything that I longed to achieve was lost. I was slaving at the hot stove of Paolo's life while my music career went on the back burner. Now I was ordering onions, not sound engineers.

I made the call and sold the grand piano to pay the hospital bill. He wouldn't mind, wouldn't miss it. I couldn't play it anymore. From the sale I got 110,000 patacas and the bill was 98, so there was 12 spare, which got swallowed up straightaway in running the joint. I was wrecked as an amateur restaurateur. What ugly words. Blame. The. Romans. The pizzas and the Latin languages of love and crappola.

Two days later, I got Thaew to drive us to São Januário and we picked up Paolo and his things. I signed another goddamned piece of paper saying that I was discharging the patient out of hospital against medical advice. Dr Raj shook his head, course he would, ouch. He sighed and said that now Paolo was off the mechanical ventilator, he could not speak.

'Paolo has flaccid dysarthria. It's a complication from the venom.' He waved his hand as he knew I didn't want to hear any more detail than necessary. I looked like hell. My eye bags were spacious enough to store travel accessories. My perm had gone from Kabuki to kamikaze. I had nuff stuff to tackle of my own.

'As I told you, he has hypotonia, his speech is slurred, low volume, low pitch and intensity, his breathing thoracic-clavicular, which is to say he has very short breaths, his tongue movements and mouth opening restricted. Li-an, he can't speak. When he can, he has gaps of involuntary silence in his conversation. He should really go to the Speech and Hearing Unit at the Otolaryngology Department.'

'Well, I'll consider it. How long does he does he need this… this therapy?'

'An hour for three months at the minimum. Daily.'

'Like I say, I'll think about it.' I looked at my watch. 'He has the best care at home from his *amah-cheh* who has looked after him and his family for about four hundred years,' I said.

'She's not a clinical specialist.'

'No, but look at him. He's stick thin after staying here—'

'He can't feed, Li-an.'

'No. She'll take care of him and he will be fine soon,' I rattled off, just to get out of the place. I beckoned to Thaew.

I knew stopping Paolo's treatment was risky. But the more guilt one felt, the less shame. Paolo slumped into his wheelchair, which, incidentally, I also had to buy at some grand price. His drooping eyelids lifted slightly. Even that little action exhausted him completely. His hand was still very distended from the bite, stretching his skin like a red balloon and making it look like he was wearing a rubber glove. It seemed pitiful rather than comical that he was wearing the Billy Flynn party clothes that he came here in, having returned the gown to the hospital. Seeing his impairment brought out a guilty sadness in me I didn't know existed. I wiped my tears away absent-mindedly but more kept coming. Had I not suffered and laughed at myself? But only out of bitterness and desperation.

Thaew took the wheelchair handles and pushed Paolo out to the car park where he would be transferred into the Benz and then to his bedroom, which Auntie had prepared for the new captive. Paolo was now dependent on me, totally, yet I did not know who was imprisoning who.

'How long we keep him here like this? How long?' demanded Auntie.

'Until we've got enough money to pay for more treatment. So not long.' I had been telling the doctor and Auntie this not to convince them but to assure them and myself that it was true.

'He's got neurological damage, Auntie. He's better off at home.' I pursed my lips.

I watched her blank over the big word, unable to decipher its meaning. It was Auntie who was reassuring me, not the other way round. 'Is fine, sneck bite not new thing, he will get better at home. I know use what herbs.' I'd misunderstood her vacant stare. She was actually considering the plan of rehabilitation. Having handed Paolo to Auntie and wiped my hands clean from the greasy handles on the wheelchair, I went back to my pavilion, where Ben was waiting for me.

'Ben, I have to see Paolo's lawyer. Remember that guy you overheard outside the restaurant? His name is Alex Richardson.'

'And?'

I had arranged to see Alex on Wednesday, January 28. I needed him to get hold of the accountant as the corporate accounts deadline was looming. That was the only date available. Business here was still done on auspicious dates as the Chinese were naturally superstitious. Chinese New Year was on February 4 on the Western calendar which meant that meetings needed to be conducted on any dates with an

8 in it to counterbalance the unlucky number 4. The Chinese word for death was the homophone of the number 4. It was a crazy time. All accounts had to be cleared by Chinese New Year. Year of the Golden Rooster. The metal rooster year was supposed to be a proud and ambitious year. The Chinese superstition was that it was bad luck to share bad news, so I'd told Alex that Paolo had had a little 'accident', but was fine, he fell in the pool, but he was going home already and he said he would send flowers. A few associates or customers actually sent Get Well Soon cards and flowers too. Not many, because the restaurant was still relatively new. Besides, those who knew him did not know him that well. Some called. They were given the same update. Those who were rivals were secretly pleased. All they knew was what I knew and I was being fairly optimistic. Alex was sympathetic but fairly distracted. He never offered to come round to visit Paolo. I assumed that their relationship must be purely business. So now the partners had found out through Alex too, but they got the news secondhand, which was that he'd had a little accident and was fine and had gone home already. I explained to Ben that, according to Alex, I couldn't liquidate my assets because I had to pay some kind of corporate tax (didn't quite get this myself). They were in my name but without Paolo's signature and consent, I could only reinvest the profit in the friggin' pizza business. I could take nothing out except for wages.

'So we can't leave for New York, no recording deal, no two hundred and fifty grand, not even fifteen, no deal memo. The only thing I managed to do was sell the piano to pay the medical bills.'

'So now what?' he said.

'Johnny's has to make more money. It's in my name, right?'

'And how will you do all this?' he said.

'Turn Johnny's into something else. A club. Disco's big, pizza's small. When I get my first fifteen grand pay rise, I'm Audi here.' Alex said I didn't need the partners' decision in reinvesting the profit, if I wasn't going to use their financial assistance. Neways, they might not agree to me turning Johnny's into a club.

'Do you want to see Tai Gor?'

I'd heard about this guy, 大哥, Big Brother. He worked hand in hand with the casino in the VIP rooms. He was a 疊馬仔, *dip ma zai* or dead chip dealer or chip roller, whatever you wanted to call it, in the bate-ficha ('beat chips') business and the kingpin in the 白鳳, Pak Fong (White Phoenix) gang. The bate-ficha business only existed in Macao casinos and nowhere else in the world. You rolled or exchanged chips between the customers and the *dip ma zai* or chip rollers. A dead chip was one that was non-negotiable, could not be exchanged for cash at the casinos, only by bate-ficha dealers like Tai Gor, for commission. The chip rollers carried dead chips and walked around the gambling rooms seeking customers. They exchanged the dead chips for cash chips or cash with their customers. In return, the chip rollers got a commission for this kind of exchange. I was hesitant. 'You sure about this?'

Ben said that he was. The guy was a good bad guy, not a bad good guy, and that was better, right? I sighed. Despite my reticence, I went along with Ben because he knew the guy already, and I knew games had rules. Las Vegas was for families. Macao was for the super high rollers.

I paused and thought about this. If I just borrowed the money and flew off somewhere, Tai Gor would probably track me down and kill me. It would be safer and make more sense to borrow the money and invest it in Paolo's business until I personally had made enough to get back on the plane.

'We could just meet him to talk about the rates,' said Ben. 'Think he'd give you a good rate. I borrowed from him before—'

He stopped himself. He didn't need to say it. He saved interest by borrowing from the Bank of Li-an. 'I'd lend the money to you if I'd got it. I think you'd do well. You're ambitious and young and the club is hot. Disco is what people all over the world want now. Or you could just go back to the States with what you've got.'

'Ben, we've been through this. I've got nothing. I don't even have Dallas now.' I hesitated. I said nothing of the fact that the real reason I would not leave was that I didn't want to leave Paolo. I couldn't. If I did, I would have failed. As a piano-player, a worker, a friend. Yes, even a friend. My heart was here. I didn't want to be my mom, a quitter. She left Chicago, me, Dad. I failed as a daughter then. She did not take care of us and she got sick herself. She twisted and trashed my spirit. I didn't even know if she had once loved or still loved me. No one knew. Chinese parents did not tell their children they loved them. They could only show it and my mother did not show it because if she did, she would not have left. The only time I wanted to quit Macao was after Christmas. And it was only for a second. It was after Ben got Dan Shapiro down to fifteen grand plus deal memo. But I did not say this to Ben. 'And plus,' I said to him instead, 'what would I do if I went back?'

'Get a friggin' job like anyone else, Li-an! If you don't want to take the risk then you ain't opening a club. You go nowhere. You go home. You get a dead-end job. You got a chance to go now.'

I dismissed the idea at once. I was prepared to take the risk of going with a loan shark for Paolo to be well again. I wanted him to have the treatment that he was deprived of now. I took many risks before when I was with Dallas. I could have rolled a big time crook but I never met one.

'Cash in one hour. No paperwork, no questions, all credit histories accepted! And you have no credit history so you'd probably get approved in one minute!'

'You sure about this?' I said. It was a gamble. I knew it. I felt dragged into it. But the only way out of our situation was to do it. What I was doing for Paolo, I would do for Dallas. Ben was confident we would pay it back and I, by extension, felt it was a doable deal.

After Ben made a call, we made an appointment to see Tai Gor. We could only do this after the 15th day of the Chinese calendar as it was again bad luck to get into debt at the start of the year. On Thursday, February 19, we found ourselves in Rua dos Mercadores in a large European apartment with arches and potted palms on the ground floor. Apparently, this was one of Tai Gor's offices. We waited for Tai Gor to see us in a 1950s glitzy room with mirrored cocktail bar, jeweled ashtrays and boxy lamps on every piece of table, to create that low light ambience. Low light was ideal since I didn't really want anyone to see me here.

Tai Gor came out when his Macanese manservant, henchman, bodyguard or butler, or whoever it was, opened the door. Tai Gor was in a navy-blue suit and looked surprisingly benevolent. There was no choice but to trust him. It was not so much trust as honor or resignation. It was like you were in the dentist's chair already. He was almost like an old friend, a family dentist or accountant. And those were frequently bent here too — so what was the difference? The whole business of bate-ficha dealers was to 'befriend' customers. The only means of honoring the deal was the title of 老朋友, *lo pang yau*, 'old friends', polite words for good old-fashioned 'honor', or 'understanding', which were in turn nice words for 'we will make you'. Since there was no contract, the only lines to read between were the lines between his eyebrows, and you needn't be highly literate to do that.

I borrowed just a teensy, well, just 80,000 patacas from Tai Gor, at the bargain bottom rate of 46 percent, to top up the cappuccino with the froth. We talked about the rate for only about two minutes. We got it down from 58 percent, which, I was told by Ben later, was low anyway. Sharks could charge 100 or even 1,000 percent interest. A slight shudder came to me, which I expressed in a big sigh. It was not that bad. We were young and the young were brave, weren't they? In the romantic old days of the mid 1800s, 'agents' or middlemen, someone like Tai Gor, preyed on hard-up naïve gambling novices. If the debt could not be paid at all, the debtor would be sold off as a coolie to the USA or UK and worked as a slave forever in order to repay the creditors. 'Til debt do us part.

Most of the meeting was the business plan, which was when I would be required to pay what amount back. There were to be three monthly payments, each for 20,000 patacas plus interest. The first payment was in two months, which he rounded off to April 30, the second on May 31, and the last being June 30. Twenty taco shells plus interest was… My math was not so good at this point so the henchman brought in a huge calculator and gave me the staggering total of 29,200 patacas.

Tuesday evening. February 24. I picked up the papers from the doormat and popped in to see Paolo for two minutes to make sure he was OK. Auntie propped him up like a rag doll in his wheelchair next to the bed when I came in. Auntie and Thaew had to heave-ho his body around just to feed and wash him.

The lighting was dim, only slightly dimmer than at Tai Gor's. A low-wattage ceramic bedside lamp lit his cavernous room. A few layers of curtains were all drawn tightly shut. The lamp was mushroom-like with its enormous shade and cast grotesque shadows like a forest of trees in the room. It was beginning to resemble an opium den. There was a pleasant soothing Chinese smell of camphor and nutmeg, from the oils that Auntie had been using to massage his muscles. It was the smell of my childhood bedroom too, when my *amah-cheh* rubbed the very same oils on our sore tummies. He could not speak or move very much, yet he was awake with his droopy eyelids.

Ben turned Paolo into this monster. I was mildly shaking and he could see that. I cleared my throat and sat on his bed. This wasn't Paolo anymore, let alone the Paolo I met in Chicago.

I sat very near the lamp so that I could skim the headlines. 'Britain in recession,' I mumbled over my trembling voice, 'Sir Geoffrey Howe says the British budget will be announced March the 10th, taxes to be raised…' I looked at him. He was listening as a snail listened to the rain. I sighed and flapped the papers as I turned the page.

'I need to transform the restaurant,' I started to say, but I couldn't think how I was to say any more without revealing the plans. It was my last chance to play, my only chance. A very mild stab of 'what would Paolo think' pulsed in my veins, but it was only a momentary surge. More guilt, less shame, I reminded myself. He could not say in writing or in speaking whatever he thought, and he would not hear of it anyway. I was not a gambler like Ben, but I placed my bets on the restaurant. I consoled myself with the hope that with my grand plans, we would soon be flush, oh yeah.

'What I mean is, make it much better, you know? I'm keeping your joint going. I'm going to make plenty of mazuma, you'd like that, wouldn't cha.' I was getting used to my monologue. I might even start to believe it myself. I returned to reading the papers aloud.

'Hmm. The Grateful Dead playing in Madison Square Garden, New York, in, like, two weeks. March 9th. What else.'

I finished off with a few items of disaster news so that he wouldn't think he was missing out on too much. 'Earthquake in Athens. 6.7 on the scale.' I rushed it but he was creeping me out by then. I was talking to a living corpse. This was Ben's work. I put the papers down. 'Good night, Paolo, I will see you soon. Tomorrow. Maybe. You're gonna get better, I promise.' I was so cut up, I couldn't go far from his door. Outside his room, I sat on the floor, buried my face and wept. I was sure he could hear me.

In my room as I got ready for an honest night's work at the restaurant, I felt exhausted from seeing Paolo. My vision was still for Ben and I to go to New York to resume our life together when Paolo was well again.

We had a big gaping floor space in Johnny's where the grand piano was, which we naturally filled with more tables, but already we were no longer drawing the crowds. It was time to turn the restaurant into something else. It was too fancy for here. Too much razzmatazz. The piano was a joke. Then there was the competition. Johnny's was the first. Other pizzerias have since cropped up. How could we compare with a global pizza chain for prices and its bottomless salad bar and hopelessly ersatz Tiffany pendant lighting? Besides, the tourists preferred American food and the locals preferred Portuguese, Chinese and Macanese. Where did Johnny's fit in?

After closing one night, when I didn't feel so wrecked, I went in to see Paolo with the papers. This time he was in bed. He was lying down and Auntie had not come in to prop him up. 'Brought you a present.' I put a new bottle of JB and a straw down on his bedside table. And after that, I said nothing for a long time. I looked around the room and it was exactly as it was a few nights ago. Time hadn't ticked a second by. I put the papers on his bed and sat in his wheelchair. I had no tears to cry and no words to say.

Finally, I got up without looking at him. 'Paolo, you'll get treated and get well. We will have enough money soon. I could get on a plane now but I am not gonna.' Said all that in one breath and then I left. The papers were still on his bed.

...and if not... there is no 'and' or 'if not'... you couldn't put him down like some sick dog. I'd done enough for my contract. I hadn't quite seen what was at the edges of the big pic, but essentially that was the big pic.

I made appointments with three building contractors to get quotes. We were going to start works around the end of February.

I knew Paolo would hate the idea, but I was moving with the times. Jazz is dying. Jazz is dead. At last and at least, I would be meeting and playing to young people. There was no need to keep him informed on every detail. He would be happy if we became successful. A club would make money every night on drinks and bar snacks. It didn't cost much through Ben's connections to hire or buy lighting and audio equipment. I wanted to party forever and I was so sick of eating pizzas and playing piano.

'Johnny's is doing very well, Paolo,' I said. 'I'm sure you're glad to hear that.' I had closed up for the evening. It was way after 12 and Paolo was still up. I was almost pleased to see he was up, waiting for me. Thaew had moved the TV from the lounge into Paolo's room. It was too darn gloomy to read the papers to him when the TV was on. Neways he was catching up on all the news so why'd he need me to read. The TV was on most of the time now, I heard Auntie say. The bedside lamp would have to be off when the TV was on to keep the lighting low. I noticed that the bottle of JB on the bedside table was empty and the straw next to it. I had brought him something he could enjoy. I exceeded my own expectations. I would help him more next time — callous of me to just dump the bottle on him. Auntie must have had to open it, hold it and help him with the straw.

Paolo was ageing rapidly and wasting away after his discharge from the hospital. His skin was looking as white as the belly of a serpent. He was on a semi-solid diet since he could not open his mouth wide. Auntie said it took time. Traditional healing and medication always did. It did not upset me to see my prisoner anymore. I looked at him as I would an old friend, remembering who he had been. Thought back on the last two weeks and I realized I could not speak to him about any of it. I was protecting him. He had been tortured and maimed enough.

Johnny's was closed for two weeks from Sunday, March 1. I sold all the kitchen equipment and ovens and pared down to the basics. In return, I bought more drinks' fridges. The Italian chef Paolo had hired at great expense was given his one-way ticket back to Naples. Ideally, I had to change the name of the club. Ben and I spent many nights in bed fantasizing about names. The club would be our baby and naming it was more than half the fun. In the end, Ben thought of the name Estoril, after the region known as the Portuguese Riviera between Lisbon and Cascais.

'You know what? I got you something you might like.' I grinned. It must have looked sinister in the flickering colored light of the TV. 'Only the best, Paolo.'

I fished in my jeans pocket for something, anything. 'Course, I found something. I cut him some lines and helped him use the tiny straw from a Vitasoy child-size carton of soy milk. I watched his ageing skin relax and his eyes tense up with real hot tears, not reptilian tears.

I was impressed that I had stood by him so stoically since his hospital discharge, keeping his business afloat without any business acumen or experience. As they say in Macao, *não há outra mais leal.* There is no other more loyal. He once made me work for peanuts, tried to kiss me when he was drunk one time and he hated the 'hypocritical hippie piece of junk' that was John Lennon. You could say we were square. At last guilt and loyalty were one.

Dallas and I were used to 'medicating' guys who were well, not guys who were unwell. Now here's one who couldn't breathe, couldn't snore. He hissed away like an animal in the dark. He was photosensitive and Auntie kept the curtains partly drawn all the time. He slithered about in his wheelchair or in his bed, slobbering and gasping. Almost every night, I'd cut him some lines, before or after I went out for the evening. It cheered him up. He was my pet snowbird. It cheered me up. I had to see him every day or every night.

I had to give Auntie a raise because she could not possibly cope with so much care for Paolo. In the end, she roped in a niece from a destitute village somewhere. I agreed to another pair of hands and to feed another mouth. This gave Auntie time off to buy her packs of Double Happiness and indulge in her favorite pastime of Pai Gow dominoes at the Ruby Luck Luck on Saturday nights, while the poor pockmarked girl stayed in, nodding off in the kitchen, waiting for Paolo to nod off too so that she could switch off his TV and the soup pot.

When the venue was completed, Ben and I were absolved of the usual restaurant-running jitters of food, food, food. Johnny's became Estoril on Saturday, March 14. We could permit ourselves the pleasure of songwriting, music-making, lovemaking, snow-ploughing and drink-nibbling again. I was looking swell, so my customers told me. My hair was re-permed and colored and I went to Hong Kong for my caposhi new dresses from London's clubland. We changed gears. New wave punk pop moved over for disco. We were playing 'He's the Greatest Dancer' at least once every night of the week. We didn't even have a 'Saturday Night Fever' multicolored lit dance floor. Those were 'Good Times'. 'Everybody Dance', said Chic, and we did.

I had Paolo's wheelchair fitted with a drinks holder. I bought a child's non-spill drinking tumbler (blue, for sure, cos he was a boy) and slotted it into the holder. And hey presto, things were beginning to look up for my old friend and me. Let's just call them more gifts from clubland, along with what was in my purse. Whatever chilled half-bottle was opened was brought home. I poured myself a glass and I filled his bottle. I chatted about the night in the monologue that was now my part, unself-conscious, unrehearsed, as natural as my voice was to myself. Forget the papers. He had the TV to read him the papers. I had a deep urge to spoil my snowbird. It was our little secret. I watched his yellow eyes under the hooded lids dance as though they were candle flames on a dark night. He could do nowch, but oh yes, by golly, could he suck and snort from a straw.

I persuaded Ben to move into the pavilion, but he said no way. Technically the pavilion was not the same building but I got what he was saying. I didn't blame him and I didn't want to pressurize him into anything, for I feared he would bust out on me. 'Don't wanna be in the same building as the retard—' said Ben.

'Ben! Don't call him that,' I snapped. A nerve in me struck like a gong. Suddenly I did feel like barfing.

'Whassamatter witcha,' he said. 'Gone all safty-pafty?'

'No. You made him what he is,' I said. 'He lived. I look after him.'

'Don't you dare,' he said, jabbing me. 'I did it for you. For us.' I missed Ben when he was all caramel-voiced Chet Baker; that seemed like a million years ago, when we were indeed happy and actually sat and sang together in thirds, sixths, chromatics, whatever. Now whenever we were not in the club, we were like alligators having lunch.

'That was what came back to me,' I said to Paolo that evening on my nocturnal visit bearing gifts. 'Dem days.' I took a gulp of Comfy after I topped up his non-spill tumbler. I closed my eyes and listened to the tinkling ice cubes like they were magical wind chimes. 'When I was playing every night. It was like a dream, like living in the Thirties. I was happy, Gatsby-style. It was a party that never ended. Except that it did, and it was 1981. You know what? I'm gonna take you out there. Yessirree. Out of this damned room. You got wheels, right? Ain't nothing stopping us. Not like we got neighbors or anything.'

The servants were in their quarters. I put my drink down on his bedside table and Auntie would kill me but there were no coasters and I knew the wood was teak. I got up, undid the brakes, and pushed my snowbird out of this damned room. He had been here for months. It was surprisingly heavy and required my undivided physical and mental concentration. The hall was totally dark but I loved that. There was no question that I could play in the dark as I could play with my eyes closed. I was now so relieved that Ben hadn't moved in. I ran back into Paolo's room to get my drink, and I wiped off the watery rings with my own T-shirt. Each time I came back from the Estoril, I would jump in the shower and get changed into what I called my home clothes, old T-shirts, jeans, that kinda thing. He had no idea Johnny's was history. I didn't want him to see my glad rags, diamanté earrings, stilettos, or he was bound to get suspish.

It was almost silent. You could only hear the clock tick and the roar of the sea. I even instinctively tiptoed. I parked his wheelchair and lifted the piano lid. I sat down and I sang and played whatever came to my mind. 'Long Ago and Far Away.' 'Can't Help Loving Dat Man.' 'But Not For Me.' His favorite had to be 'We Belong Together'. I knew he preferred the older musicals but I didn't restrict myself. He liked a few Scott Joplin rags, usual Gershwin and Cole Porter stuff, all played in stride style. 'Someone to Watch Over Me.' ''S Wonderful.' Stuff from the Great American Songbook. Must have been at least sixty songs. And that was just one night. I couldn't recall the list. My brain was alcohol-soaked by then and yeah, his was too. He totally swallowed it. The music and the drinks.

That night, he passed out first. I wheeled him back to his room and much as it grossed me out, tumbled his ass back onto the bed as Auntie showed me how, without doing damage to my own back.

Things were not so cozy in the club.

I had my other life now to lead, the one in reverse, the 150mph one. Ben and I slipped off into the bathrooms for our little treats that Ben got us from his pure Chinese white collection, which we cut into neat rows using Paolo's razor and my compact mirror. Don't Stop 'Til You Get Enough. It was easy to forget about the grand piano and Benny Goodman and Paolo Giametti Russo. When I looked up and grinned, the only thing reminiscent of the pizza parlor was the blue and white Amalfi Coast decorative tiling on the eye level of the cubicle walls. I blotted the image out by shutting my eyelids to enjoy my euphoric calm. Portuguese, Italian, Spanish — what was the difference? I was sure the customers here, wired on jittersauce, Ees, Cees and big fat Mezzrolls, would not be offended by Italian tiles in a Portuguese disco. On Tuesday night, a traditionally quiet one, I warmed up the evening with live playing. This was a night that I would not be going in to see Paolo because at the club I would already be playing live and was beat by the time I got home (if you could imagine that even I, a night owl extraordinaire, Queen of Magical Journeys, got beat once a week). We performed my songs, sometimes with my Les Paul and sometimes without, and Ben on the Roland TR808 drum machine, rarely without. We had the Korg DW8000 synth to mess around with for simple organ sounds, echoes, bleeps, that kind of stuff. At last we were doing the music we wanted, and we were performing. All minimalist, all good. We were paring down the sounds as disco had grown omnipresent and all-consuming.

We were charging covers of 20 a head, 30 on weekends. Not

exactly dirto cheapo. We were the newest, funkiest club and the lines forming outside made up for the lines inside. We were making the mazuma in drinks and drugs. Ben got two guys called Mah Sing and Rocco to work the floor and the booths with a variety of meds. We got another couple of black belt Kung Fu heavies from Hong Kong for bouncers. Two specialist cocktail waiters were hired from Singapore just to further meet the sophisticated demands of the modern social group and to justify the cool cost of 50 great patacas a Mai Tai or Black Russian. Our specialty was a cocktail made from cimbalino coffee from Porto. A little cymbal. That cute enough for you? We'd like to think of ourselves as refined to a T.

Each time I started to play, he wept. There was no telling if it was with joy or sadness. Must be both. This was what he wanted and now it was all he got. How cruel was fate? Everything else — his other senses, his speech, his motor skills — had been taken away. Only his hearing and his ability to suck remained. Now I was no medical practitioner but I'd like to hear Dr Raj tell me all that. How could he have made Paolo happy? That's what I'd like to know. Auntie, Thaew, the village girl whose name I didn't even know, and me were looking after Paolo round the clock.

When he wept, I sure knew how to cheer him up. I started playing John Lennon, Blondie, Talking Heads, Chic, Stevie Wonder. Oh I could go on, and I did. He knew what I was doing as well as I did. His yellow eyes stopped moving completely, focusing on specks of dust on the floor. He must be exploding inside. I was Sunday Girl.

Some nights, I'd pass out first. Like a tired child at a school desk, I would lay my arms in front of me on the keys and rest my head on them. He'd sit in his chair dozing until Auntie appeared from her quarters at 6am. 'Weck up! Weck up!' she'd whisper to me and send me to my room like my own childhood *amah-cheh*. Then she'd wheel him back to his room and put him to bed.

Other times, and these were considered the best nights, I would complete a pianothon. You could only do this alcohol-free. I played until the sun came up. First, you'd hear the sunrise: the dawn chorus of gulls and it was still dark. Then, minutes later, the room turned from darkness to a dark, warm pink. I could only say that sometimes it felt rather stirring, like when you saw the words The End at the end of a movie and they switched on the lights. You didn't actually want it to end. You woke up from a dream. The owl in me preferred nights. The first rays were the sign for us to call it a night because of his photosensitivity. I never wondered what would happen if we stayed on. What exactly was photosensitivity? What if he was like a vampire and melted like plastic into a heap? Already he looked like a vampire with his widow's peak and his yellow eyes. I took him back to his room.

The Estoril was really bouncing. Every night I was getting down to it and it was hot. But all things soon passed, Cosmopolitans, snow, Good Times, nights, hopes. I had got offbeat. I didn't notice such things as the empty cash desk. It was a week to the end of May, coming up to the first payment with interest, back to Tai Gor. It was the first time I was even looking through the books. I had the strangest idea that I should be looking into a more substantial wine list for our clientele, who seemed to be tourists and yuppies in their twenties and thirties. Wine drinking became caposhi. I was interested in those from Porto in Costa Verde, Portugal.

Immediately I thought: the cocktail waiters from Singapore. My nerves were shattered. The first payment to Tai Gor was the most important. If we could not even do that, there was no mention of further payments. The club would have to sit on its shades. Plus they'd do some bad things to us, I would so not like to imagine. I was doing the hoola, upside down, inside out, and I was looking at Ben to supply me anything, some mezz from his stash would do. Nothing primo, he didn't have to make calls or anything. It bugged me, and I wanted to calm down quick.

I said nothing to Ben, for deep inside I didn't want to disappoint him. Hell, we were tight. We had never had success before in anything and here he was DJing the shit he loved so much, I was performing, I was getting any drinks and drugs I wanted and Paolo had become a family pet. My emotions were as mixed as drinks and I was confused. Times seemed to have changed overnight, over a few months.

Disco was all about playing very few or no instruments. It was a self-entertaining lifestyle. I was lucky enough to escape, unlike Dallas. I'd achieved what I wanted — which was to be sophisticated. Didn't come here to eat pizzas and hot dogs or to sit down. I wanted to dress up and get down. I only just started enjoying the 'new wave' style. I used lots of mousse or gel in the hair, far-out makeup, loud colors. It was a blow. Everything could turn into a car crash if we couldn't pay Tai Gor back the first payment.

I told no one and I called the original contractor to fit a closed-circuit TV. It was completely normal and should be done anyway. How did we get away without it all this time? I didn't want to be clamped down like Studio 54. I wasn't dealing or pushing. I wanted to see every room, but I told him, I especially wanted to see the cash desk. I didn't tell him I wanted to see for myself why we were making less and less guacamole when we were pulling in more and more avocados. When I catch him or her, I am going to be making a steaming Red Hot Chicago Dog out of the grifter, oh yeah! With sliced dill pickle spear, nuclear green relish and what else? I swear I will burn more calories with a squeeze of yellow mustard.

Ben was playing Lipps, Inc.'s 'Funkytown'. It was like a good bitch slap in the mug. When I saw the footage for myself in the office room at the back of what was Johnny's old kitchen, my heart sank. It told me what I feared most, or rather what I had hoped I would not see. The dirty rotten scoundrel was refilling his drinks at the bar and his pockets at the cash desk when the place was hopping. No one saw what he did. And if they did, this town sure ain't funky. I'd been the biggest dumb ass schmuck.

Now to kick his kop in and his tush out? In the middle of 'Just Once', or should I wait 'til the evening was over? Yeah. Like I knew what I was doing. I thought maybe later. I couldn't have these cats leaving now. They were still coming in and paying their covers and their 10 pat-a-cakes a mojito, fo' sho.

It was bad. And that ain't good. I was grossed out and hellacious and beat. I could barely stand from the discovery. I rummaged in the desk pen caddy and voila! Produced a pill. Stacy, is you is or is you ain't my baby? I swallowed it and shook my dyed tresses. My lurex sweater-dress clad knees and my knuckles were white. I could feel my infamous ivory-tickling talons growing into ivory tusks, ready to spear my love. I breathed out fire like a dragon and my muscles tensed, poised to take flight. What a discovery to make! Could Christopher Columbus have done the same? No. What about Galileo? Unlikely. Could I wait 'til 2am? It ain't necessarily so. Next thing I knew, I charged into the DJ console and sunk my pre-grown talons into his jugular. He choked, grabbed my wrists and threw me off. I fell back and hit something — I thought perhaps my thigh or butt — on the mixing desk. I screamed.

'Whoa! Ssup? Li-an!' He wrestled with me and my dilated pupils.

'I'm gonna kill you,' I gasped. We were in the cozy acoustically sealed console environment of the DJ's private jet so no one could hear us. Outside, the music thumped on. Harvey Mason's 'How Does It Feel'. I knew and loved all these numbers but now they hurt me, I felt jacked and cut up. They were my lovers and they were my enemies. Because of music I was in this room, trying to kill someone.

'What is wrong with you?' he asked calmly, looking gravely into my eyes, as if I was under hypnosis.

'You! You!' The dragon in me spluttered, I could not speak, I was so incensed. The fire-breathing paraffin in my voice melted as I gasped, 'You friggin' stole from me again. We cannot pay it back in four days.'

'Sure we can, Li-an, I—'

I screamed and covered my ears. 'Don't touch me! God, I hate you! I hate all your lies.'

'Calm down. I have it. The money for both April and May. We have it! We're doing good! You see? You never asked me. You put in cameras instead. Here's most of it,' he said, lifting the false panel from under the mixing desk. 'The rest… er… tomorrow.'

'The rest?'

'I'll get it to you tomorrow. I gotta loan the guys, man.'

'The guys? You're loaning the dealers?'

'Mah Sing and Rocco have got their guys to pay. Li-an, we are making twice what we owe. Do you know math at all? We're in profit! We got no problem paying Tai Gor back. And you know why we are in profit? Cos of the guys! Li-an, Li-an, listena me.'

I kept shaking my head, closing my eyes. 'Lies! Lies!' I moaned inaudibly. I could feel my diamanté ear hoops tangled in my hair.

Like some kind of choo-choo train, he just carried on. 'I got them in just to supply jellybeans and joysticks to the cats. And in return the guys give us half. We go half-half. Those covers and 10 taco shells a mojito ain't gonna help pay Tai Gor back, let's be honest. For a start, the taxman'll be having a few drinks on us.'

I was talked out of my misery. I breathed in deeply and inhaled the next song, Who's a Funkadelic? Good question. I had no answer myself. 'OK,' I said finally. 'Sure we going to get the rest back from the guys?'

'Positive. Or else they don't work here again. They know the skinny on the deal.'

'Oh God. I hate you,' I hissed. I buried my face in my hands.

He put his arms around me. I fell into them like some kind of injured animal. The fire died in my eyes. I was weak and further weakened because he had access to the cash and to these so-called guys. *Não há outra mais leal.* There is no other more loyal. Who was I but the tai-tai in all this? I had no choice but to believe him. If I threw him out tonight, I sure as hell wouldn't see the rest of the cushion. The cash desk was thinner than a lettuce leaf on rye.

That night, I wept openly in Paolo's presence. I should not have been drinking before I saw Paolo but I did. I sobbed and pushed my face into the sheets so that Auntie would not hear. My tears fell in thuds onto the bed like gumdrops. I hate him, I whispered. 'Course, no one knew how a snake got into the house, cos you know, we're surrounded by acres of wild parkland. Wildlife, in from anywhere, right? They're out there searching right now. Oh, but they won't ever find anything. I know. See, I've had run-ins with the pigs before. They can't link a—

Within seconds I knew I'd said too much.

I used the corners of Paolo's sheets to trumpet my rhino juice. He must have thought I was weeping for him, for he wept too. I held his hand in mine. The poor deluded soz. Who's sorry now? We both were. Happy together in our misery. United at last.

Within a few evenings, aware of my indiscretion, I sobered up. The secret was not to be drunk with Paolo, in front of him. The ghost galleons sunk by dem loose lips would haunt me forever. I said too much the last time. He must have wondered why I never got jelly-pinned with him again, despite my consistent generous offerings. A sober girl was a supergirl.

Indeed, the guys returned the balance. Ben and I went back to how we were when we first met. We focused on the music again. The beat went on. There was a subliminal feeling that if we surfed the disco wave, we would need to survive. Immediately after the payment to Tai Gor, I was tense again. We still had to keep up the payments and the next one was in a month. Who was to say that we'd meet the target? We barely made it this time. I couldn't keep track of the guys' cabbage patch. I didn't even know if it was all true or not, yet it was believable in every sense: we made more money illegally than legally.

Toward the end of May, just when we were about to make the second payment, we were threatened by the drug squad. It was holiday season soon for the Chinese and Taiwanese, so we didn't want to miss out on extra profits. The DS said they were going to shut us down because they'd been tipped off by our competitor, the Incognito Club in Three Aces Casino, that we were doing, like, major-major pushing. Ben said it was easy to shut them up. The fee was about two thousand patacas.

That was the only obstacle we faced — for a while. We paid the DS and the Tai Gor instalment. Back home, Auntie complained that Paolo was still sick. A long time had gone by for him with insufficient medical treatment. If I didn't do something about it, the *amah-cheh* wanted to report me (to who?) and she even threatened to quit (from service?). She didn't want to look after him. I was appalled by her ingratitude. In Cantonese, I said, 'Listen Auntie, if you quit, firstly your two sons will stop private schooling. Secondly, you will not get any more opium for your pipe.'

Immediately, the *amah-cheh* backed off. She sought instead a different Chinese 中醫師 *tsung yi si* out of her own pocket to get him some boiled-up roots (清熱解毒 *tseng yit chit tuk*, she said which was literally, 'extinguish heat neutralize poison') because she was sorry for him It had a list of 13 ingredients including herbs starting with angelica, dandelion, chrysanthemum and ending with scorpion, centipede and silkworm! These were supposed to calm nerve damage. Que melodrama! She was spittin' real fast how he was like her own family now. He used to be a person, you know, she said, impressing me with her use of 'used to', meaning he was not a person anymore. 'Do you think I do not know that?' I said. I held back my own tears as what had happened to him was unspeakable and I could hardly talk about it without somebody biting my head off. First Ben, now Auntie.

'Paolo, I think we are in a stable situation at last,' I said to him. In private, 'course. 'I hear you're getting better. Soon you can even open the curtains. You don't have to live only by night.' I knew that it sounded lame. How could I put it to him? I took away the telephone in the hall outside Paolo's room and the kitchen. It was now a liability. He could suddenly walk like those pilgrims at a miracle healing and phone somebody.

Auntie became more cooperative: helping him get better by making him stand up every day. 'No need doctor,' she said. 'Is better now with the new medicine.'

'OK, you think?' I said.

'Yup,' she said, with a hint of confidence. 'I talk to the *tsung yi si*. He say, this medicine is just for krait bite. Is working. Snakes been around long time in this place. Longer than hospital. No problem.'

I was somewhat cheered by her prognosis. Once again it was more than trust, it was more like honor. You put your fears with the *tsung yi si* and hoped for the best.

That meant that Paolo would improve his leg muscles. He was weak all over, and he still didn't speak except in barks and gasps when calling out to Auntie. She said he was better and he could stand on his feet now for a minute. She criticized me for being impatient. 'What you know about snake bite?' she said, quite rightly.

When it came down to it, I just paid her and her niece more. They were addicts. As long as she had her Saturday nights at the Ruby Luck Luck, she was cool. They were hooked on easy money. And there was no easier money to be gotten than wiping the ass of a strong silent jumbo jet like Paolo Giametti Russo.

'When I get my first massive pay rise, you will have your rehab,' I said to he who was silent. 'You owe me good, and now I owe you. Screw the contract.' I stopped to think how he was not in rehab right now because I was still working on the club. I wasn't even paying myself.

'I'm using money to make money, right? You understand all that, doncha.' Once he recovered he might shut the Estoril down, just like the DS tried to. Johnny's was his baby, not the Estoril. He still did not know about it. If he did, he would know that it represented everything he hated about music — deafening, stand up, drug-fueled disco, and the world changing — ditto.

The race was on. There was little time left. I would be paying Tai Gor back in full and returning to New York with Ben for my deal memo and big fat recording deal check, and all this before Paolo was well again, and he could be, with Auntie's homemade healthcare routine and a rehabilitation procedure with the professionals.

I was feeling OK enough not to look at the closed-circuit TV footage. The time toward the third and last payment neared. It was a week before the end of June, very humid, and temperatures touched the nineties. Ben had another of his 'trips' to make to Singapore. I knew he was the man for this leg of the journey, in some long demand supply chain that stretched from Asia to Europe.

I even looked forward to him coming back laden with gifts of gold for me, preferably a smart-looking cuff that I could wear to the Estoril or the chain-link drop earrings I'd seen and coveted in Vogue. They would enhance any outfit and I was bored of all my clothes. He was good at gifting. Like me, he was a traditional romantic, into old Hollywood cars, old movies, old songs. He said his father was the kind who would open a door, any door, even a kitchen cabinet door like it weighed anything, for his mom. But the gold dust seemed to have disappeared. The only cuff I could expect was one I should like to give myself — behind the ear.

The air was very still and I knew I should try not to freak but I was about to. Ben was not answering the calls. Was he even back? If he was back, where was he? I leaned forward and back in the office chair, I was mental. I was scratching my eyes, my hair. I was opening and shutting the pen caddy drawers in the office room, looking for pills or coke he liked to leave lying around for us to relax with during the never-ending post-club hours. I searched the cash desk and the DJ console. If there was enough for Tai Gor's payment then I'd relax. I said I'd relax. In this room we now mostly lived and in this room I must now ride the beef. There was not enough. There was nine. We needed twenty nine and two hundred. We were twenty gees and two hundred short. I was shook. History was repeating itself like a bad hit. For a second I thought he must have OD'd. But it was crazy. He hadn't touched stuff for months.

There was no one to DJ. I managed to get a stand-in from an entertainment agency. He sucked. His musical pedigree and taste were rather questionable but he was available. In general, he was not aware of the dance beat and the BPM of the songs he chose was simply too low. I found any excuse to blow up at him, usually no good reason. Poor guy, it was not his fault he was stuck in some kind of war zone.

Ben was AWOL again. I got in the Benz and made Thaew drive to the Bela Vista. It was all coming back to me. The unanswered calls, the endless messages I was leaving, the sweaty palms, sleepless nights I endured. It was too much for me to eat up. He knew the time had come to pay Tai Gor. He was avoiding my claws. Every scenario went through my mind — if the trip to Singapore ended well, then he would have gone to the casino and had a party. If it didn't go well, then Ben was fried. If Ben was no more, the Estoril was kaputski. How could I run this place without him? Mah Sing and Rocco would just walk out, taking the customers with them. I needed to get to the bottom of it. I was a not so hepcat now and things were gonna turn ugly, I swear.

Thaew waited downstairs. I was already on Ben's corridor, outside his room, when I heard shuffling noises. Muffled shouts and some thuds. I hid behind a column of the many arches, opposite a red fire extinguisher in a glass case like it was a museum. Then there were dragging and kicking sounds quite nearby, along the corridor to the fire exit. I couldn't hear exactly what was going on, but it ain't a good groove. The noises faded. I waited 'til there was quiet and I popped my head out. His door was open.

I knew something shady was going on — how many men were there? I crept to Ben's door and I whispered his name twice. My heart thumped like a couple of bongos on acid. I waited. There was no reply. There was no one in the room. It was a total wreck. I went around the bed. The sheets had been pulled off. The bathroom had blood trails on the tiles and drips over the vanity. I freaked. His Wayfarer glasses were broken, and they lay like a little dead bird on the floor. My instinct was to run, but I resisted. After all, there was no one here, right? Ben could still be in this room, unconscious or hurt. I had to find him.

After a frenzied search of no more than two minutes (the room was quite bare), Ben was clearly not around. I glanced at my Casio LCD watch. I had to be quick — Thaew was waiting downstairs. I'd looked in our secret space, which was really a concealed riser cupboard full of main lines, heating pipes and valves, piles of cobwebs and dust and that kinda stuff. The door of the cupboard had been papered over with the same 1940s peacock feather design as the wall itself, torn and stained to camouflage the cupboard edge. Only a thin black line gave away that it was a door but the wallpaper pattern was busy enough to take care of this visual barrier. Inside the cupboard, of course, it was unfinished, unplastered and unpapered. Messy cement hundreds of years old smeared the naked rough brickwork. It was a two-inch thick real wooden door, none of this cardboard Disney cutout modern garbage. Ben once told me he'd found original 1950s Old Gold cigarette ends in this cupboard. Ben's private stash in his *The Empire Strikes Back* children's lunchbox was gone — either he'd used it up, taken it, or he'd been robbed. A wild itch of panic spread across my arms, forehead, thighs, everywhere. I didn't want to entertain the thought that he'd got iced. When I heard guys spittin' real fast in Cantonese from the corridor, I jumped into the cupboard, breathing in so that I would fit.

The voices were muffled once I was in the pitch black of the cupboard. On top of that, I could understand more Cantonese than I thought, having spoken in roast pidgin-with-everything to Auntie.

I think there were two voices, with a third interjecting every now and then. They mentioned the word 金, *kam*, which was gold, several times. Insulated in my lagged cupboard, contorted against pipes and powdered with ancient dust, I could not hear the context in which they were speaking, but the name Ping Chau came up too. As to who this was, I had no idea. Why was Ben involved in all this? I dared not breathe in case they heard me. There was so much dust and the urge to sneeze was overwhelming, even painful. If my good Catholic God could hear me, I prayed that I would not sneeze, or even move a hair. It would surely be followed by a slug in my face. I would not even blink, in case blinking brought on coughing or sneezing. They came specifically for something, I heard a drawer open and shut. They left as quickly as they entered.

I burst out of the cupboard and let off about six or seven enormous sneezes. My eyes and mouth were watering from the itch. I wanted to leave in a hurry and I made sure that no one was around. I looked both ways in the corridor and it was all dormy except for a ticking grandfather clock on the landing and the cascade of water from the fountain in the courtyard below. Gently I shut Ben's door and locked it, soundlessly putting the bolt and chain back on. I went through the drawers to see if anything was missing that they'd taken. Ben's clothes were all still there. I grabbed a bunch and inhaled his scent deeply. It was stale cigarette smoke and Halston Z-14. It brought me back to a million light years ago, before the Estoril: when we got dressed here together, teased and sprayed our bangs and folded our sleeves, ready to hit the casinos and the bars and the clubs. I felt my blistering tears pouring out onto his Banana Republic shirts, piano keyboard braces and acid-washed Jordache jeans. Seeing the stains, I swallowed and wept more. I wiped my nose on them, further imprinting them with my rhino juice and shutter water. I crushed his jeans against my neck as tightly as I first held him.

I heard crinkling sounds of receipts left in his jeans. I dreaded to think what he had been spending of the Estoril's. I removed the receipts hurriedly like a crazed 1950s housewife suspicious of her husband's extra-curricular activities.

They were not receipts at all. It was actually a single sheet of folded paper, Bela Vista writing paper. It was a letter… to me! It was dated just last night. I read it without blinking, faster than I could scarf down a plastic cup of spiked punch.

> Dear Li-an,
>
> You may or may not get this. Ain't good. Got back from Singapore and they came and totally banked on me. I couldn't face you. Honestly, I was way bad, man, you wouldn't have known it was me.
>
> If you get this at all, please forgive me. I may already be in Ping Chau. I'm going to be paid there at midnight. I will have the balance of Tai Gor's payment. Gotta be quick.
>
> I love you.

Oh Ben, Ben. Why did they hit on you? Why had they kidnapped you? I asked him aloud even though he was not there. I didn't understand what happened on his Singapore trip and he didn't explain much. I was relieved to read his letter but I started to feel very anxious.

There was only one person who would know about this place called Ping Chau and he was downstairs.

It was nearly 10 when Thaew took me to the jetty. My dinner was a cup of Java brew at the Estoril. I told the staff I would not be there that evening and I hoped that it would not be used as some kind of alibi. I told the head bartender that he had to cover for me. Tod Wong was my most trusted guy in the club these days. I could rely on him to make sure they did not have to wing it without me. I was feeling very reticent suddenly.

I was going to see the only friend that Ben ever mentioned, João. Ben said that João owed him big time, because, as usual, João had a beef with someone he had to pay back and Ben got him 'over the rut'. For that he was infinitely grateful and had to kiss Ben's ass. I quickly learned that in Ben's world, someone always owed someone for something or other. *Conhecer alguém é dever alguém.* To know someone was to owe someone. It was a permanent and solid understanding of mateship, of favors, to be done and given in perpetuity, for one always had to be returned. It was an infinite process.

João was a Macanese oddjobber with a glossy little speedboat. He lived in the 118-year-old hostel called the Sailor's Palace in the Inner Port area. It wasn't easy to find him in the dim cobbled alleyways obscured by hanging laundry and staring young children running around without pants. Battered flasks of hot water lined the walls and cubicles for hire branched off the narrow passageway.

I paid him upfront. He wanted 750 patacas and I got him down to 650. About 90 US Dollars. I had no idea if that was cheap or steep. He told me he had Irish ancestry, but I just thought, like, whatever. Whistling an Abba melody, he put the notes in a rubber band, strapping it tightly as though he was rolling a joint with a satisfying ping. He said nothing, not that he needed to. His whistling about being funny in a rich man's world was grating enough.

I hired the boat and João became my crew. Sha Tau, Ping Chau island's largest village, was a creepy spot with a ghost-town feel. Many cottages were boarded up. We shot under the canopy of mangrove branches like an arrow into a diagram.

Here in our camouflaged cave, João and I hid. The only shimmer in the moonlit sea was from our helmets. We sat like statues in the narrow cabin, which allowed little freedom of movement. We waited in a secret bay at the island's south end across two huge rocks known as the Drum Rocks, or Watchman's Tower Rocks.

The speedboat was painted black, equipped with two powerful 100HP Johnson engines specially assembled and mechanically assisted with turbo jets, making it silent and fast as a sea snake. We would be unseen and unheard, which was customary for a gentleman of his profession.

A large part of the island was country parkland, explained João. There were footpaths overgrown with orchids, wild mint and morning glory. On weekends the place was crawling with trekkers and nature addicts. At the north end of the island was a chunk of land that had broken away from the island. The Chinese said it represented the head of a dragon.

The dragon's head was where João's team would be headed ultimately. He stopped at the Watchman Tower's Rocks, waiting for the one-ton four-wheel-drive Mazda laden with trays and equipped with tools, hooded lamps, a couple of spare tanks of gas for the journey through the parkland. The Mazda would drive all the way back up north to the dragon's head where another boat would be waiting to go back to Hong Kong's main island.

Expeditions like these by speedboat only took place at night. It used to be guns and opium, but today it was mainly cocaine and gold, said João matter-of-factly. He didn't even use any nicknames for his goods. He was not coy or cagey about any of it; he'd done this now for about four years, on and off. He waited and waited in the boat for gold pieces of all shapes and sizes and coke packaged in sugar paper sacks to arrive via the Mazda. Over the years he had seen typewriters with gold space bars, weighty salmon, bottom-heavy hens, and hi-fidelity systems with portly speakers. That would be Ben's department. Ben had made all those trips supposedly delivering and receiving audio equipment.

Once the Mazda arrived, João told me, normally the driver would help him unload whatever was on the boat onto the truck, and reload the boat with what he would take back to Macao. On his next trip out to Ping Chau, he would then have to transport the 'processed' gold, now recast into bars for smuggling back to Hong Kong.

It was a relay. He was only a boatman, he said, shrugging, only responsible for this leg of the journey. What happened after his boat set off was not his problem. Once in Hong Kong, the gold went into the vaults of some two hundred Chinese banks. The cocaine went to eager distributor kingpins whose suppliers, dealers, agents and so on were waiting. 'Not for me,' he said. 'Me, I like the quiet life. I would not give up my day job,' he laughed. We watched the sea-cave where he knew Ben would be. After a few minutes' silence, he said, 'If your boyfriend's been sent here, heh, now you know what he been up to. He never told you about it?'

I shook my head and, realizing he couldn't see me, I made a negative-sounding uh-uh. Ben told me so little of the golden world he inhabited that I was embarrassed to admit my ignorance to myself, let alone João.

'*Desgraçado*. Heh. And you come all this way for him? Tsk. I'd do it, cos I owe him one, but why should you? *Que pena*.'

'Don't be sorry. So what's the day job?'

'Jeans. I work at a wholesaler's. You know Lai Kwong Pereira Textiles?'

'Nup.'

João had made this trip innumerable times before. Tonight had not been timed with his own cargo 'delivery' back to Hong Kong because of the likelihood of us bringing Ben back, dead or alive. He removed the lids that concealed the boat's cabin cupboards to show me that they were empty, but I could not see a thing anyway.

He'd waited for hours in darkness before and I wasn't going to try to imagine what he could be thinking about during the long waits. It was not like he could read or listen to radio. I didn't bring the Sony Walkman. Perhaps his patience was more intense than his imagination, and he'd learned to meditate, not medicate. Not even nicotine was allowed: the glow from a lit cigarette could attract customs officers. What an ironic contrast. To think that he was handling such a shiny commodity yet we were sitting in an unlit time and space.

I had already learned to be calm just being in the boat, where my sense of hearing seemed to have improved when I had thought disco had damaged part of me forever. I was rocked and soothed only by the cradle that was a narrow cabin, in the womb-like movement of the waves. My shutter lids got real heavy and I wanted nothing more than to collapse and sleep, yet I was still sitting upright. My head rolled from side to side like I was a buoy…

'Ay! Wake up, wake up. They're here.'

I strained to see. The sea-caves were lit by hooded lamps. They'd arrived here by boat from the cove and I could see Ben's outline. He was taller than all of them, but cornered by a wolf pack he seemed dwarfed. Like the bounty hunter, he'd been lured by greed to shady ventures, and greed had pushed the water high. I counted. There were nine men prowling, all armed, four with Uzi machine guns and the other five with stick-like weapons. The view was faint, and I had to use my old skills — an acute sense of hearing, perfect pitch, musical training, a disco heart.

Somewhere above the sea-caves, bats fizzled with distressed squeals and over-flapping wings. On skids of the higher terraces of the grotto were an Ali Baba's wealth of white powdered coke in bags and opium in plastic boxes of brown cakes and other substances in pouches and vials, resembling a vaulted bank guarded by a secret band of thieves and hoodlums.

Four implacable-looking men, cradling their Uzis like handbags so that they could carry their hooded lamps, dispersed to the back of the caves, checking if all was in order, as they should be. It was like a giant fridge door had opened. Temporarily lit, the cave was deeper than I first thought. Further still in the cold dark corners was more loot, en route somewhere. Boxes of electronic equipment, whiskey, radios, stoves, fridges, typewriters were stamped, sealed and labeled in at least two languages. Most of this stuff would contain gold some place deep in its construction, yet nothing was glittering and nothing was good.

The four men came back to the foreground, like it was a theater, where lights simply faded in and out. I was knocked out by the countless wealth in smuggled goods. These were not pizzas or pianos. Ben had been sucked into the lucrative filth of deals and more deals. He must have been thinking the same, as he stood, head down, between the four men, who also carried radios. The boss seemed to be a bearded nastafied dude who actually did look like a wolf dressed in combats. He could be Nepalese, Thai, Cambodian or any other six nationalities I could think of. It was hard to say as he had so little in the way of skin or eyes showing under all that hair.

The Wolf patrolled around as though Ben was a pair of boots he was considering buying. Then he shook his head slowly.

'What you doing?'

'I gave you back—'

'No! Shut up, music boy! You come back from Singapore. Something missing. Either your brain or 285 ounces or 10,000 US dollars.'

'I have it, Leandro. I told you I have it.'

The name told me he was some kind of Indo-Portuguese mongrel, probably dealing since he was three in the favelas of Goa. But here was the speech. I knew it was coming, like at a wedding… or a funeral, more likely.

'You got plenty warning, music boy. You don't play with the music. You playing with the fire. We been so good to you. You work hard, we pay. But what happened? You keep losing at baccarat. Cos you're shit. And still we nice to you because I like you. Now I don't like you.'

Simply said. The Wolf's speech was probably no different from the ones he made in the playground as a dealing toddler. Silently, I said a prayer and goodbye to Ben. This was it, I said to myself, this was it. I stole a look at João. Arms folded, frowning, he looked like he was watching a serious play, calm and tense at the same time.

The Wolf flicked his chin, giving the signal. The other three Uzi-toting men grabbed Ben's shoulders and tied his hands behind his back. 'What the? Hey!' said Ben. One of them slapped his face. Ben roared, twisted and squirmed, falling over rocks and wriggling his protest and indignation, but the three kept him pinned. They seized him around the waist and grabbed his collar. Each time he resisted, they jabbed his stomach with their guns. He was rained with slaps on his head and ears, which immobilized him.

Ben screamed and cried but the three, now assisted by two more men of the stick-armed variety, dragged him to a wall of rock. They lashed his wrists together and tied him to the wall, hands high overhead. They removed his Puma sneakers and pulled down his Hang Ten jeans. I closed my eyes. I was feeling very sick at this point. João nudged me. Stay awake, he whispered, like I was falling asleep.

The Wolf licked his lips. 'I ask you again, music boy. Where is the two eighty-five? I am happy to take ten grand US, if you don't have the two eighty-five.'

Ben shook his head. 'I'll get it to you. Next week. I swear.'

Four men came forward and slapped him all over again and struck his shins with the sticks. Ben screamed and screamed in the semi-darkness while the lamps flickered, as if in sympathy. They kept hitting his shins and his feet.

'We will now break your fingers one by one. So make it easy for everyone and just tell us where is the missing gold from Singapore.'

No, I hissed, no. My breaths were short and pained. My heart was beating rhythms I never thought I had in me. Ben cursed and prayed to Yahweh, the Jewish God he never believed in, in a language I never heard him use except in swearing, and now he was praying in it too. A twig snapped in the darkness, but there were no twigs. Ben screamed and screamed. They'd broken a finger. I didn't dare imagine how. He started to breathe heavily.

'What do you say, music boy?'

But he didn't reply as he had passed out after hyperventilation. I thought back on my time with him. Those fingers had whanged a guitar and spun a few decks and caressed my cheeks and were now being violated. They might as well be crushing me. I could not picture a time when I had been happier than when Ben was the axman and I was the canary. How it was always meant to be. Ben would be maimed even if he survived the night. He would never play again.

They tried to revive him by splashing water from a bottle, for it was no fun torturing an unconscious victim. Well, I coulda told them that wouldn't do. If he were asleep, yeah. Ben just hung there, eyes shut, limbs slack. They prodded him with the ends of their Uzis and kept on for a minute or so, until Ben opened his eyes.

'Good morning! We are not finished. Another finger we break now. So. Start again. What do you say, music boy? Where's the two eighty-five or a dime?'

Two men with sticks started to bend his fingers back again and I couldn't bear to watch.

I couldn't think if I had seen any gold lying around. Certainly no cash. There was none in the secret cupboard at Bela Vista and none in the club. The ten grand was the money we were supposed to pay Tai Gor back in the current instalment. Could I have missed something? A fleeting lapse of concentration as I jogged my memory. No. Nada. Definitely no gold.

Ben shrieked, 'OK! OK!'

I waited, as did the others.

'With my girlfriend. She's got it.'

The Wolf grinned. I couldn't believe my ears. They'd got so good in the course of the long night I must have heard wrongly. But Ben repeated it.

'She's got it. Cash. You know where the Estoril club is, Leandro.'

'See? That's why I like you. Let him go.'

Several hands unshackled Ben and he tumbled like a piece of scaffolding from the rock. They dragged him to the edge of the sea-cave.

He shivered loudly. He didn't have his Hang Ten jeans on, or his sneakers. Across the bay, a stuttering engine rose above the roar of the waves. Salty sprays flew over the bald head of a boatman who approached the mouth of the cave as elegantly as an eagle. Ben wept freely as he was lowered into the powerboat.

'Where are they taking him to?' I asked João. He put his finger to his lips to say shhh. Then he unwrapped a towel that had been in his cabin cupboards. It was a gleaming gun, as snug as a baby. I could not see what sort it was.

'Don't hurt her, please,' Ben pleaded in a pained voice. 'Don't hurt her, Leandro.'

Three of the men hopped into the boat. They propped him like a rag doll and used a rope to tie his feet and his hands together. Ben groaned. Starlight sparkled over the black horizon, indicating it was dawn soon. How many times had I taken off my heels and had breakfast at the all-day diner with Dallas minutes before dawn after a hard night's partying? How many times had we said 'cheers' and clinked our paper coffee cups at the first rays of the sun? I could not remember.

The Wolf started gyrating and dancing in a lewd way. He put out his lower lip in a pout as though he was a pole dancer. The other men humored him by tittering like birds. 'Women, eh? You can't let them get to you, music boy!' laughed the Wolf, now standing huge, arms akimbo, tall, a long way up from the level of the boat. 'Adeus Amadeus!' he sang.

The three men got ready and were hoisting Ben off the hull of the boat. They were done with him! It was a pesky task. Ben was writhing, screaming and struggling like a baby who refused to have his diaper changed. The Wolf nodded to one of the gunmen, who then aimed his Uzi at Ben from the watery stage that had been the venue for Ben's gig.

I said another little prayer for Ben. Juice fell from my shutters openly. I kept them open in case I would not see Ben again. He didn't want them to hurt me. I knew that he loved me then, but he had to squawk. It was only natural when he was being tortured. I didn't hate him for bitchin' on me but something inside me cracked like a brittle cake. Of course he'd want to save his flippers, but I feared for both of us. They were sure to come and get me now.

A gunshot exploded into the marine calm of dawn. I looked around, unsure what I should be seeing. João had opened fire. He shot one at the armed men in the sea-cave, but he had missed.

Yet more rapid explosions of machine guns followed, erupting into smoke and flames. The men on the watery stage had opened fire into the darkness, though they did not know what or who they were shooting at. There was a great deal of confusion and it was getting light soon. Customs, the Wolf yelled to the others. Customs. The bald boatman of the powerboat tumbled overboard. The three men with Ben jumped off into the sea. I put my hands over my mouth so I would not scream.

João had kept us hidden well, for the men could not tell. 'Don't worry, I kill nobuddy,' he drawled to me, unperturbed by the commotion in front of us.

There was panic as each jumped into the sea by which they had arrived. Like a wolf pack, as soon as they saw one doing that, each followed and did the same. They swam in all directions, some toward the rocks, some toward the boat they first arrived in, hoping for a quick getaway. The engine started. Water seeped through the holes of the bullet-riddled boat. Not long after, they would be sinking.

The name of the boat Ben was lying in was *Nauti Girl*. It was also in Chinese characters. I wasn't too sure if it was the translated name or just any other Chinese name so that the boat name was bilingual, as was the regulation in Hong Kong. Although a contradiction in terms, it was in faded neon paint, like a pair of favorite jeans. I could see to read the words, and realized it was already light.

White herons soared from the mangroves, their branches unburdened from the weight of the birds. Soon the morning sky was alive with whirring white wings and chattering, as if the birds' cries protested the invasion of their roost.

João and I waited until it was clear and there was no one around. The swimmers had dispersed. They had either drowned or they'd taken off. It took a while, and it seemed like an eternity, though it must have been only fifteen minutes max. João was so keen on repaying his personal debt to Ben, and I could not bear to leave Ben here in the *Nauti Girl.*

João started his quick and silent monster and we shot toward the *Nauti Girl.* Ben had lost consciousness and he lay there in his Uncle Sams, stuporous. I'd seen that same look on the greaser too, when he went into his coma. It's odd that I referred to it as his coma rather than the coma. I just saw it as his, and his private world of frothing darkness.

All that was left visible in the sea-cave were the hooded lamps abandoned by the men. In rosy daylight, indeed they looked like pretty gold pendants hung up and strung along, but they might as well be parsnips. We had to take the exit pretty quick. João said, 'Hey, mate, how you doin', you gonna be just fine.' He groaned and heaved Ben's battered body into his black speedboat. I carefully examined the broken left index finger and tied up his flipper in rags I found in the boat's cabin. 'Don't worry 'bout that,' said João. 'I got a guy to do that. To do anything. Well, almost anything,' he grinned, and I saw then that he had gold teeth. He didn't smile once all night. That is, until now.

When we got back to the Inner Port, João called a traditional bone-setter. Here we were in the safe house of the Sailor's Palace because we were nowhere near the Estoril or the Bela Vista. Seagulls flapped their wings and squawked from the harbor. When the bone-setter had left, João made us some jasmine tea and I sipped it as though it was the finest and lushest cocktail I ever had the pleasure of putting down. Ben was running a hothead and we were treating him only with Chinese medicine. He probably had an infection from the injuries he sustained. He opened his eyes after a couple of hours and thanked me. He reached to hold my hand and I grabbed it and held it tight. I shook my head and my tears fell. I pointed at João. 'Don't thank me,' I said, choking on each word. 'your buddy here saved your life. He fired a gun and they all jumped off.'

'I guess they were fraidy cats.'

'Nup,' said João, wiping dishes from the drainer with a filthy blue towel that looked sketchily like the one in the boat's cabin cupboard. 'They ain't got enough to pay off the customs dudes,' said João. I was right, it was the towel that the Luger handgun was kept in. He wiped it a bit with the same towel, wrapped it and tossed it back under the sink cupboard like it was a sink declogger. After that he had to go. He had his own stuff to do. He patted Ben on the back. 'You're OK, buddy. You doin' fine. You doin' fine.'

'Shouldn't we take him to the hospital?' I said.

'Nup,' he said, shutting his door behind him, 'he doin' fine.'

But he ain't actually. Ben was in a spaz state. His front teeth were broken and jagged. He had rips along his skull cave and his forehead and eyes were red and had blown up so much his eyebrows were in the wrong place. I couldn't look at him. This wasn't Ben anymore. My handsome New Yorker from Harlem was now in hell. Tears came to my eyes again. He was striped for life. He should be on a drip, jeez even I knew that, he was in so much pain it was making eating or drinking impossible.

'If they survived they'll be back to get me, Ben,' I said, looking away from him at a Chinese zodiac racing calendar, with Arabic race-horses and English ads for Player's cigarettes on the margins, on João's wall. It was Wednesday June the 24th, I noted. I would never forget this day. The bells from the cathedral rang their hourly peals. 'You remember what you told them? That I had the money you owe them?'

'I'm sorry I did that.'

'No. It's cool. I get it.'

'You do?'

'I don't hate you,' I said, wiping my shutter juice with the backs of my flippers. We were all alive thanks to João. Ben had already got a raw deal. 'Anyway, you remember what you told them?'

'Yeah.'

'Well, where is that money? Don't tell me your tomb at the Bela Vista. You ain't got dust. Just dust,' I wept.

'Li-an, I'm gonna get it, when I can get up—'

'No, you stay down,' I said. 'We'll do it later.'

I could not keep up with what he was saying and I made no attempt to reply or even acknowledge it. My eyelids were determined to shut. What was it I had? Oh, yeah, right, I remembered. That boob of a doctor had first hissed out that vile word — ptosis. I was so exhausted

I fell asleep right there, in João's split rattan chair (his only chair). I curled up and put my heels to ass in a fetal position. The room was cramped and smelling of curry, tea leaves, stale coffee, cigarettes, sweat, deodorant, Chinese herbs, plus a hundred intricate little secret scents woven into the fabric of the building, I could not care. Those scents had already permeated my skin and my other vital organs and it would not bother me if I had to breathe João's room for the rest of my life.

When I woke up and looked at João's bedside Chinese alarm clock with the chrome bicycle bells on either side of it, I guessed I must have been asleep an hour and a half. I'd lost balance and nearly fell out of the rattan chair. I looked over at Ben. He was breathing very heavily, his eyes closed. He was running an even hotter head than before. I touched him. His head, neck. I held his hand. He was like a kettle. It was not good. His mug was white as cigarette ash. There was no phone and João had not returned from whatever he was doing. I had to get Ben to hospital somehow.

But I also needed to be back at the Estoril later. One night without me and the place must be in shreds. Just my luck, I seemed to be able to land two guys in hospital. I didn't want to bump into that South African creep, Dr Raj. No, wait, wasn't he Australian?

We could be stuck at the hospital for hours and hours, just like the last time with Paolo. I could think of nothing but Ben's long guitar fingers and how he was gonna get fixed up real good again. But my head hurt. I hadn't slept much and had eaten nothing. My tummy was rattling like a roulette ball doing 90mph.

My eyes were hooded and puffy from crying. I hoped he would wake up soon. I was gonna get some pork chop buns for our breakfast. Coffee. For our picnic at the hospital. It would be a nice surprise for Ben when he got better in a few hours, with any hope, by the evening. I opened the door a little and put my peepers out. I could hear the sound of children playing, dogs barking, nothing spish.

I checked my jeans pocket and I had enough patacas for about ten buns, but I thought two would do us fine. I had plenty of change to call Thaew to pick Ben and me up and take us to the hospital. I had to go find a phone booth. I drifted in the direction of the barbecue smells and the shacks, hovering so close over the stench of the blocked drains and harbor sewers.

I got caught in one of the flapping sheets of laundry. I thought the sound was from the teeming crowds of seagulls. The next minute, I felt myself strong-armed into a car. I glimpsed that it was black with blacked-out windows. I guessed it was too late to grab a bite. I gasped at the shock of being abducted. A massive hand that stank of sweat and smoke covered my mouth to prevent me from screaming and I could hear the scuffle of feet (theirs) and some clever little dance involving me being lifted by my ass, swept off my feet and into the vehicle. The hand was so large it covered even my nose, paralyzing me. I could not breathe and for a second I pictured myself as Paolo with an ineffectual mouth that gaped like a fish. The maneuver to get me in the car was so quick it was almost as though I was weightless, since I could struggle so little. As soon as I was seated my hands were tied and I was gagged. I went cold at the fear of being raped or maimed or killed. I was totally unarmed and unprepared for this. There were two cats in front and two at the back, sandwiching me in between. All were pretty hefty toughies wearing shades. The view didn't last. One of them blindfolded me with a synthetic-feeling rag. He was so rough, his fingernail scraped me on the temple. My head was damp a while later and I knew I was bleeding where I got injured.

The car sped off, taking sharp turns and Chinese angles. Nobody said a word. I had no idea where we were going so they needn't have taken the trouble to go jujubes at it. I was a better driver and parked even better that one time when I filched that Chrysler. To be fair, it was for joyriding, and joy was to be had in easy rides. I was one classy number, as Dallas had said. My stomach was not OK but I was not going to toss up bile and lining onto their upholstery. It would only get caught up in the gag I was now sporting. I was feeling lightheaded and travel sick from the roller-coaster twists and turns.

We went down a steep hill and the car stopped. I thought I heard a ship's long, low horn. Birds screeched over us. I thought we were near water. This is where I would go down, for sure.

Front passenger (Macanese accent): So you know, babe. This is about music boy. Where is he?

Me: arrgkgh arrghkgh...

Back passenger removed my gag. I gasped. My poor Ben was so injured and sick and now they wanted more of him.

Me: He's at the Sailor's Palace. He's unconscious. He's very sick, has high temperature and can't speak. If you don't believe me, you can—

Front passenger (laughing): We don't want your pretty bwah-friend. You can keep him. He says you have the ten thousand US dollars or two eighty-five ounces in gold at the disco. We take you there now and you give us the money, then we let you go.

That would be from the stash I had been keeping for Tai Gor's payment at the end of the month, which was Tuesday, June 30th... Haysooz, Santa Maria, it was six days' time. So not only would we owe Tai Gor 20 gees, now it was another 10 so that made it 30. Thanks, Ben, you sure are awesome to do business with.

'That's not my problem!' I found myself crying out. 'It's Ben who owes you that money! I need the money for something else. Listen to—'

'No, you listen. You get the money now or you get out of the car now. We got a fridge in the trunk we goin' to tie your neck to. Then you jump into the sea, just like music boy supposed to. You can swim but you not goin' far. So. Is it your problem or is it not.'

What choice had I at this point? Like a mouse on barbs, I obeyed every instruction to get them what they wanted. When we got to the Estoril, they took off my blindfold and untied my hands. I got my keys out, disabled the alarm, went in with my two chaperones, the backseat boobs. I reached for the false panel under the DJ console and started to count 10,000 USD, which was about 80,000 patacas. Of course there was not enough. What was the magic monthly figure to give Tai Gor again? I remembered. It was 29,200 patacas. We were 20 short anyway before Ben was whisked away to his moonlit rendezvous. We had 9,000 in the DJ console. It was a total joke. The baboons must have been laughing at our pathetic little industry. My math was getting so good now, somebody give me an award. They slapped me real hard. I saw stars and stripes. I was sent flying and I steadied myself when I reached ground zero. I sat like a glass-eyed teddy bear on the floor with legs outstretched while they took all of it and said they'd come back for the rest, which was 71,000 patacas. Otherwise: fridge, neck, sea. I shook my head and cursed Ben all the way, under my breath. Right now, he needed to get to the hospital. The 'splainin' can come later. He owed me mega big time, if not the money, the explanation.

God, I was crunk. I got sliced near my eye. I was slapped on my face, which had drawn beads of blood near my skull cave. I was sitting in the DJ console without a pork chop bun. When they had gone, I counted the money left. I was wondering how to top up 20 gees for Tai Gor. The cash desk had almost nothing in it. Two hundred. Great. I took it, folded it nicely and pressed it into my jeans pocket. I rummaged in the drawer for the mirror that we used for cutting lines in the golden age. I used it to check my injuries. Was nothing. A nail mark. I tossed the mirror back into the drawer and leaned back.

I was away for one night, and the goons had shut the place. No wonder no roughage. Tonight I just didn't feel like opening, but I must. There was Mah Sing and Rocco to fog. Ben had been good to them, they must have been selling enough joysticks and jellybeans to choke a million sailors all the way down to the bottom of the South China Sea. It was almost 12 noon, neither night nor day in my mind. Using the phone in the office, I called Thaew. I said to him to take me to the Sailor's Palace. I just wanted to check up on Ben. I didn't tell him that if Ben was at all conscious, I was going to scream. I was so mad I couldn't think straight. Thaew looked at me all weird, but said OK when I yelled, 'Drive.'

'Wait here,' I said to Thaew as I ducked in, past the elderly doorman with the Dr Fu Manchu beard. Actually, it was more like Fu Mancini: it bore the ballroom elegance of a bygone era. João wasn't his usual 'doin fine' self. In fact, he looked a little cagey and distant, like he'd never seen me before. His face was pale and harshly shadowed by the dreadful yellow light of the tungsten bulb in his room. I said, 'what's the matter.' He said Ben had gone into hospital. He called for a meat wagon when Ben's temperature hadn't gone down on its own. The paras said to him there was some kind of infection, which João didn't understand, and internal bleeding, which João did understand. 'Ain't good, man, ain't good,' he concluded in a plaintive voice. He was nearly in tears. 'Is my fault, Li-an!'

'No, no.' I shook my head. 'He's sick because he got banked on by those dicks. It's his fault. João, listena me. It's his own fault he owed them good. That's all.' But I was crying too. I couldn't hear the conviction in my voice. Whatever I was saying was meaningless and after the fact. We both didn't know if Ben would make it.

'I shoulda taken him there sooner. And not tried the bone-setter this morning. I thought he gonna be fine.' João's tears fell and his eyes were wide with anxiety. 'Sorry, Li-an, sorry,' João wept. He reached over and clung onto me as though I was his mom. I didn't want to hug him back, so I gave him stiff little pats on the back as if to say, 'well done' when in fact I had no more words of consolation left in me for myself, him or Ben.

All I could think of was people like Ben and I wouldn't ever have insurance. I sighed. I knew there'd be a bill coming. I wanted to forget about that because I had my own Big Ones to worry about first. As long as they kept him alive there, I could try to trace his family in New York. They were like, MDs, right? 'Course they had money. He'd be flown back first class if it was up to them. I put that on my ever-growing list of things to do.

João's paws started moving over my back like a bug infestation and he tried to kiss me. When he sensed that I froze, he stopped. What a nerve! I wasn't in the mood for any more funny business.

I pulled away abruptly and said, 'See ya.' His arms fell to his sides and he wiped his eye juice on his diesel-stained T-shirt sleeves. I didn't look back once as I got back into the Benz, where Thaew was asleep quite comfortably with his mouth open. He woke up straightaway and started the engine. Once home, I called the agency to book another DJ for tonight. I called Mah Sing and Rocco to get their asses down here too, but they were not there and I helplessly left messages. How much did I realistically think they would be selling tonight? Ben wasn't here and they worked for him, not me. I couldn't be serious if I thought we'd clear 20 gees after wages.

I needed Auntie's bright green soup to wash down a Tagamet and a couple of Brufen for luck. I was beat and needed to crash and to clear my head, spread some Vaseline on my cut. I was A-OK with OTC (over-the-counter).

I got back to the pavilion and set my clock so that I wouldn't oversleep. When I woke up, the usual routine of green soup and putting on makeup took over, except that it took a little longer using industrial cammo on my zebra face. I thought about Ben for about a second and my blood warmed again with fear and anxiety.

Just so that I was clear: Ben's boating boys were owed seventy-one grand and Tai Gor was owed twenty-nine. Total debt a hundred grand. At the most we'd make 4,000 tonight from juice and jelly-beans. Was I any good at blackjack or baccarat? People gambled just to win back their debts. The risk was being in even greater debt. I wasn't that dumb. I'd take a flapjack over blackjack any day.

Where was I going to find the money in six days' time? It was all going to end for me. I could feel it. I said to Dallas I'd come clean but I was a bunny. I never thought I'd meet someone like Ben. I was sucked dry, and I was the sucker. I didn't know what he'd done or what other promises he had made to me. All I knew was that he had promises to keep to these cats and he'd taken the Estoril's dough, my dough, for baking my bread.

I slurped the soup and I remembered something. Speaking of el diablo himself, didn't he once say that the record company had an offer on the table for me? A deal memo. How could I forget that? We didn't take it at the time. Ben said I needed 15,000 US dollars. I would ring New York straightaway. What was the name of the A&R cat? I had to think hard. Did I write it down? I fished in the pond that was the inside of my chain belt quilted handbag. I could be in the caboose for the stuff that was in here. I looked at my notebook of lyrics, chords, songs, scribblings, taking care not to be sidetracked by my own sentimentality. It took a while to find it but I'd got his name. It was Dan Shapiro.

I checked the time difference. I called international directory assistance and the operator. I was put through about a million people, though I didn't mind — it sure was nice to hear familiar American voices again and to be called ma'am. Finally I got to speak to Dan

Shapiro's assistant. I was so astonished I couldn't speak. There was no deal memo. There was no 15,000 US dollars mentioned. All he said to Ben was that he liked my tape. Very much. OK so I should be happy that a) he liked it and b) I didn't need to come up with 15,000 US dollars now.

Or I should be totally slammed that I had no deal after all. After that piece of appalling discovery, I made the obligatory check on Paolo, as though I just wanted to make sure that shocking news wasn't automatically followed by more. Still there, still in his wheelchair, still drunk or drinking. He had his whiskey in his plastic tumbler slotted into the chair's drink holder and he was slurping from a straw, hands-free. It went everywhere as he could not even use a straw properly. His chin and bib were wet. He moved his head jerkily like he didn't have a neck. It tore my heart to see him being transformed into a reptile. It brought hot tears to my eyes. I rushed to him and used the towel on the back of his wheelchair and wiped his chin dry. I sighed and shook the tears away like they were flies. *The Young and the Restless* was on TV at low volume. He saw me and raised his dead-as-a-button eyes. I didn't know where to begin. Just as I was about to speak, he spoke. He slurred just one word, Li-an. It sounded outlandish and bestial, like a talking animal in a kids' show. I was speechless. He was better? He must be better. I just survived a mental night and all drug-free! It wasn't a hallucination. What if he could move again? Could he? I held his head with both my hands. I stared at him for a second or more. I checked both his eyes.

But it was time to leave him and get ready anyway, dressing up, glittery adornments, quick snort. 'Paolo, I will be back, you're doing great,' I said at last. I had to be my alter ego again, just like I was before João and I went on the moonlit sea like the owl and the pussycat. Getting ready had started to grate on me, it had become a farce, especially as I didn't have Ben, my fellow narcissist, getting ready with me. Alone, it seemed vacuous and unjustified. I had cuts and bruises. My skin was like a tomato's. I was going onstage without the boost of offstage passion that was my true drug. Together our egos must have kept us buoyant. Just for that night, I wanted to stay in and be with Paolo. We were both injured and hurt.

I was being optimistic that night. Wednesday night, June 24. We hardly sold eighty covers. That was not even twenty-four hundred. Mah Sing and Rocco laughed in my face. People were here to see and hear Ben, they said, as if I didn't know that already. If they weren't here, they added, it was because Ben wasn't here. How were they supposed to push enough jellybeans for me? Even the Singaporean bartenders had minutes spare to polish the mojito glasses. I was dreaming of a white Christmas when I hoped we were going to make close to four thousand patacas. By Tuesday, June 30th I was to have a hundred-grand ready for Tai Gor, or else... they would use their alternative means for honoring the deal. I wasn't afraid of kicking off. I was afraid of the big bad wolf of torture. I'd end up a slab of meat like Ben, but worse.

Thaew came to pick me up as usual when the Estoril was shut.

It was late when I got back to the pavilion. Took a big hit of substandard Vitamin Ex. I looked into his room and the lamp was off. I couldn't see his hooded peepers. I shut his door very quietly.

I started to search again. I started in Paolo's study, the womb of depravity, where everything had begun. The safe with its burned-out lock. The couches, the paintings, the Persian carpets. All his album sleeves one by one. I worked methodically and in total silence. No music for once in my life to distract me. I just wanted to find the money that went missing originally on New Year's Eve — quarter of a mill, which Ben had tried to nick but failed. I went through the living room, the crockery and glassware armários in the dining room, between the stacked limão baskets in the kitchen, under crates of tomatoes, in the ceramic lid of the manteiga dish for butter, behind the many queijo boards for cheese, under the heavy mahogany banco and the toalha chest for linen in the washroom with its basket-weave patterned wicker lid. It surprised me what I found: how much food we were getting through. Auntie never reported to me that the food allowance was too much or too little. We just carried on after Paolo was taken ill. There was food everywhere, but no dough. Nothing. Diddly squat.

In Paolo's old bedroom on the first floor, I found that he had so few clothes and was so tidy, I could barely remember that he actually lived in this room for a short while.

I was drenched in pore juice and my noodle was in shreds. I looked at myself in the mirror and I saw Dallas beside me in the reflection. She had that purple boat-neck dress she bought on sale at Harlem Irving. Madison, she shook her head, what have you done? She smiled a sorry smile, one that she gave for her best 'customers', good boys, those that she had decided not to scam after a long night. 'Did you come all the way out here to do this?'

'To do what?' I said, genuinely confused by my own actions.

'To put a guy on ice downstairs and to put another in the icebox,' Dallas said. 'Ben didn't make it.'

The moment I pictured Ben, I sobbed. I rummaged through Paolo's vanity cabinet drawers, slamming as I was shutting them. My heart was breaking with each crash of wood on wood. Cotton wool, bars of soap and little towels fell out because I couldn't shut the drawers properly. Doesn't he have any shit here? They did it to themselves, both of them. My hands were shaking and banging like a washing machine. My fingers got caught in a drawer and I screamed. I pulled my fingers out. I ripped tissues out of the bamboo tissue-box holder and jabbed my eyes and nose with them.

'Uh-uh,' Dallas shook her head again robotically, like she was dancing. I was not used to seeing her shaking her head all the time. I mean, she never liked taking Es as far as I'd known her. 'Paolo was bitten. Maddie, he'd been poisoned. By you. By all the stuff you've been giving him. And Ben! He's been living in casinos. He's been smuggling gold to make more to pay for more debt, which in turn meant he could owe more and gamble more. Were you blind? Remember the gambling addict's holy grail? Betting on anything. Now he's paid with his life—'

I couldn't listen without cutting in. I slammed both palms on the vanity counter and leaned forward toward the mirror. 'I'm in debt for both his and my shit, Dall. I couldn't keep him afloat when I'm sinking myself.' I found some pills at last in the drawer and recognized them as ones I gave him. I rocked my head back jerkily and swallowed a couple.

'I did nothing, I swear!' I blew and wiped my nose noisily. All I wanted was to run a club, be a musician, playing to people. 'Showbiz! It was the biggest buzz I ever got!' Showbiz also made me crunk with greed. I didn't say it. Pretty obvious. I was not myself and I looked like a corpse. I pulled a face at the mirror to make sure it was really me that I was seeing. My face was gray, my tongue yellow and my eyes red. All the colors of great health, so complementary to Paolo's bedroom color scheme. Yeah, I sure was an oriental lily now.

I took Paolo's shaving knife from the drawer. I ran out and downstairs without saying goodbye to Dallas. I suddenly thought of somewhere that the money from the safe might have been hidden. Somewhere obvious! Yes! Somewhere Paolo thought no one would think of. I couldn't believe I was so smart at gumshoeing and never thought of this before. My sense of elation was overpowering and I felt I was in those dreams where your thighs and calves were weightless and wherever you tried to run you ended up soaring in the air.

I went to the pool cabañas and the pool itself. I jumped in and swam, gasping and choking and kicking rather than front crawl, until I got to it. I grabbed it like a goat. I slashed The Kissers to pieces. Panting, I watched them collapse and waited for the 250 wet large bundles to tumble out of the bottom lip. Instead, the unidentified, formerly inflatable object bled into ribbons of red vinyl, before the strips themselves floated as flat as the pool surface in radially opposite directions to each other.

I kicked and paddled back to the pool edge with the knife in my hand. I climbed out and just sat there watching the beast disintegrate. Nada, not even two-bits. Now why did I think there was lettuce in The Kissers? I clutched my hair with both hands. I was going crazy. I knew I was. I knew I'd lose my mind out here. I tossed the knife to the side and hugged my knees, head down. I didn't know a soul here and not a single song could cheer me up now. All those damned anthems we danced to — they didn't march Ben back to life, did they?

I returned to my pavilion, dripping like a sewer rat. The household was fast asleep and even Paolo's TV and lights were off. I got changed out of my navy and gold party outfit from the club tonight. It was colorfast! I swam in it! I morbidly cheered myself up as I grabbed a towel to dry off my hair roughly. I was wide awake and I had no idea what time it was. Someone like me wasn't a day person, that's for sure. I changed into T-shirt and shorts and crept down to Paolo's study. The place was all dark but I knew it well.

As soon as I was in there, I shut and locked the door, preparing myself mentally for the very last time I would search this room. It was the first place I had looked before snake and the last place after snake. I tried to be methodical, but who was I kidding? I was not a logical person and I started randomly on his bureau and the armário, the shelving, in between and inside every record sleeve, anything that caught my eye, really.

I sank into his leather chair and I thought back on the first day when I arrived here in this house. I shut my eyes. I sat in this very chair and listened to Jan Garbarek until the greaser came in. When I opened my eyes, there it was in front of me. The painting I gave him, of a blue elephant on a gold background.

I once liked that painting that I bought Paolo, but now I detested it. I wanted to take it down and destroy it, but when I removed it from the wall over Paolo's desk, there was another painting behind it. A man pushing an old-fashioned cart in Europe. It weirded me out. Did he mention that it was worth money? I'd sold the grand piano in Johnny's. The one here was on rental. I couldn't sell it. I thought back on the night when I first saw this painting. No, not here. It was in the baroque room in Chicago where I woke up to be told I was going to Asia.

Then I saw the painting a second time. Still it was not on a wall. No, where had I seen it? It was here in Macao after I'd arrived. I remembered now, it was an album cover. I never forget an album cover. It wasn't by anyone famous but it was inspired by a piano piece and that was why Paolo liked it... now, what was the name of the composer?

I jumped to my feet again. I poured myself a whiskey from his decanter into a glass. It didn't come to me. It would involve me going through all the albums again, which I didn't mind because I really missed the greatest hobby of all — browsing through music without any aim or time pressure or care in the world. The album was here somewhere, and I remembered that Paolo showed it to me.

At last I found it. I whipped it on the turntable. It was the most rebellious thing I'd done since I'd known Ben, because he never allowed me to spin a disc, let alone a classical one. I was his lamb. My finger was still in midair, lifting the stylus, when I heard a sound. I stopped. It was the softest shuffle, like rope being pulled. I listened but there was no more. Surely it couldn't be him. His room was upstairs on the main floor. And even if he could stand up and shuffle like some penguin, he couldn't make it down to the basement where his study was without breaking his flippin' flippers and about a thousand bones. I didn't want him hurt. If he broke his flippers he'd be back in the krankenhaus. Paolo? I called out softly, a little tentatively. No reply. These old houses had plenty of weird sounds. We also had mice, Auntie said a few times. I relaxed and dipped the stylus down like the beak of a precious bird.

It came back to me. I'd heard it just that once when I arrived but it was lost on me because I was impatient to go out, I didn't even see the album cover when he put it on. I couldn't remember the circumstances in which I'd heard it, but it wasn't right at the time. It was the most beautiful piece of piano melody I'd ever heard, far superior to Chopin or Beethoven or any of the big boys. It was so simple I wanted to cry. It had the same name as the painting, 'Siciliano', Opus 42 number 2, from *Trois Morceaux Poétiques* by Moszkowski. I read on the back of the sleeve that he was a relatively obscure Polish Jewish German living in Paris (life was naturally multiracial for millennia before racial purification a few decades ago decided it shouldn't be), a composer from the Romantic Period.

Normally I hated everything that Paolo liked, but here I secretly shared his passion for this piece. The melody in A major was poignantly lilting, formed by the 6/8 time triplets, and a little melancholic because it was lifted with a rogue F#minor to C#minor chord change in the third and fourth bar, a daring and modern move for its time and place. That was the 'hook', as they called it nowadays. I pictured Paris in the late 19th century. I didn't bother to read any more of the sleeve notes, I just listened with my peepers shut. It reminded me that I was a complete wastoid. I started with good musical education and now I'd abused it all. They told me I was good. If I was to go into songwriting or classical, I'd be sailing through like the Valkyries' ride. Things had changed long ago for me because I dropped out, because mommy left, because of Sherylanne wanting Dad to kick me out, now Ben, because because because. I inhaled the music as though it was a hallucinogen. My fantasy of being a musician was just that — a fantasy.

I had a strong hunch about this painting. After all, why would he have hidden it behind a piece of junk that I'd given him? Just as well it was small enough to fit behind the elephant painting, like a card into its matching envelope. I went and got big sheets of newspaper from the pile in the corner of the study, still dated just a few days before New Year's Eve, before the snake incident, as though they were waiting for their rightful owner to come back and read them or turn them into scrap.

I carefully wrapped up 'Il Siciliano' with the newspapers and taped it securely. Only a few hours to dawn. I seemed only to have any energy at night. Daytime filled me with terrible sadness and longing. Daytime debilitated me, ever since I worked with Dallas. I reserved my special daytime despondency to taking the Sicilian cart to a Hong Kong auction house. Whatever money it fetched would do me just fine. At the very least it would buy time with Tai Gor and Ben's debt collectors. For a few hours now, I wanted to lie down as it was my only chance. How much were all these albums worth? All his furniture? I could get a valuer to come in. The painting would be quicker.

I had to raise a hundred grand. The painting wouldn't be that, I didn't think it was the Mona friggin' Lisa or anything. Plus all the furniture and the albums? I was so relieved I'd be able to do it after all. There was no junk in this house except mine. Everything that was Paolo's was bourzhee, from the albums to the furniture. It was upsetting to check all this stuff. I thought back to the good times. When it was just piano and pizzas. Something died the day Ben and I sold the grand piano at the restaurant to foot Paolo's bill. And similarly, this house would not be the same without the stuff in it, even I could see that.

I couldn't go back to Chicago leaving Paolo here, and leaving *bohcoo des debts* behind, as I knew the animals would just hunt me down. If they didn't have a nose for it, I'd be dead already. They knew that I knew that they knew. I had to pay up or pay the price. You couldn't run from these guys. Their web of international connections was bigger than Donna Summer's hair.

On Thursday, June 25 1981, I got the 11.15 jetfoil from Macao Ferry Terminal to Tsim Sha Tsui in Kowloon. I couldn't wake up any earlier. I had popped a couple of tabs to get me to sleep quicker. I stepped out like a phantom, careful not to wake Paolo. It was drizzling and gray. The ferry took an hour. I fell asleep. I dreamed about Dallas and João and Ben and Paolo in front of all these people on the ferry, who hadn't a clue what I was up to. I was all alone on this trip and even Thaew wasn't aware where I was going — I got a cab to the ferry terminal. When I woke up, I had fallen on the deck. I got up and stood on the deck without holding onto the railing. I buried my hands and my chin deep into my windcheater. I sandwiched the painting between my feet. Wrapped in newspaper and two sheets of plastic, I made sure it was waterproof even if my club-worthy shoes and jeans weren't already soiled from salt spray. I had my Sony Walkman for company. Caught my gray-green reflection in the glazed indoor seating section and god I thought a LeVee junkie I'd once seen was actually on the boat. Then I realized when I saw my own bright blue headphone sponges that it was only me frightening myself. I looked so horrific and almost beatific that I thought this must be what people look like toward the end of an exquisite and worthwhile life. I wept again when I thought of Ben. At least I knew love. At least he loved me. I thought back on Led Zeppelin's 'Whole Lotta Love' live in Chicago in 1975. Going to the concert was a birthday gift from Dallas. I wiped my tears with a scrap of tissue I found in the windcheater pocket. The jetfoil blades cut through the water, leaving a wake as good as toothpaste foam. Something in me felt kinda lawless and impetuous but I felt free as the sea for the first time.

Every few minutes the Star Ferries departed from Tsim Sha Tsui's Star Ferry Pier to Victoria Harbour in Hong Kong Central or Wan Chai. I knew I needed to head for this area full of art galleries called

Wyndham Street, opposite the old Central Police Station. Somebody would buy this piece of junk. Anybody.

I knew I looked like a tramp who'd just broken into a loaded house to bring this painting here. I went to four galleries and wanted to give up. The painting was weighing me down and I was so tired of carrying it the corners were already dented from being lifted and put down so many times. I wasn't a professional art thief or mover (the same, as far as I was concerned).

Richard Whitfield Gallery finally gave me a chance. It was owned by an oldish bearded English guy of the same name. I thought he was more likely to give me a chance cos he looked kinda like a hobo too. His leather sandals were like he'd been walking the streets for fifty years. His clothes were mismatched and the wrong size. He probably thought I was artistic. I'd heard that the English were less fussy about looking perfect because one could always just be eccentric.

'Interesting.' He put away his reading glasses after he was done looking at it. 'Where did you acquire this?'

'Um… It's my uncle's.'

'I see. This is the second of two, called *The Flower Cart*, by the renowned British artist Charlie Hughes. Il Siciliano #1, *The Horse Cart*, went for… about six thousand US dollars in New York a year ago. I can't remember. I'd like to check that figure and get back to you. Do you want to leave this here and I'd give you a receipt for it?'

'What's that in patacas?'

'You want that in patacas?'

'Or Hong Kong dollars. Sorry, I can't work it out.' I made a hand movement, indicating that I was shtoopid. What did he expect? I was an artiste, not a storekeeper.

'About 46… 48,000 dollars.'

Jeez! In my mind that was nearly half what I owed Tai Gor and Ben's boys, since HK dollars were roughly the same as patacas. It would solve half my problems just like that.

'Can you make it fifty?'

'Like I said, I'd need to check first.'

'Can you make a call now and check it? I don't want to have to come back because I live in Macao and I have to come back by ferry again.'

'You have to come back, I'm afraid. You have no papers, no documents, nothing with you. I need to verify stuff and authenticate it first. If you want to put it on auction, you'd still need to do this. You can't get the money today.'

'OK. How long will it take before you call me back?'

'Three working days at the most. Monday.'

'Three days? That's outrageous.'

'Well, you can't have it.'

'I want to sell it today.'

'Well, you can't.'

'Can you at least give me a letter saying how much it is worth?'

'Oh. You mean like a valuation?'

'Whatever.'

'Yes, I suppose I could. But it will cost you 50 US dollars. Or 350 HK dollars.'

I made a face. What could I do? I gave him an annoyed shrug and wave, a gesture that only an American could pull off.

'OK. Wait here.' Richard Whitfield spoke to me like I was a six-year-old waiting for candy with my hands outstretched. He disappeared into the back room and came back with a form. He filled it out, signed and stamped it. I read it briefly and it said that he thought the painting was worth about 48,000 HK dollars, pending a more detailed valuation. He wasn't going to value it at 50,000 and that was that. The friggin' hippie pig!

I yanked the form out of his hand and picked up the painting. 'Are you going to help me wrap this back?'

'It's 350 dollars, please, for the valuation. You need to leave it here if you want to sell it.'

The sly friggin' hippie pig. I unzipped my windcheater pocket and fished out an assemblage of crumpled notes that resembled a little rotten cabbage. I dumped them on his desk while he peeled off the notes and counted them out correctly. 'I'll give you a receipt for this.' He opened a drawer and wrote out a receipt, which I shoved into the pocket I'd just unzipped.

'Thanks,' I said, not committing myself to anything. I needed the valuation to buy me some time. Should Ben's boys or Tai Gor harass me, I'd show them the piece of paper, that I had the money to pay them back as soon as I sold the painting to the gallery, which was in three days when the formal and more accurate pricing report and verification was done. I wrote down my name and phone number in his book. He sighed and made a note in his diary to call me once he had the final deed done. I could theoretically be paid for the painting in three days! That is if I accepted his offer, which by his grubby calculations could be theoretically lower than his estimate.

But no need to spoil it with so much negativity. I had the same mentally and physically relaxed feeling I'd get after a joint now that I was free of the painting. Every time I'd like to smoke, I should just sell a painting, except that there was no shortage of Mary Janes and I couldn't get my claws on enough Mona friggin' Lisas.

As I was leaving, I caught a reflection in the glass window and it was Ben. I jumped. I was still thinking of him and my heart cracked a little as I left the shop and the bell tinkled above the self-closing door. In the streets, in bars and in the Estoril, I sometimes thought I saw him, or someone looking very like him. I hated that. He was still very much alive in my world, even if Dallas had said to me in my dreams to 'cut the crap'.

I schlepped back to the station and to the ferry terminal for my longish trip back to Macao. Thoughts of Ben came in waves, like the sea. I felt reasonably well and upbeat. You see, Dallas? I'm getting through this all on my own. I want to show you I can do it. And you see, Ben? I found it hard to forgive you for what you did to me but I have already. I still felt the cutting feeling, pangs of weakness for his voice, his humor, and of course his crazy optimism. He haunted me every few hours. I could not stop thinking back to the night in the cave when he had pleaded in his pained voice: 'Don't hurt her, please… Don't hurt her, Leandro.' Now I feared for myself.

When I got back to the pavilion I needed to get ready again for the nightly routine at the Estoril. We couldn't afford to shut any nights at all. The show needed to go on, without Ben's talent. I worked hard and I deserved to get this overbearing debt thing out of the way, thanks to Ben who got me going and who got me stuck here. I looked at my Casio LCD watch. I had a couple of hours left, so I went to Paolo's study again, looking for album covers to fantasize about the music life. And that fantasy, as far as I could remember, was the best thing that my daddy ever taught me. Just you and your music, together always, happiness in your hand. My reverie was interrupted. There was a call for me when I was just sitting there in Paolo's leather armchair like some kinda Buddha, figuring it all out. Auntie said she didn't know who it was. She said a Mr Wheat Field.

'Mr Wheat Field?' Oh! I struggled out of the heavy armchair. My heart tripped along slightly. It was the ape from the gallery. My damp fingers reached for the glossy red phone receiver. The spiraling cord had become so entangled, like instant noodles, that I had to put my face about two inches from the phone itself.

'Well, Miss Donohue, interesting news, interesting news. I just made a call to New York. You know what I said about that British artist Charlie Hughes? Guess what? Il Siciliano #2, *The Flower Cart*. This is a very rare painting, his last in fact. He painted it when he was ill in Italy. We valued it at 12,000 US dollars.'

I could say nothing. No words came. It was double what he told me. You didn't need a math major to work that out. That was about 96,000 patacas, which would completely free me of Ben's and my debt!

'The only issue… what I'm trying to say is… how did you get hold of it? It's not in your name and you don't have any evidence that you own it.'

'What?' I paused and went over in my mind what he just said. 'What are you talking about? I told you my uncle owns it.'

'What is your uncle's name?'

'Paolo Giametti Russo.'

'Mmm. I'm afraid that is not the right answer.'

'Well, maybe someone gave it to him.'

'Can I speak to him?'

'No. He can't speak right now. He's not feeling too good.'

'I have to speak to him. He needs to authorize you to sell this wonderful painting.'

'He's done that. I'm allowed to sell it.'

'Well, I need to see it, I'm afraid—'

'What do you need to see?'

'What we're looking for is provenance. A signed letter from Mr Russo, witnessed by somebody official, like a doctor, an accountant or a lawyer, stating that he was given the painting by the owner, that he is the owner now and that you are authorized to sell it for him.'

'Mr Russo is the owner. I told you.'

'He's not, I'm afraid. Well, not officially, anyway.'

Afraid, afraid, afraid. I was sick of him being afraid of everything. I should be the one who was afraid.

'Who is this official owner then?' I said officiously.

'I suppose there's no harm in telling you. Il Siciliano #2 is owned by Jack Ray Simmonds and Il Siciliano #1 is owned by Alexander J. Richardson.'

The name Alexander Richardson rang a ring-a-ding. It was Paolo's lawyer and partner! I didn't care about Il Siciliano #1, which was not in my possession anyway. I was curious why this Jack Ray Simmonds's #2, *The Flower Cart*, was in Paolo's house. It could be on loan. In my fitful dreams, I remembered the baroque room in Chicago where I lay and this very painting was hanging on the yellow fireplace wall, which no doubt I only glanced at in a Venetian mirror reflection.

I could not dwell on all that now. I must press on. With the new valuation, the entire debt would be paid off. Just on the back of one painting, or should I say the front of it? Kewl.

'The new valuation is ready for you, Miss Donohue—'

'Right.'

'Any time you would like to collect it, along with the painting—'

'No. I'll leave the painting with you. Please just fax the valuation to me. I'll give you the number in a sec, Mr Whitfield, when I put the machine on. I'll get you the statement of authority. My uncle would definitely like to sell this painting. Thank you for getting back to me so quickly.'

The only way to get this letter done was to forge it. Forge is just forget without a t. There were no signatures of Alex Richardson or

Jack Ray Simmonds available to me. I'd have to search the entire study again, and hell I'd searched enough drawers already to last me a lifetime.

I spent some time going through Paolo's Rolodex. In my mind, the little cards of accounting were whirring too. It was unlikely that I would be able to sell the painting. Here I had been thinking all this time that I was some smart-ass business bunny. I felt defeated, senseless and centless.

I looked at my Casio and it was already 7.23pm. Normal people had gone home. Only the night owls like myself were getting ready for flight toward the bright lights, thumping beats and the stage. I had to get changed and ready for the night's usual festivities at the Estoril.

My thoughts were interrupted by a loud crash from Paolo's room upstairs on the main floor. Auntie's voice immediately shouted out, help, help. There were quick running footsteps coming from the corridor above. I looked up, unsure of what to make of it. Rather slowly and warily I rose from Paolo's desk. I left his study in the basement and went up the stairs.

Paolo had collapsed from his wheelchair onto the floor. Paolo! I shouted. You OK? No reply. His drink, whatever it was, had spilt. The bottle on his bedside had shattered. There were glittery shards everywhere and the floor was wet with ice and the drink that he was drinking. Auntie! Auntie! Call an ambulance, I shouted in Cantonese. The *amah-cheh* ran off to the phone in the hall. I checked Paolo's eyes and they looked dead. I felt his pulse. Nothing.

If he died, it would solve my debt problems. But I did not want him to die. I did not want the Estoril or Paolo's assets. I realized I had been living out what Ben wanted. All that glitters. All fooey. Didn't Debbie Harry sing about dreaming being free? For a start, it wasn't free. I didn't dream of being a cold-blooded blipper like Ben. Wasn't I an immigrant twice? My first new start was in the States. I tried hard not to be like my mom, who could not take in new experiences or feel happy about anything. The second start was here. It seemed not so long ago that I first arrived here and lay on a pool chaise longue and didn't know a soul or a thing. Well, that was the dream. It was a time of innocence, a time when feeling amused was a form of self-protection. As Dallas once said, whatever she did, she did out of amusement, desperation and self-protection. 'Kid, that's all you gotta know,' she said. But nobody protected Paolo and I felt kinda responsible. We were all 'people from abroad' and the creed was that we had to look out for each other. An immigrant isn't in control of life all the time, my mom said. Sometimes you just get washed around like garbage in the sea, ending up where you end up.

These thoughts occurred to me while I stayed by his side and waited 'til the meat wagon arrived. I told Auntie to stay in the house while I went with Paolo. The ambulance took twenty minutes at a guess and arrived at 7.48pm. It was all coming back to me. Hadn't I done this many moons ago? The hospital staff should be buying me drinks. I kept bringing them new business. Knowing my luck, I would meet that Oz croaker again, what was his name? Dr Back-in-the-days-of-the-Raj.

In the ambulance, the paramedics did a quick once-over. They asked the usual stuff, did Paolo do the Holy Trinity: drugs, alcohol, smoking? I thought, dang, you bet. But I just shook my head instead. They frowned. 'He's lost consciousness,' they said.

'Well, I gathered that,' I nodded sagely. They checked his blood pressure.

'We think he's had a stroke.'

'I don't know anything about strokes.'

'We need to take his blood to do more tests for cholesterol level, irregular heart rhythms, diabetes, blood clots. He has to have a brain scan — a CT scan or an MRI — as soon as possible, to work out what type of stroke he's had and which part of his brain is affected. He may also need to have other scans, of his heart and blood vessels.'

'Is he going to make it?'

One of the paramedics cleared his throat, readying himself to reply to my question. He took a deep breath. 'We don't know right now. Nine times out of ten, after the initial intense pain the body goes into a coma to shut down from the stress. Some are so severe that instead of physical paralysis the heart stops and body function fails from lack of blood flow. But we are getting a pulse, so that's a good sign. One in three people die within a year of having a stroke. So he still might make it.'

My heart was torn. We were all in that limbo state. 'You will be OK, Paolo,' I said. 'You will be OK. Very soon.' Everything would be OK when they fixed him. There was something very special about starting again. Like I did in the States, like we did here in Macao, me and him. Like he did after the snake bite.

I left the hospital doing their thing on Paolo. I said I'd be back but had to get to work. I'd come back the next day, if that was all right. I could not afford to shut the club or leave it to run itself. I had no painting and no Paolo so I was still in debt.

Friday night. June 26. I had already seen Paolo. He was same-same. They were doing tests on him. The consultants would be back to see him. I picked up a new deck of Luckies on my way in to the club that evening. It felt like the best and freshest thing I did all day, in my current state of mind. Lit one straightaway, before I was even out of the store. The stand-in DJ played a lot of garbage that night. It was OK. I wasn't in the mood to yell at him. As long as he stuck in some of my favorites like Harvey Mason's 'On and On', Patrice Rushen's 'Look Up!' and Heatwave's 'All I Am'. All I could think of was where to get 100,000 potatoes from. Twenty-one for Tai Gor and 79 to settle Ben's debt. Indeed, it was an obsession and the time bomb was ticking. My head itched like mad and I was scratching like a dog with fleas. These cats knew where I was and would be dancing on me or my grave soon.

Thaew never came to get me that night. I was tooting the ringer since I shut the club at 1.50am and I knew the screws had tightened a few rounds. I didn't want to see what I had to see when I got back to the pavilion. I took a big slug of my strongest juice before I called a cab. I made him wait outside.

My head spun like a seven-inch on 33.

The torpedoes had squirted metal into Thaew and Auntie.

They were lying face down in pools of blood. I was frozen hard like a daiquiri made too early. The TV was still on. Thaew must have been in here having his midnight snack with Auntie when the assailants came. It was the 26th, I kept reminding myself. Four days before the deadline for paying Tai Gor back. That means, whoever came was not Tai Gor's White Phoenix gang. It must be the Uzi wolf men who were after Ben. There were too many cats to consider and Ben had led me into their lair.

The entire contents of my stomach emptied like a bucket and I opened the kitchen window as I did not want to overload the floor with any more color. What had happened and was gonna happen here? Should I call the cops? My only experience of the Macao Polícia was from after the soup job when they found nothing. If it was anything like in Portugal or China, everything could be arranged. *Não se preocupe, nós somos amigos.* Don't worry, we're friends. I could not pay them as well. God, how many more people were to be paid? I couldn't even pay myself. After what seemed like a long time, I unfroze. I grabbed a couple of dish towels to wipe my face and tiptoed to my pavilion across the lawn. My legs felt like old rubber bands that could not stretch back. I did not want to see any more. I had to move out tonight. I grabbed all my gold pieces, my tapes, my clothes and shoes. As an afterthought, I ran into Paolo's study in the basement. The place was run through clean with a rotavator. They would find nothing. There was nothing here. Had I not looked long and hard enough all this time? I glanced frantically toward the albums. Thank God they were left alone. I grabbed the first record I could see, the last one that I played in this room: Moszkowski's 'Siciliano'. It would be my memento of this place. I used the phone to ring Alex but again there was no answer so I hung up. I got into the waiting cab. I could not help thinking that if the pimp-dog was here, he'd be plugged up too, wheelchair or no wheelchair. Mary, Mother of God, bless the souls of Auntie and Thaew!

'Where are we going?' said the cab driver.

I was lost in my thoughts with all my stuff in shopping bags. I was sitting like a doll until he spoke. 'Er...'

'I been asking and asking.' He flinched. I was breathing heavy. He could smell the liquid laughter that had just come up from my stomach. He probably thought I'd overdone the partying tonight. He could not have known any better.

'Sorry, I didn't hear you. We're going to...' I thought hard where I'd like to be. The hospital came to mind. Paolo could still hit the wooden kimono. I had to be close by. Think. Think. Quick. '...to Largo do Senado. Hotel Central.'

He rolled his eyes. Yeah, so it was a nine-floor brothel in Senado Square with a casino at the bottom. It was what they called in modern times a budget hotel. I'd be surrounded by gangsters and their molls, therefore a safe house. *Para viver é ser*. To live is to be. Central, one of the oldest hotels, was built in 1928 and was once the gambling hub in the city. It would be a tour de force. The whole place was dark and dank and needed cosmetic surgery, so I wasn't expecting crisp white sheets and fluffy towels. I did not care as I needed some rest tonight. I knew I had to face Paolo at the hospital the next day.

Saturday, June 27. Three more days and I would turn into chopped tomato if I didn't meet Tai Gor's deadline. I was up early in my room at the Central. By early I meant 10.20am, according to my Casio LCD. I grabbed a cup of Java brew and a crispy pork bun at the nearest roadside quiosque. How hard it was to have a lie-in with hookers for neighbors, snapping caps from dusk to dawn, at their clients or each other. Their jaw action alone had the acidity of pure poetry.

In the familiar waiting room with the forest of orange seating, I ran into Alex. The hell was he doing here? Was it his wife, Gillian, having the baby? He had enormous gray luggage under his eyes and looked so crunk that I was not expecting any bouquets.

'Listen, I missed the call last night,' he said in a distressed voice, 'I knew you or Paolo had called from Paolo's office... and I came over straightaway. I'm so sorry about what happened. I am sure you have moved out.'

My thoughts skipped to the call last night. 'You know what happened?' I asked, dubious.

'Yeah. Looks like another armed robbery. I'm sure they got what they wanted before they gunned down Auntie and Thaew. Don't worry, I've called the police. They'll be here soon. They have to talk to you. The... corp... the bodies... have been cleared away. Haven't you watched the TV this morning?'

'No. I've been in the dive known as Hotel Central,' I said. 'It freaked me out and I could not stop throwing up. I didn't sleep at all last night.'

'Poor you! I totally understand. It's all over the news. The whole house has been cordoned off with police tape. You must come and stay with us, it would be much better than that dump… if you don't mind being woken at 5.30 by a yelling baby… we'll be up pumping anyway.' Alex made a sorry attempt at smiling.

'Pumping?'

'Oh yes. Expressing Gillian's breast milk using a pump. I have to help her unload the sterilizer pot, you see. Her let-down reflex is often slow.'

The hell was he talking about? I was having a let-down crisis! An entire warm and toasty vista of his domestic life opened before me like a meadow.

'You are so good to have saved Paolo's life. If he had been there when they were there…'

I gestured a wave to mean it was nothing. I felt a little electricity of guilt but it passed. We sat in the waiting room for a good half-hour until we were called. We were both exhausted and we said nothing. I thought I was going to pass out. Somebody give me coffee and a donut! I snuck a peek at Alex's expensive but crumpled Santa Barbara Polo Club weekend clothes. I finally broke the silence by making conversation.

'Is it a boy or a girl?' I asked.

'Girl.'

I said nothing because I at once realized I changed my mind about making conversation as I was in no mood.

We went in to see Paolo. He was asleep. He was unable to swallow, and had been given fluid through a drip in his arm and all the nutrients he needed though a nose tube. The nurse brought us a couple of polystyrene cups of coffee and I gulped mine at one go.

The consultant came in and said that Paolo did not need an operation. They had done a CT scan, which established that Paolo had a subarachnoid hemorrhagic stroke. That meant he had a burst blood vessel in his brain. They'd given him nimodipine, which helped keep the blood flowing to his brain. He would have to take this for about three weeks more. He was also put on high blood pressure medication. It would take weeks or months to recover.

Once he was well enough, Paolo could be discharged, but he'd have to work with a rehabilitation program that the hospital devised for him, a care pathway, designed around his particular needs. It might involve physiotherapists, speech and language therapists, occupational therapists, I could barely listen due to my exhaustion. My eyes and ears had drifted off to another world, but I saw that Alex was taking it all in.

The consultant flipped through the sheets in his file. 'I see you signed off a self-discharge form in January this year. The burst blood vessel could be because of the snake bite, you know. A complication.' He shut the file.

'He had a snake bite?' said Alex. 'You said he had a pool accident.'

'…'

Before I had a chance to reply, the consultant interrupted us. 'I have to go now, will you excuse me, please,' the consultant said, as he left the room.

'No… I… hadn't been in contact much with Paolo at all…' continued Alex, 'since Gillian's had the baby it's been chaos.'

'It was on New Year's Eve.' I said. 'Paolo had a snake bite and fell in the pool. I thought he was going to be OK. I took him out of hospital and he came home. Since then we've been caring for him round the clock. The only time I saw you was January 28th but it was just before Chinese New Year and it's unlucky to share bad news.' We had not seen Alex since then, which confirmed to me that he and Paolo were at a professional distance. They had a business thing going, or these so-called partners were only around for the good times. And there were many. After I had informed the guests and the restaurant customers that Paolo had an accident and was recovering, there was no more news from except a few phone calls, flowers and cards.

A nurse came in and announced, 'Inspector Lei Chan from the Macao Polícia' He was a tall middle-aged man with a moustache. He was in a dark suit. I remembered him from the other soup job 'robbery' but I said nothing.

'So we meet again, Miss Li-an! Do you know anyone who could have done this?'

'No.'

'Why did you not call the cops straightaway?'

I hesitated before replying which was not good as I was trying to be pretty damn polite considering I did not want them to find out about New Year's Eve. 'I was gonna. I was afraid they were still there. I called Alex to call you and then I left as quickly as I could. I checked myself into the Hotel Central.' They had found nothing from the soup job and that was something to go by. Everything was gang-related here, mafia-style, and that was the unspoken fact. The numbers in gangs were unseen and growing and the cops couldn't do anything about it. Everybody in the Estoril was in some gang or other and like hell I was gonna pipe up.

'Do you know what they are after?' he said.

'No.'

'This may or may not be linked to or carried out by the same culprits at the New Year's Eve incident. But it is highly likely.'

Great, I thought, but I remained schtoom. They couldn't be more wrong but they had no more leads for now, the reason being, robberies and burglaries of the rich were not rare in Macao due to the gambling trade, black economy and of course the culture of warring gangs. Yes sure, the police would take down details and investigate but they knew for every cop there were two bent cops and about a hundred or more suspects. When Inspector Lei Chan had left, Alex and I walked to the hospital exit together.

'Yes, I saw you at the New Year's Party…' said Alex, 'and I left after midnight. God, I'm so rubbish, it was only a few months ago. I just thought he was ill, and then recovering and then busy… The baby just took over our lives… Why didn't you call me? What happened?' He was rattling on like a steamer.

'There was nothing to call you about. Look, it's a long schmory, Alex. I am so, so beat. I will tell you soon. Maybe even tomorrow. I need to crash real bad.'

Alex gave me a lift back to Central and I picked up my things, checked out and paid for one night. We drove back to his apartment in Guia Hill. It was a 1960s block on six floors with original green terrazzo tiles and decorative iron bars on the windows. In the courtyard, there was a mosaic-tiled fountain. You could hear birds singing in their cages suspended from apartment windows. You could say it was vaguely Mediterranean except for the sight and smell of woven trays spread with dried salted fish and red chilies sunning in the courtyard.

Alex made us ham sandwiches but I declined. It was already 1pm. Tai Gor and the White Phoenix gang would not catch up with me yet. They meant business. And business wasn't business until Tuesday. I'd be turned into a ham sandwich myself. Alex's wife, Gillian, and his baby, Barbara, were having their lunchtime nap together. I couldn't stop thinking of Auntie and Thaew's carks lying there iced with dark sticky blood. The thought of it came as a blow to me. They were the most genuine and loyal people you could ever meet. And we might not have liked each other but we were tight. There were five of us in that house. Paolo, Thaew, Auntie and me and Auntie's niece. Who knew where she was? But she had survived. She was given the night off when the meat wagon came for Paolo. None of us were from Macao. Day in and day out, we were looking after each other and Paolo. Not a day went by when we didn't need each other.

I said to Alex that I really needed to put my shades down for a couple of hours. He showed me my room, which was dark and comforting. It was small, strewn with odd pieces of teak Sixties' furniture, including his desk in the corner. 'It's a spare room,' explained Alex, seeing my eyes float around, 'and my office too.' After that, he went off to have his ham sandwich, which I was sure he was looking forward to in the peace and quiet of the apartment. I felt the hammer of sleep strike me — I went down straightaway in the unmade bed (probably Alex's) and I must have slept a very long time.

When I woke up and opened the bedroom door, it was already dark. The songbirds outside had stopped singing. I could hear the TV from other apartments, playing Cantonese soaps. I knew my body had gone into shock, and I hadn't recovered from the recent events.

'Oh good,' said Alex from the kitchen, terribly bright with pendant lights. 'You're up.'

I squinted and put my hand up to shade my eyes. A baby was in a reclined seat, kicking at an arch full of dangly colorful toys, bells and mirrors. She was as innocent as a kitten, especially since I had only seen the scum of human detritus recently. I could not imagine this baby all grown up and going to a club, buying drugs from Rocco and Mah Sing.

'Hello, Li-an,' said Gillian, looking up from the chopping board where she was dicing onions. Her jaw was taut and her eyes hard. I sensed that she wasn't too pleased about having me appear in her apartment and staying for an unknown period. There were bags, lines, impressions, hues, everything… under her eyes, like somebody had scribbled an essay in pencil on her face. Her hair was tied back in a messy half-ponytail and the gray roots were showing. She had completely transformed into what I had long suspected was the 'mom' look. Yet in her chaotic appearance, she was peaceful and unhurried. She sighed, which I knew was not a good sign, and returned to the onions.

'Sorry,' I said, 'I was totally wiped out from last night.'

She looked up again, shrugged and smiled to say, so what?

'Bad news,' said Alex. 'While you were asleep there was a call. I don't know who it was, but they know you are here. They said you know the music boy?'

Uh-huh. That meant it was the gang of Uzi-toting wolves. 'The music boy is Ben,' I said.

'Who's that?'

I took a deep breath. 'He's… he's my boyfriend. There's trouble. He owes them 79,000 potat… patacas and on the square, I haven't got it. It isn't my debt but they are now pursuing me.'

'I don't really want them coming here, to my house… to my baby,' said Gillian shakily and making a real effort to be calm, not looking up this time from her chopping. 'I took the call myself.' She shook her head, unable to say any more. She breathed rapidly and fanned herself with her fingers as if to cool down.

'What we're trying to say is you can't stay here,' said Alex, clearing his throat, 'because they know where you are.'

'Where will I go?' I asked, vacantly, dazed. For a second I felt like that baby.

'I don't know, back to the Central, perhaps?'

I sighed heavily and put my flippers on the kitchen table. I looked at them, remembering the easy livin' they once had, though I didn't think so at the time, making melodies, holding pizza slices. Now they had a helluva job making a livin', any livin', let alone melodies. I hadn't had a song in my heart for a while.

I went back to the room to gather my carrier bags of possessions. I felt like a hobo. I looked up from the bed and there was the painting, Il Siciliano #1, *The Horse Cart*. It was in the same style as the second of two, which had been in Paolo's house. A sweet, stellular idea came to me. I opened the door quietly and gave Alex and Gillian a hairy eyeball to check what they were doing – by the look of it, some kind of disagreement, probably about me. They looked too preoccupied to care what I was up to in the room. I had a few minutes spare while the couple were getting dinner ready.

Dallas, you know that this was what we were so good at: grifting. I searched through Alex's desk and contents, and the filing shelves over his desk. All I needed were two signatures: his and Simmonds. I would be free of debt. It was most definitely rinky-dink-dink. The place was littered with signatures. After all, the files were full of letters and nothing else. As soon as I spotted the signatures on them, I took two documents randomly, not even reading them.

On second thoughts, I took the whole damned file, just in case the signatures on them ain't right.

I selected a couple of blank sheets of Alex's headed notepaper as well, from the top pigeonhole of writing material. While I was there, I crimped the pages with a sort of official-looking seal. Maybe it needed an official inked stamp too. Art and craft were natural pleasures to me. I rummaged around for the most ace rubber stamp dangling from Alex's rotating wheel of stamps. Now also from the pigeonhole, a couple of nice stiff office envelopes with Alex's cred printed on them. That should do it. I'd write the letter later.

Later, letter.

After slipping the file into one of my shopping bags, taking care to bury it as deep as possible into my clothes, I enjoyed a most humiliating dinner with Gillian and Alex where I only managed to scarf down a potato. Alex offered to whizz me back into town to what was apparently my new home — Hotel Central, where dreams and lies were one.

In the car, I began to explain what had happened, and what I was trying to do by turning the pizzeria into a club so as to make more money, and my delusion of being a recording artiste had vanished like the money Ben had control of, and so on. I never intended to keep Paolo ill for so long. Auntie and I simply thought he would get better. He was only bitten by a snake and didn't have any real illness.

I was rambling a little, as I had trouble remembering the actual sequence of events. It seemed like twenty years ago that I met Ben. It seemed I lived in dreams, like Sunday Girl.

Alex listened attentively but his expression had changed from calm to nervous, like his wife's. He looked pale green, like a cabbage. He kept looking in his rear-view mirror.

'What's the matter?'

'N-nothing. Did anyone know that Paolo had been ill for so many months in his own home?'

'No, I don't think so. Even you didn't know.'

'I've been so caught up with doing everything to support Gillian after Barbara arrived… Anyway, probably best for him to be kept in low profile.'

We had arrived at Central. The moment I got out of Alex's car, I changed my mind about going into the hotel. You could say it was the mere sight of the place that put me off. I flagged down a cab. I had to get back to the Estoril. I needed somewhere to put my shopping bags down. The handles were almost worn through, they'd never survive another night. On second thought, perhaps it would be me that would never survive another night.

The shutters were down and a hastily made sign had been stuck up on it: 'Closed temporarily due to staff shortage.' The deadheads. I knew I could not rely on them. When Ben went, the Estoril went. There was no one to keep this place open. People came to see Ben. They did not come to see me or the bartenders or Rocco or Mah Sing.

I used my keys to unlock and slide open the shutters. I found myself inside the cavern that I had grown into, like Alice in Wonderland. Now it was not ''S Wonderful' and there were no made-for-me Manhattans with cute tags saying, 'Drink Me' as I swanned in. The place was screaming with silence. It was a sound I had never heard before in the Estoril, even when it was Johnny's. It had become a graveyard… a cemetery to Ben and all the songs we danced to.

I helped myself to the bar, pouring out a large amber-colored fly juice — who cared what it was, I'd paid for this and I was goddamned having it and it'd better be strong, I thought. I wandered deeper and deeper into the night that was the back office. I snapped on the lights and began my search through the file. Documents with fewer words were preferred — I had no aptitude for reading schmaltz and I wasn't exactly requiring some light bedtime reading.

I found a fax memo dated three years ago that said:

>Jack, here's the contact you need for Chicago. Ask for Ellen Krantz. Say you're Johnny. She'll know.

(There was a phone number, scribbled by hand.)

>Alex, thanks. p/s I got the keys to your apartment today. I'll get UPS to drop them over to you. Enjoy your vacation.

>Appreciate that, Jack.

The address of the said apartment was in the title deeds along with carbon copies: Alex's apartment in Guia Hill was owned by Jack Ray Simmonds! Here were the signatures of both parties.

Just this document alone would have done me just fine, but hey, I was being cautious and I took the whole file because it was there and I didn't want to screw up.

Another letter seemed mysterious:

February 11, 1981

Dear Mr Richardson,

My name is Chiara Russo and I am a journalist from New York. I am writing to you again regarding a painting that you acquired a year ago called Il Siciliano #1 in a series. I wrote to you about this a few months ago, but you did not reply.

Can you please help us in any way?

Thank you.
Sincerely,
(signed)
Chiara Russo
For the Russo family.

Three things: the Johnny of pizzeria fame was Jack Ray Simmonds, Alex owned the painting #1 and someone called Chiara was looking for Jack. But why were all these linked?

Midnight. I was spending my Saturday night in the Estoril. I was feeling too hellacious and beat to return to the Central. Come to think of it, this was quite a comfortable back room and couch. There was not much time left for my own little project. I must not forget that I had to go to Hong Kong first thing Monday to rid myself of debt at the gallery. It was time to begin the forgery. I wrote out the letter roughly first, then I typed it up on Paolo's olive-green Olivetti sitting in the corner.

Dear Mr Whitfield,
RE: Sale of Il Siciliano 2 to Richard Whitfield Gallery
I am the owner and with my lawyer as witness, I authorize Li-an Donohue to sell Il Siciliano 2 on my behalf.
Thank you.
Sincerely,
(signed)
Jack Ray Simmonds
In the presence of
(signed)
Alexander J. Richardson

It took an eternity; it was like I bled each word out drop by drop. There was not a minute in which I did not remind myself that I was doing this for Paolo and Ben. Not a cent of it was for me, unless there was spare change at the end. Hell if I knew how to do business I'd do it! Like most people, the only ways I knew how to make money were firstly to earn it and secondly to sell stuff and man, I was doing both, like, already. Repaying debts was not making money. Debt repayment was a non-profit organization. I had never used a typewriter before. When all was done, it looked like a friggin' poem. All I had to do now was practice the signatures a few times and sign away. I put my wringers behind my neck and did a sort of stretch.

I shut my peepers in the Estoril, on the battered couch in Paolo's back office. I used sheets of cardboard for my blanket, like a true hobo. All the time I was waking up because I feared that the debt collectors would appear any minute. Any of them in the wolf man's gang, Ben's sharks. They worked 24-hour days and round the world. On Sunday I went back to see Paolo, and he was a lot better. I read the newspapers to him and damn, there was a lot to read. It was the Sunday papers, after all. When I left him, I decided to stay in the Estoril for the rest of the day as I was definitely aiming to open that night. A quick stock-take and a clean. I could do all this without thinking now. I could not let disco die in my own hands. I once said jazz is dead, was dead, and now I was trying to save disco.

Monday. I caught the 7.15 jetfoil from Macao Ferry Terminal to Tsim Sha Tsui in Kowloon. I was so early that I had to wait outside the gallery until the lesser-spotted bearded pig trotted up to the door to open up. There was a helluva wait while he checked signatures and made calls and Xeroxes and whatever.

By 12.30 on Monday, June 29, just as he said, I got my big fat check. I cashed it straightaway and bought two batik bags from a roadside vendor of tourist junk to put my newly acquired Hong Kong dollars in. The ape took a chunk of commission from the sale, which left me with only 82,000 Hong Kong dollars.

On the ferry back, I went to the women's room and contrary to what I usually did in bathrooms, which was to put my compact mirror, a hundred pataca bill and a razor to good use, I counted up 21,000 Hong Kong dollars for Tai Gor and 61,000 for the wolf gang. It was not enough because I owed him 79, but my debts came before Ben's. I put 21,000 in one batik bag and 61,000 into the other. I would explain to the wolf that it was still 18,000 short. I did not know if I would make that up quickly, but at least they could see I was trying. The only way was drip-feeding payments. It was more than Ben ever managed. One deadline at a time, that's what Paolo used to say, I remembered with a sharp tug of sadness and guilt.

First, Tai Gor. From the Macao ferry terminal, I cabbed it back to that 1950s glitzy room in a large European apartment block on Rua dos Mercadores with arches and potted palms. A blind accordionist was sitting in the shady arcade pumping out some fuzzy wheezy sounds while his dog slept on the stone floor next to him. Children were drawing a hopscotch diagram in colored chalk, ready for their game.

I got upstairs but already I knew something was wrong. The door was ajar. It had been crowbarred or kicked in. I hesitated, not knowing if I should go in or not. I heard grunts and soft thuds from inside… and then a baby's cry! It stopped abruptly and turned into a sort of whimper. Why was there a baby in Tai Gor's apartment? I pushed the door very gently but it was yanked open suddenly.

I was face to face with a familiar-looking Uzi, lovingly handled by one of the wolf men from Ben's moonlight rendezvous. Somehow they were now linked with Tai Gor and I dared not think how. 'Get in and don't move,' he snarled.

I dropped the two batik bags and put my hands up as I entered the room. The view opened. Who should be sitting there but João in the Fifties' high-backed winged teak chair. He was gagged and tied up. He kicked feebly at the legs of the chair he was tied to, which was the sound I was hearing, the soft thuds. He grunted in pain. His mouth and lips were cut, the blood dried dark. His eyes had been socked black and I had trouble seeing if they were open or shut. I gasped.

'João?'

'He dunno nothing about the money.'

'I know,' I spoke shakily. 'What Ben owes you. I have it here. Why get João involved?'

For that, I got a hard, sharp clap on my temples from the edge of the Uzi. My skull clattered momentarily under my perm. I screamed in pain and swerved from the force of it. I glimpsed the big black beard of the wolf man, steadied myself, and put my hands up again. He was still in his combats, I didn't think he had changed his clothes from a week ago. 'It is this piece of shit who been tailing you cos he always got time for music boy.' He prodded at João's temples now instead of mine. 'Lucky we got him, if not we not finding the lawya-sar or you. Understand?'

I looked around. Alex's baby was crawling on the floor. She had found some apples, which had fallen from Tai Gor's crystal fruit bowl. It lay shattered nearby and no one had thought to pick up the pieces in case she got hurt.

The baby picked up an apple and peered at it before trying to put it into her mouth. I shouted: 'Stop!' She dropped it on instinct and looked confused — she didn't know if she should cry but she did not. I wore my maternal instincts like a karate belt. The baby looked at me, unaware who I was, but she knew the word 'stop'. I shook my head rapidly while staring at her. It's dirty, I said, it's got glass all over it. Dirty. Glass. I repeated. Keeping her transfixed, I rushed over to pick up the baby, which distracted the wolf man.

I was dizzy and overwhelmed by the Rembrandt-tinted vision of what was happening in this flat. 'You got this— this baby? From Alex?' I said to him, grabbing the baby by her torso.

'The lawya-sar. He got nice apartment.'

'What about Tai Gor?'

'Don't worry, he's here.' The Uzi didn't move, but the wolf man did. He took a few steps to the window where Tai Gor's silk carpet was rolled up like a doner kebab. He kicked the carpet open to show me that it was Tai Gor inside.

I held my breath. They must have thought Tai Gor was hiding me. My heart pounded. I shook my thoughts away. There were so many, they were like a cloud of hornets.

'Where is Leandro?'

'He gone to find you again, they don't believe this little shit boatman,' he nodded at João.

I cast my chin at the batik bags. 'I give you the 79,000 and I take the baby away right now,' I said. It was the same amount in patacas as in Hong Kong dollars. I had already moved the baby away from the glass. I had to put her down in order to raise my hands and I had not figured out how to carry a baby with one arm like experienced moms. This was only my first time carrying a baby, after all.

The Uzi's unholy hole followed me all the time while I crouched, still with hands raised, and opened one of the batik bags. I didn't need to pay Tai Gor back now, so in fact I had saved a few bucks. I counted and took out 3,000 Hong Kong dollars, all that was left for me. I stood up and kicked the bags to him. I put my hands up again.

The wolf man emptied the bags, still aiming the Uzi at me, and counted the rest of the money with one hand. Satisfied, he kicked the bags back to me. I picked them up. Then I walked over to the baby and picked her up. 'Hi, beautiful,' I said to her. It was easier than picking up the batik bag this time round. João shot me a panicky look from his half-shut eyes that said what about me, bitch?

I ignored him.

I walked out into the sun, feeling free as I should. The baby stank like a toilet. The men had not changed her diaper for a friggin' long time. I stepped into a drugstore off Largo do Senado as soon as I could and bought the first thing with my 3,000 patacas: an 'economy' pack of diapers. I needed some help from the drugstore assistant with guessing the baby's weight in order to buy the right diapers. She was a mother of three and took pity on me. She washed and changed the baby herself to save me doing it. God had been kind to me today, Dallas.

And only after that did I get a cab straightaway to Alex's.

I got the cab to wait with my carrier bags in it. I carried the baby and her new pack of diapers in. I said I would have come sooner but I'd had to go to a drugstore to get new diapers first. It was no surprise to me that Alex and Gillian looked like zombies. They had been up all night. After Alex had dropped me off, he returned home to learn from a hysterical Gillian that Barbara had been kidnapped at gun point. It was the most terrifying evening of their lives. They had been crying continuously. The gun-toting masked men arrived asking for me. They said that I had gone. On the table was the remainder of the potato meal that I ate. Everything looked exactly as the night before.

Gillian was so relieved she took the baby from me and was speechless for a long time. She rocked the baby like a boat, her eyes shut. She drank in the moment and sighed long and easy. Alex, feeling left out, kept saying thank you to me. 'Let me pay you for the diapers,' Gillian said, sniffing and drying her tears on her sleeve. I'd heard that personal hygiene was no longer a priority when you had a child. 'I must say I underestimated you, Li-an.'

'You didn't. Everything you thought about me is true.'

They laughed nervously, not sure what to make of what I said. They knew me not. I explained what had happened that morning in the least complicated way that I could. I was at Tai Gor's to return the money and to rescue the baby (though strictly that was untrue, since I didn't know of the kidnap until I got there).

'Where did you get the money from?' asked Alex shrewdly. I didn't want to tell him about the painting that I'd sold because I had to forge his signature plus one other in order to do that. But I was ready for the question. I had already been thinking about this in the cab.

'I got paid back by a couple of my debtors, thank God, from the Estoril. You know what it's like— business,' I laughed vacuously.

I left Guia Hill in a hurry. There was nothing further to be said. Alex was tired and I didn't want him to ponder what I'd been saying. He had not suspected anything because his mind had been pulverized by the terror he'd been through.

I was done now. I had 3,000 Hong Kong dollars or 800 US dollars (enough for a plane ticket to New York), my demo tape, and some sentimental shit like my shoes, clothes, pirate tapes and the Moszkowski *Trois Morceaux* record from where this whole brainstorm regarding the painting started. One more trip before my getaway: back to the pavilion to pick up my axe, the beloved wine-red Les Paul. 'To Coloane,' I sang to the cab driver.

I felt light as a feather as I gathered my shopping bags on the floor of the cab. In my haste and focus on getting the baby home, I'd forgotten about the file I'd filched, used and now didn't need. I rearranged the documents and replaced them carefully in the file. I intended to sneak it back to Alex's study on the pretext of having left something behind while I was asleep in there. The Plan of Li-an had fallen apart. Now I was stuck with a file I wanted to be rid of, at rocket speed. It was evidence against me. I was still thinking if I should chuck the file away when a letter I had not seen the night before fell out:

June 20, 1981

> Dear Mr Richardson,
>
> Regarding the whereabouts of Jack Ray Simmonds. Since you were his lawyer, you know him. We've been looking for him for 22 years. Jack made friends with my wayward junkie uncle Paolo Giametti Russo while vacationing in Positano, Italy, in 1959. He had confided in Jack, who was working at the resort, that he had a house in Portugal. They were both 24. The house had just been left to my uncle by my grandfather, who just passed away a month before that.
>
> But my uncle Paolo died of an overdose. Jack took everything of his, the fine clothes, the leftover drugs, the passport, money, the Italian leather shoes.
>
> Do you see what I am saying? He became Paolo. He went on to Portugal and sold the house.

I paused here. Wait a minute! She was saying the Paolo I knew was actually 'Jack Ray Simmonds'? I found it hard to imagine Paolo doing all these things she said he did when he was 24. I mean, it was possible, but I wanted to believe that she must be wrong!

> With our characteristic Italian family squabbles, and the fact that my grandfather had left so much property, we did not realize that the house in Portugal was missing. By the time we got around to claiming it, we were told it was already disposed of. Can you imagine our rage?
>
> There was a painting in this house called Il Siciliano #2, The Flower Cart. We are looking for it. It would lead us somewhere.

She ain't getting it back. This was the painting I just sold. I dreaded to think that it was true what she said about Paolo being an impostor — otherwise how did this painting come into Paolo's possession in the first place?

> Yet last year, on October 14, 1980, Il Siciliano #1, The

> Horse Cart, was sold in a gallery in New York to the scoundrel.

That was the painting hanging in Alex's apartment! Jack a.k.a Paolo must have given it to Alex.

> Twenty-two years it has taken us to get here. Of course, you probably assumed that he was the real Paolo when he came to you to sell the house in Portugal. Why would you think anything else, especially with his expensive clothes and a passport photo that matched his appearance. He is like a snake that has just slithered away in the long grass and disappeared. We despair that we will ever see our money or the painting again.
>
> Please say that you are able to help us in any way. My family are offering anyone a reward of US$150,000. We want to prosecute this scoundrel and we are serious.
>
> Thank you.
> Sincerely,
> (signed)
> Chiara Russo
> For the Russo family.
> Telephone: (212) 326 XXXX

'Sorry, not Coloane, Hospital São Januário, please,' I cried.

I had to get to Paolo pretty pronto. Think fast and act zippy. There was no Ben to strip me of my cash and my dignity. I had nothing now. Not even that *Flower Cart* painting. I would rather just tell Paolo the truth — that I sold his painting. He could take it or leave it. It was OK. We were square. If he was cool with it, then he was cool. If he got all spaz, I would show him the letter. I could call his bluff. I just had to mention the name Chiara Russo. My pockets could be so well-lined with the reward I'd hardly be able to walk. I could do whatever I wanted in music at long friggin' last.

Why wouldn't Alex sell the information to these guys? I knew now. It became clear to me. He'd been paid. Those memos that I found confirmed it all: that 'Paolo' gave Alex the Guia Hill apartment and the

Horse Cart painting hanging in Alex's study, and that Johnny's (Jack's, in fact) Pizzeria was set up by some deal between Jack and Alex in Chicago. Therefore Alex would never trade 'Paolo' off for the reward offered.

But did 'Paolo' not change the deeds of the property and the restaurant to my name? Oh, that. I shook my head. I was deluded to think it was love; it was more like an infection of anthrax, as sang the Gang of Four. I saw myself as queen of his castle. The treacherous knight Sir Ben rode on my white horse with me because of his greed. Now I knew the name transfer was only such that the name 'Paolo' did not appear on any documentation. That was why I could not liquidate his assets.

My esteem for 'Paolo' had been raised high as a flag. Just like I had been, he was a total pro flimflam artist, an impostor, my prized possession too. And now it seemed… my dear snowbird was worth one hundred and fifty grand. When it came down to it, did it bug me that he was actually Jack Ray Simmonds? Hell, no, things could be much worse and I swear they had been.

I thought about it but I could not turn him in. I didn't want to go back to Chicago. I was his carer, wasn't I? Had to be here until he was well, and then I would love to press restart. For an immigrant, there were no endings, only beginnings. This time, I wanted to get an apartment in Greenwich Village, start writing music again, play in a band, and of course start touting my demo to record companies. My vagabond shoes would surely lead me to New York, New York.

Oy, vey ist mir. I really didn't want to sell the painting. If I hadn't needed the cash so urgently, I would not have sold it.

When I got to the hospital, the staff said it was too late. 'Paolo' had bought a walking stick, paid his bill and discharged himself. 'What?' I said, barely audibly. 'He's outta here?'

'Did he not tell you, Miss— Sorry, I don't have your name here.' The Filipina nurse pointed her finger to the visitors' list. I noted that Alex had not been again either, since we met up here. Two bearded men had come to pick him up and help him out of here, she said.

I bit my fingernail. 'Where'd he go?' I was so surprised that for a moment, my mind was blank. My snowbird had opened the cage door himself? I was too late to warn him of the letter.

'We don't know,' said the nurse. 'Do you not have his home address?'

'Oh yeah, sure,' I said with a bleak smile.

I waited outside the hospital for another cab. When I went past the Estoril, there was a 'for sale' sign on it, and some realtor's phone number, and a shiny new lock. The shutters were still down, but already handbills were stuck on them. There were dead leaves and garbage gathering like a funeral pyre in front of the Estoril.

Who'd put up this sign? I thought it might be one of the three partners. It was gonna happen as soon as they knew we weren't raking it in. Business was business and art was art. It was outrageous. The Estoril was my suckling, my infant, fathered by Ben and mothered by myself with my own blood, sweat and tears. It was heartbreaking. Grief choked me. I asked the cab to drive on. I would get back to the pavilion, grab the remainder of my stuff, and call the airport.

My hands were shaking as I got my keys out. It was a bright evening and I knew all the crevices and all the doors well. The sun hurt my eyes. After all, I lived and loved the night life. There was nothing wrong with my night vision. It was the day vision that I had trouble with.

My key still worked. There was a strong smell of disinfectant. The Polícia had got the evidence they required. I ignored the blue striped Polícia tape everywhere. I expected to see Auntie and Thaew on the kitchen floor in an advanced state of decay, but there was nothing there. It was like their murder had not taken place. The floor tiles glowed from being cleaned.

I ran into Paolo's study. I was shaking so much, I could not stand up. I sat for a minute or two, listening to my heart pound. Was he here? I heard nothing. I put down my carrier bags. I was confident that he would be here. He was weak and I was strong. All he needed was piano music and he would be mine.

I scuttled out of the study like a cockroach and headed upstairs. The stairwell was entirely wood-paneled so it was dim even though it was daytime. When I was halfway up, the damned stairs creaked but I realized it was not from my weight. I looked up at the top of the stairs.

It was Paolo.

Jack.

He had his walking stick and his double-gusset Ermenegildo Zegna travel bag, probably belonging to the original Paolo. He looked scalier and yellower than the bag itself. His head seemed shriveled and cupped his increasingly hooded eyes. The black widow's peak that used to mark his forehead distinctly had been combed absent-mindedly away from his face. I suppose you could say he was once handsome in a vampiric way, like a faded photograph.

'Five months you kept me here. I should kill you but I won't,' he slurred in a mechanical voice. He was still a cat from Sha-town who looked Italian and said ciao. A whole lifetime of music education left me with ears that heard but never listened. I was listening properly now and it was still Paolo. Not Jack.

Paolo hissed 'excuse me' and stepped around me. He tried to make his way down the stairs with his silly stick and his leather bag. I could not let him get away. He was my last chance to earn that reward.

'I… kept you well… here, didn't I?' I said. 'It's… your own home. Wait!'

I shot out my leg to stop him. He caught me out. He waved his stick with one hand. It distracted me. I thought I was going to be struck like a stray dog, I who had no weapons, tools, nothing. Using his other hand, he opened his Zegna bag. He pulled out a roll of canvas. With a flick of his wrist, the roll unrolled. It was the elephant painting.

'This thing. You gave me this,' he said. 'I don't love it but no one had ever given me anything in my life.'

'Yeah, I did, and?'

'And yet you cut off my phone, my life,' he droned. 'You put me downstairs. You played me choons night after night that made me weep in pain.'

'I thought you liked those damned choons?'

'See, dat's why I like ya. You are totally naïve and innocent—'

'You never paid me a cent for the music.'

'And thick-skinned! I couldn't pay you. You were giving it to Ben.'

'You can't say that.'

'Sure I can. You left mikes in the grand piano. I heard more than your recordings.'

I paused and tried to jog my memory to when the piano parts were recorded.

'I worked hard for it. It was my money.'

'You were not born in '42. Whatdju know 'bout hard work?'

He almost seemed to chuckle like some spazzed tractor. I reminded myself he was sick. He'd just had a stroke. It wasn't a laugh, more a wheeze. 'You were blinded. After Ben, you never wanted to play piano. You never wanted to eat pizzas. You just wanted money.'

My blood surged with rage. I took a couple steps to be higher than him. Since he was limping on his stick at the rate of a pace an hour, I raised my arm to grab and stop him.

'You cannot leave!' I shouted. 'Where are you going?' I fed him the best trusted stuff from my handbag that I would save for myself or Ben. 'I've been taking care of you. I've been taking care of Johnny's.' I stood up tall, though I was on a higher step than 'Jack' was.

'I know,' he said. 'Thank you. I'm not… you don't belong to me and I don't belong to you!'

But something happened inside me. My weakness and indecision. What he said was true. I detested it. I feared it. He showed me the elephant painting. At that moment, he gained his advantage. I gave him a worthless piece of painted fabric from the market in exchange for his 9,000-dollar work of art.

Paolo saw my shadow, cast by daylight from the upstairs landing. He saw my vulnerability. I lost him. I lost my foothold. I gripped both his hands. I was dancing the tango and he was leading. I did not want him to leave. This could not be goodbye. Where was he going? Oh jeez, how it reminded me of mom. I also tried to stop her on the day she went to the airport. 'Cept that mom was steeped when we tango wrestled. To let her go that day meant I had failed as a daughter. It was complex then as it was now. A real Broderick. I fell like eggs into a bowl. I breathed the strong Italian leather aroma of his polished Ferragamos. It was almost therapeutic. I turned myself over like a turtle.

Paolo sensed that moment, the moment my mind let him go. Physically, I was strong. Mentally, mincemeat. At last he managed to pull his fingers away from my dukes — long, slender, smooth, my pride and joy. Did they not bang out enough choons for him? His breathing was short and shallow now. I kicked his stick away. I heard it clatter down the stairs to the bottom.

'I needed you, I... but I need to go now,' he whispered in pain, in the softest voice I had ever heard from him. 'Here's your return ticket.' Paolo slurred like a machinoid. 'Thank you for helping me get back that money. Li-an. I know I can count on ya.' He was weeping. His tears fell. He swooped up his travel bag (which must have been poured with iron and cast in lead) and swung it. I tried to run after him but I was caught up and lost my balance on his damned bag. It was my turn to dust down the stairs so-fa-mi-re-do perfectly in rhythm, bounding like a dog on a beach.

When I got to the bottom, Paolo had limped and semi-slid his way down using the handrail as support. Slow motion. In a beat I'd be up, I'd be moving like vapor. I felt the gush of a cool breeze. I groaned. I was hot and I felt wet. Blood oozed from my temple into my hair.

I heard a car pull up, then footsteps advancing from the driveway onto the front step. 'You ready, boss?' a familiar voice called out from outside the door. Where had I heard that voice?

My peepers were half-shut. It didn't make sense to me. I was flopped out with my gams folded like origami.

'Ciao, bella,' Paolo said, tearfully. 'I'm sick. I have to get well first. I will make it up to you. I promise. Arrivederla.' He smoothed back his black hair. He picked up his travel bag and his stick. He rearranged himself into some kind of order, as though he had just got out of bed and was shuffling into slippers. He took one long look at me. I first saw that look when I played 'On the Sunny Side' in the Drake Hotel the night Reagan got in, when he was still Paolo, tanned and chiseled like a doll, when he said 'we're celebrating', when it all began. The look that made me say yes to whatever I was saying yes to. I didn't care what anybody said. He was Paolo. If he was some English duck called Jack, I'd eat my sequined beret. I did not even get to tell him about the letter from Chiara Russo. He was a wanted man! He opened the front door and limped out. The door slammed.

I rocked myself into a crawling position. I wiped my blood onto my sleeve. I hauled myself up and clung at the window sill next to the front door. I looked out. An unfamiliar jeep with dark windows was in the driveway.

Paolo was being escorted toward the jeep by a long-haired guy in combat trousers, to whom he had handed his travel bag. He leaned and limped on his stick to the jeep. The beardo weirdo was the one calling out 'You ready, boss?' from outside the front door. He turned around to open the jeep door for Paolo.

I gasped.

It was the wolf man I met in Tai Gor's apartment. That meant it was the White Phoenix gang that squirted metal into Auntie and Thaew, not the wolf gang. I was mistaken all along.

Four men with guns jumped out to greet Paolo. One of them was Leandro. All five made up for the wolverine chopper squad at Ping Chau. Their footsteps and voices were inaudible. They were full of smiles.

I came to my senses. Ben thought he'd been smuggling gold and opium for Leandro to pay his gambling debts. But Paolo was Leandro's boss. No wonder Paolo was pleased to see me, wept and everything. He knew I was ultimately paying him back. Now I got it. I had been a total mug. I had worked hard paying Ben's debts only to pay Paolo back. The realization was way harsh, man. And for that I got a plane ticket. I looked at it in my hand. It was to Chicago, not New York. But it was cool. I could drop in on Dallas downtown first. I'd find my way to New York after that.

Slow motion. I crouched on the floor. I didn't know for how long, because I blacked out after that.

1982

11:59

Was always more of a consumer than a producer anyways.

My taste in music was too wide-ranging for me to be a musician. In all the time I was in Macao, I had written only 12 songs, of which eight were on the demo I did with Ben. What was I doing the rest of the time? Paying debts, partying at the Estoril, getting the boot. Like I said, music was my passion but being a musician was my delusion.

I made it to New York in one piece. Via Chicago. After I woke up from my Big Sleep, I climbed back upstairs and dressed my wounds in Paolo's bathroom where the lighting was best. I could not get a flight for another four days. I left Macao on Friday, July 3, 1981. I was home again, celebrating the Fourth of July in New York.

There was no way Paolo was 'Jack'. If he was then he was the best one-and-only impostor I'd ever known. I didn't know what to do with the file I had filched from Alex's study and I didn't want to leave it behind as evidence of my forgery, so I took it back with me on the plane, along with my Les Paul, my tapes, Moszkowski's *Trois Morceaux* and just one bag of clothes, which I'd never unpacked since New Year's Day, the day I was supposed to run away with Ben, when I left it under my bed.

I didn't look too bad now, but I was right, I couldn't get on that plane the next day, let alone a stage again. I was not quite the canary I'd been. My map was a little messed up, that was true: it was only an inch, but a scar was a scar always. I never got stitched and in fact I shoulda. I was rattled by my own snowbird whom I had hand-fed the very best dust and Southern Cees.

When I arrived in New York, it was all over for disco. I thought, hey, wait a minute, I'd missed out on a revolution! It was time to get a job.

The anti-disco backlash had caused record companies to shut down. Rock music producers did badly out of it, and rock musicians were losing the spotlight. There had always been something holy and at the same time sinister about rock.

Disco was music for brain-free bunnies. It was being blamed for the new mysterious epidemic called AIDS, for gays enjoying themselves in public, for blacks enjoying themselves in public. I blamed Reaganomics.

That was the trouble. I had most fun when I was back in the clubs, in my fancy rags, dreaming, smoking, drinking, snorting. It was a social thing. Disco was multicultural and rooted in funk, Latin and soul. I was reared on white music and white bread sandwiches. It was my daddy's record collection. Beatles to Blondie, it was all good. Sho'choons. The piano playing that made me a living was proper old-fashioned rags, stride, rock 'n' roll playing, not that modern thing that everybody was doing now, ballady Elton John augmented fourth chords or Billy Joel's descending broken chords. Did we already mention Billy Joel's arpeggios? All great stuff. I loved them all, traditional, modern. Thinking about chords was still my favorite thing to do before I went to bed every night, like a prayer for little girls.

But disco was pure fantasy and freedom. It fitted me like a sheer, flowing Halston dress. That 'sound', which I had tried to perfect, left the dance floor for even higher BPMs, more synthesized effects and guitar accompaniment. It was getting stripped, more naked. Disco moved its bell-bottoms in the direction of dance. Just one word, one syllable: dance.

I had planned to be in New York for a year. I ended up staying a year and a half. I joined a couple of 'dance' bands and started one, but it didn't work out. I never found this new sound that Ben and I were playing quite naturally in Macao, and yet we had less equipment then. Ben and I must have floated in a balloon of innocence. It had now popped. Music wasn't about bands or instruments anymore.

I never found the simpler, funkier big beat that I was supposed to pick up, that was dance or dance-pop. And it wasn't fun. I was 25 and deep in my trashy heart of glass I breezed off music, my original, my one true passion.

I got a job in a record store on 48th, thanks to my wide-ranging taste in music from Moszkowski to Motown. I did quite well considering I went out to Macao with the six dollars I had in my purse the night Reagan got in and came back with 3,000 patacas (minus about fifty for the cabs I had to take on the last day), which was 800 US dollars. Of course, there was the Sony Walkman with the pool-blue ear sponges, a gift from Paolo. I would always cherish those. Not a day went by that I didn't think of Macao nights.

In the summer of '82, somebody walked into the store. I was putting up the Closing Down Sale signs.

I heard the little Santa bell ring over the door and I looked up. He said hi and went to the back of the store. At first, he appeared to be just another bored cat looking for something to do on a fall day. He had very short hair and a beard the same length as the hair. He wore Robert La Roche multicolored acetate glasses. They were all the shizmits now: jazzy, jewel-colored, jello-like mosaic picture frames for the eyeballs. It was his stance as he browsed the records that got me. Then, as his fingers scissored over the spines, I noticed that he could not bend one of his fingers. That was when I wised up as to who it was. My heart flew like a cork.

Ben.

Ben.

Ben Mizrai? Alive. True, I never saw him dead. Only the vision of Dallas and João's dog-howl made me assume he was dead. Despite having cut his hair and grown a beard and got new glasses, I still knew it was him. Call it a broad's hunch. He had not noticed it was me. Or maybe he did but pretended not to.

Hell, it was no biggie. I had changed my look too, and about forty times since I last saw him. I was now into lace everything, like that little Portuguese café we went to so long ago when things were sweet. My leggings, turtleneck sweater, miniskirt, were all Lycra lace. It was what was called dancewear, to go with the new dance music around. I had a new perm, short, and I had dark hair now, with blond roots. I should have had the urge to paste him, or at the very least show him the exit and tell him to bounce. The urge never came. I stared blankly. And what would I say to him? You DJing? Have you got the 79,000 patacas you owe me? That I paid back to your debtor who ultimately was actually Paolo a.k.a 'Jack'?

I would sound like such a bunny, which I was, sure. They don't make them like me anymore, said Dallas. He suddenly turned around and faced me. My thoughts must have been loud enough to be channeled across the room. He looked at me tight. He had kick-ass threads and a lean face but that hand probably could not hold an axe again, as I first thought. It was definitely him, because we were both lost in our own thoughts. My memories should be locked up like criminals, feral animals. Blondie's '11:59' was playing in my head.

Ben mumbled something like 'Hey spangler, ssup.' It went all spaz at this point, most definitely. He left the records he was looking at without putting them back.

I sighed and said quietly, almost to myself, 'Later days, man.'

He turned around and left. I was such a putz. I couldn't believe I said nothing. Vat's da matta mit chew, I asked myself in a mock-Yiddish routine. Now he was gone.

After the little Santa bell rang, I hurried over to put the records back. I was geeking out and needed to see what he was into nowadays. He was looking at new stuff. He'd taken out Stevie Wonder's 'Original Musiquarium', Survivor's 'Eye of the Tiger' and Steve Miller Band's 'Abracadabra'. So vot? He was only doing S to W before he shot out like an arrow from my heart.

As soon as he left, I couldn't breathe. It was not the sight of him but that of the albums he had been looking at. Up to that point, I was fine, I was even indulging myself in mock-Yiddish taunts. He did not affect me as much as something we once shared so deeply. Music. I was walking wounded. Geekdom hurts. Clutching my heart as though I had been stabbed, I ran out of the store, yelling. Ben, Ben, Ben, Ben, Ben. I ran aimlessly, not knowing which way to turn. I stopped to catch my breath. I put my hands on my waist, panting. I realized I was weeping. I covered my face. I must have seemed like a total space cadet. How could I have left the store unattended? If my manager was around I would have been fired. 48th Street was swarming with people, sirens, traffic. For the second time, I had him and I lost him. He was gone.

Things were changing and not just at the turntable. By the end of summer, something called the compact disc was being produced, and not just produced, but way mass-produced. We received the first batch in October 1982, which incidentally was Abba's *The Visitors*, quite an apt name. I would always remember that album. I was there when the first CD came to the masses!

I was so jacked. It was wrong. How could they ever have replaced vinyl records, which filled a room with the deep, rich mahogany sound of analog? Paolo and I at least agreed on one thing when I first stepped into his study: albums are your friends. Listening to a vinyl record was a commitment. You didn't invite a friend and then walk out of the room, but you'd do that with a CD. That was because there were too many tracks — nine, if I recall, and more and more bonus tracks to come, I was told by our suppliers, because of the storage capacity of a CD. In fact, depending on the length of each, it could have up to 35 tracks. You could leave the CD on until the end and not have heard a thing. A CD was not a friend: it was a visitor, a traveling salesman.

With a vinyl record, you had to stay in the room to listen to it and then turn it over after less than half an hour. You memorized the lineup of the musicians. You read the lyrics to the songs. Sometimes, you got a giant glossy poster that was out of this world. That would be the first thing I checked whenever stock arrived in the store: which albums had a freebie?

After winter, the store shut down. It was only a little store anyways.

I sold my wine-red Les Paul. It was a miracle I even had it for so long.

I should take my interesting times (as the Chinese euphemism went) back with me, I decided. Chi-town: you gotta live it to believe it and in my case, believe it to live it.

1984

Chicago. I'd come home. January 1984. I knew now why my mother went back to Singapore. It was home to her, just as Chicago was home to me. She explained it badly in her goodbye letter and there was no need. Being Chinese, naturally she could not verbalize emotions. They were just a giant heap of abstract thoughts. I might have once despised her inability to detangle that mound of desperation but now I knew it was her dignity, her way of handling tough times. I did the same as her when I wanted to. Instead of being all American and liberated and saying 'hey I'm angry, sad, whatever, and this is why I'm going shopping' I still favored my mother's option: 'this is stupid, I'm stupid, you're all stupid.' In fact there's even a Chinese phrase to sum up enduring hardship: 吃苦, *sek fu* in Cantonese (to eat bitter), or 'if you don't shut up, you'll be eaten up and go all spaz.' Once, home was where I put my hairspray down. Now it was a place that bugged you in a way you felt familiar.

Not only that, I had to get back to Dallas. She was where I'd leave my hairspray and she bugged me in a way I felt familiar. I got a job in another CD store since CDs were now a novelty luxury item. They gonna make me a manager if I make it to six months max. I may even get to go to CD fairs. I could now afford a phone line. I also bought a new axe, this time a five-year-old Dixon Strat. It was deadly enough. I got an apartment, not in Chinatown this time but in Lincoln Park. 2738 N. Pine Grove. In the 1920s, this 14-story building was a beautiful busy little hotel. Marble and granite lobby. Lake views, city views. Rooftop garden for those flapper parties that I'd fantasized about.

It was way bigger than a toenail, so good enough for Dallas and me. Now I would get a ginormous *Annie Hall* poster for the hall, just to make her feel at home. She would be out in five weeks three days. I was counting down like it was the birth of a baby. It kinda was. She was starting anew. No more taxing.

Rock and dance traveled like parallel lines after disco died. It might sound weird now, but dance and dance-pop became purely wallpaper, and rock became stadium level, at the Billy Ocean scale of corporate identity. It went all conservative and Laura Branigan. Yet I remembered a time, perhaps just before my last band in '77, Mrs Dixon, when rock music represented a kind of menace, and if not, then a newness and freedom, a lost world of frenzy and excess.

Not only did I work in a CD store, I was occasionally given and sometimes bought CDs on impulse, at cost. Just for the thrill and vanity of buying. Luxury is the search for pleasure, yet the most luxurious place in the world is in one's own mind. I know. I thought I should barf. A total Neanderthal being gifted such gems. Even the box was called jewel case. I was moving with the times. I took one to Dallas and she couldn't believe what she was hearing and seeing from a piece of plastic. My taste was getting rah rah, nowhere. And she thought I had class. I wasn't really a musician anymore, I told her. It was part of some weird groovy delusion.

I was tired from working and I didn't have much time to teach. I had two students. I didn't sleep with their dads, I told Dallas, and she laughed. Felt like a VIP when I gave Dallas my telephone number.

I even gave my mother in Singapore my phone number, in case she felt flush at any time. Daddy and Sherylanne — of course. Daddy was now in hospital being treated for some liver disease. The call could come anytime.

Popular music was a way of prolonging adolescence. Once I got critical, I became an individual. I grew up.

I went to meet Dallas at the MCC downtown on the day of her release. Jeez, she had aged, I thought, though I didn't say it. She said she was just looking her age now, because as usual she read my mind. She was creased like tissue. Around her eyes, mouth, neck. Even her hands. Gosh, what were they doing to her in there? Her eyes were hooded and small, and her hair was short, badly cut and gray. She couldn't do that stuff anymore. Any of it. Artist's model or grifting. Not because of the way she looked now, but because she was exhausted from being banged up.

'Losing your freedom is the most exhausting thing in the world, didja know that? Ask any new mother.'

I thought of Alex's wife and baby.

For days we watched TV, read, spoke little. I got her hair done at Harlem Irving and it weren't cheap. We got her all new makeup and clothes and stuff. She almost looked like the Hollywood broad she once did. Then we hit the town. Bars. Clubs. Stores. Movies. But she wasn't happy. It wasn't like Dallas. She wept often. Yeah, she was a baby again. She remembered places and some of them were gone or had changed. It was part of her exhaustion.

Then one day we talked.

And we talked for days, weeks. Told her everything, slowly. Paolo. Ben. Alex. Everything. Almost everything. Under my bed was Alex's file. Inside it, I had the Russo family's telephone number in New York. Something stopped me from sharing this, as though it was the last piece of a Big Apple cheesecake with the cherry on top.

We took walks. We cooked. Drank wine. Real classy we were. And she finally told me the name of her child who died at age two. Her name was Jennifer. And her husband who left her. His name was Jerome, Jerro Mister, Jerry, Jay Jay. He had many names, nicknames. We were quiet for a while. I sighed, she sighed. A long time ago, she took me in as a homeless 17-year-old. Now she had no work, so it was my turn to look after her. She said I was real smart to get a real job. Not really, I said, I was just hardworking. Now I'd been to Asia, I knew what hard work was!

'Plus, don't forget, I am Chinese,' I whispered, all serious.

'Consider yourself lucky, you got out, dintcha?' Dallas said.

'No such thing as luck,' I wagged my finger dramatically, 'dintcha say that to me once?'

'That was then,' she said. 'Now I think it's all luck.'

She was still a big spender. She loved nice things and going into nice bars. But now that it was my money, I had to be like Miss Alligator Arms. Just a tad. When I occasionally demurred, she'd ask, 'Saving up for a new mug?'

I didn't want to hear that. I got slammed and every day I was reminded of it when I looked in the mirror. There ain't good doctors in Chicago for nothing, she said. They could turn me back into the pretty tomato that I was.

'Know what, Dall? It's foo-foo. Not important.'

'But, kid, you're young.'

'I don't care.' I touched my scar absent-mindedly, like it was an old pet. 'I think it looks kinda cute.'

Every now and then, Dallas bugged me to get a loan to get the ravine on my map filled. When I had enough of her comments, I spun the question back at her. 'Do you want to get yourself fixed? Is that it?' 'Course, she couldn't get a loan. She wanted two of us to get it. That's nice. 'I don't want another debt, Dall, told you so. Had enough of other people's debts.' Was I such a dumb broad?

I realized we had both changed. We didn't agree on many things anymore. Something in her died when she was banged up, and I couldn't blame her for that. Yet she wanted to still look the part and party on. It frustrated me. Why do people want things?

Actually, I wasn't sure what I wanted but I knew we wanted different things. Sometimes I longed to be back in Macao in my pavilion, blowing smoke-rings and listening to the Cantonese radio drama on low volume drifting up from Auntie's room, inhaling the scent of fried garlic, mackerel and fermented shrimps. You can take the girl out of Asia but you can't…

I came back from the store one rather cool May evening. It was our favorite time of year when we were scoping all those years ago. A time when the city pockets and our glasses were full. Dallas was uncharacteristically in a good mood. Uh-oh. Something ain't right. She hadn't been drinking or smoking or buying handbags or shoes.

'He called,' she said.

'Who?' Every day I had been waiting for the flatfooted knock on the door. I'd be in the can for forgery. I remembered the barely whispered saying in the casinos of Macao while eyes were on the roulette ball rocketing at 90mph, 'only risk what you can afford to lose'. Now that I'd risked so much, I was prepared to lose as much, if not more.

'Don't look like you've just been shot. Your pimp-dog called,' she paused, giggling. 'He is a total god.'

'What? You're kidding.' I frowned. 'How dja know it's him?'

'It's him. We kinda had a chat. He told me where he is staying. He's going to ring again. Tomorrow night.'

'Dallas,' I sighed. 'This is not good. Why are you so happy?'

'He's going to pay for it. Me and you, sweetheart. Both. Top surgeons in Chicago. Why don't you want me to be happy?'

'Whoa whoa whoa.' I caught my breath. 'You asked him for money? What are ya, nuts?'

'Now I will say it. You are totally selfish, Li-an. When you were a nobody, I took great care of you. You were my princess, my angel. I protected you and I made you happy, every single day. I didn't care how. I just made sure you were OK.'

'Thank you, Your Majesty—'

'I am a nobody now,' she cried, unable to say any more. She put her hand on her throat and shook her head. Tears choked her and she had the dignity to stop talking.

'I am sorry—' I started. I cried too. You could say it was contagious. The crying disease. 'Dall! No. You are my best buddy, my only buddy.'

'You—' she said after a long time. 'I'm just a ghost. I live through you now. He wants me to be happy—'

'Like, no. Who does not want you to be happy—'

She shook her head, looking down all the time.

'No. I'm not with you there. You can't just accept his offer,' I said. She grabbed her newly done hair with both hands, shaking her head still, and went to her bedroom.

'Dall?' I sighed.

She didn't want to hear my tape-recorded reply anyway. Almost every day we had dramatic word exchanges. We were barneying like a married couple. Soon we'd be throwing glasses at each other and shouting 'I hatecha so why doncha leave'.

The evening after, the phone rang. I hadn't seen Dallas all day or night. Because I had said no to her, she might be in a sulk as she wasn't getting my permission. She could do what she wanted, couldn't she?

I had been waiting for him to call back. After the customary five rings, I picked it up.

'Hellow, Li-an.'

The sonofabitch. I knew that robot voice anywhere. 'How'd you get this number?'

'*Io povvo.* I try. Chi-town ain't that big.' And now he could talk. He sounded recovered. After all it had been a year and a half since he had his stroke.

'What cha want?'

'The truth is, nobody plays and sings like you. Stuck out in that bedroom for quite a grip, just so I can hear you play "On Green Dolphin Street"—'

'You're tooting the wrong ringer. Paolo. Jack. Whoever you are.'

'And for the record, I am not Jack. I am Paolo. I never stole nothin' from no one.'

'Why didn't you say that the last time we met? When you pasted me up on the stairs—'

'Doll, you did not call me Jack, I swear. If you did, I would've said I'm not Jack, trust me. I didn't think that you even could think that I was Jack.'

'OK, whatever. We don't want your money.'

'Stoo late. Dallas, bless her heart. She told me how much the procedures are gonna cost. Worked it all out in her purdy little mind. Don't worry 'bout it, it's on the house. You are after all my little China doll. Ya need a vacation. So! How would ya gals fancy packing ya bags—'

'One question. Where did you put the 250K that was in the safe on New Year's Eve?'

'In your bed.'

'At the pavilion?'

'Yeah, sure.'

'Why?'

'It was the safest place.'

I was schtoom. He had me there. It was a super platform bed that you had to climb onto, but I thought that was just the traditional Chinese design. I never thought to look in there. It seemed so terribly solid. And I believed it must have been screwed shut. I rubbed my scar again for comfort.

'No,' I said patiently, 'that's not what I meant and you know it. Why did you take the money out of the safe before the party?'

'Aw, hon, cos you were gonna give it all to Ben!'

'But how can you be sure of that?' I said.

His laugh sizzled like onions at a stand.

'Now. To make it up to you, I will pay it back to you. I'm sorry I left you there on the stairs. I wasn't feeling too damn good at dat point, thanks to you.' I imagined his Robert de Niro shrug with jazz hands as he said this. Heard that one before. 'And I have your missing wages, 2,000 dollars a month, the 250 gees and the money you paid me back for Ben's debts. I forget how much. You're the accountant.'

I should have had the impulse to hang up but I didn't. Hearing his voice brought back Macao. I cradled the receiver and I listened. Every word tingled like spicy pepperoni with extra jalapeño peppers.

'Ben,' I ummed. 'Who's Ben?'

He cackled like he'd swallowed his feathers. Snowbird was mocking me. He was even funny. I caught myself grinning before I wiped it off my mug. Yet I was so unsure of what to say that I was sittin' on it. He left me his phone number in case I changed my mind about meeting him. 'I may forgive you for keeping me sick, selling my painting which tell ya the truth I didn't like dat much, and my grand piano… now I had to buy dat back at a higher price… and in white, wouldja believe it. But for forging two signatures? You messed dat up. I could get you into serious trouble, hon. You know and I know what we're talkin' bout.'

We'd met in a restaurant and I wasn't a debutante.

It was early. Dallas never got up before midday these days. I hoped she was in a teensy sulk rather than her all-day bedtime day. I dreaded to think of those days returning as I hadn't seen her since our blow-up. But they could come back any time. I rolled out of bed like a die and made my cup of Java. I was thinking of her and not Paolo. I could help her move out. I could give her the first month's rent. Just like she did for me once, a long time ago. Cos it just ain't working out, me and her. I wanted it to work but geez, this must be like a strange kind of divorce of friends. The pain seared through me every time I thought about it. She would be totally crushed but she'd spring back, like grass on bulldozed land. The seeds to survive were there.

Hearing Paolo's voice again confused me. I remembered Johnny's, the Estoril, Auntie, Thaew and of course, how could I forget, the songs. Every song, old, new, good, bad, slow, fast, came back to me, including his favorite, 'We Belong Together'. I think of it as 'his' choon now. When I hear it, I think of him and I think of him when I hear it. It was also pretty damn hard to forget the first thing that Paolo said to me, which was 'Join us'. Something happened in that bar the night Reagan got in. I was adored. It was the first time. How I feared what I wanted, which was to be wanted, to be adored, now, always.

I could murder a pastel de nata right now — my 'little piece of heaven'. When I put the cup down, I found a piece of paper with a number written with my own chops on the side of the telephone... a Morgan Park number. Yes, I remember he had an apartment there. I didn't dream it after all. Dreaming was free then, but waking up had cost me. Of course he knew. The forgery. But only him and me. It sounded like he was trying to call my bluff.

Alex's file was under my bed. I'd need to light a fire so I could destroy the evidence. I reached my arm under.

It was not there.

It was not there.

I hopped back into bed, for it was cold. I swallowed the hot, dark liquid.

Dallas.

No.

I stared at my room, the single light globe, the floorboards painted white, the torn faded wallpaper with its bird-cage design, and just one apple in a vast bowl. Dallas was having my cake. With the cherry on top.

Double no.

But when?

Not last night, after our barney. I was in my room. It was during the day yesterday, when I was out there earning money. Oh yes, she had all day and it was all because I said no she should not and must not take up Paolo's offer of money. And if I tore into her room hissing and spluttering like an out-of-whack lawn sprinkler, it would achieve nothing. I would find that there is no Dallas. 'Course not. She would have packed up and flown our nest. I did not expect that of her. In fact, I was schtoom. How could she make a dash with everything I had bought her, and the file? I sat on the bed and I just wanted her back, with or without the letter. I didn't care. I just wanted

Dallas, my fence, my Fagin. She who asked me to Get Out of Town. The moment I realized she was gone, I missed her. It hurt so bad I could not hold a thing. It was a knife in my side. I felt the strength leave me. My flippers went cold. First my mom, and now, Dallas. I needed Dallas now more than ever. Unlike my mother when she left us, Dallas would not have left a note. But that's cos she would be back, wouldn't she? When she'd done everything she'd needed to do? Dallas, you always said we were a class act. You said I was your family.

Dallas would have believed the letter from the Russo family. She wanted the $150K reward and up to yesterday, I wasn't worried. I never thought she'd want the reward because I didn't want it, I just wanted the letter. The letter proved to me that I had what Paolo valued. A shred of dignity, he called it. A grain of integrity. What Paolo said was true. After Ben, I did not play the piano, I did not eat pizzas, I only wanted money.

Dallas would already be on the case. She had the letter. She would be aiming for the Russo reward by entrapping Paolo. I was no longer required. I was only looking after her, keeping her company, keeping her from mischief and all in the high standard to which she was accustomed, until she got her mug fixed.

My entire small, ugly, silent collection of plastic known as CDs spun before my eyes. Their silence and presence filled the space. My mind, my work, my days, my nights. You couldn't trust them. In the end, no music ever filled this bird cage. In the end, there was no song, no wisdomisms, no moonlight sonatas, no Mrs Dixon, no Estoril, no Advil. And the only straight-no-chasers I was getting these days was CD-buying, high-end customers.

CDs. They had no smell. Discs. Small flat rings, mostly consonants, zero poetry. There was a short time when that was enough. A tiny bit of ultra luxury. They were all I had.

I dialed the number. He answered. 'Your friend is here!' The time had come to put the brakes on it. I was so relieved, I gasped. The agony of not knowing where Dallas was had vanished. I just wanted her back and safe and not doing dumb things she knew nothin' about.

'Paolo. Can you go somewhere where she can't hear you?' I said.

'She's getting her beauty Zs. Drunk my best Chianti last night and now she's passed out.'

'Who is Jack Ray Simmonds?'

'Listen. Like I toldja. The English bastard.'

'And that letter from Chiara Russo?'

'She is my cousin from New York. Do you or do you not wanna hear? You who sold my painting? Damn!'

'I want the whole story.'

'OK. 1954. Positano. Charlie Hughes, the artist, was sick and dying. He and my drug addict uncle were on vacation. Aged 24. I was a child of 12, back home, in Chicago. My uncle and I were 12 years apart. We had the same name, I swear it was my mother's bad idea. She loved her brother too much. When he had an OD, Charlie Hughes got his passport, clothes, money, everything, and he got away wid it. For a short time, he became Paolo.'

'Charlie Hughes the artist. Huh.'

'Yup.'

'But who is Jack—'

'Jeez. Wouldja let me finish? Charlie wasn't sick and dying at all. He was just another drug addict. They come back all the time, like zombies, and Charlie Hughes came back to life as two people, one after the other. After he used up all the green juice like a typical con artist, he went back to England and became Jack Ray Simmonds.'

'And so Jack Ray Simmonds was actually Charlie Hughes the artist?

'You goddit!'

'And he sold the family house in Portugal—'

'Oh no, dat was me.'

'You?'

'How dja think I funded this pizza parlor all dose years ago? Damn! Sonofabitch was an artist, not a businessman. He won't know one end of a check from another. He only knew how to spend money.'

'So at some point in time there were two Paolos—'

The two Paolos were him and his uncle. The house was in his uncle's name, i.e. his name. The moment he could, which was a few years back, he sold it.

'While I'm at it, Chiara is in the dark about me selling dat house, so ya gotta keep schtoom. Ya paying attention or not?'

'OK. You sold the house to fund the pizza business. And the paintings?'

'Thanks for asking, we don't even have the second painting anymore. *The Flower Cart*. But I get it. Ya had to sell.'

'No, OK, this is true. I can't say I'm proud of it.'

He sighed. 'Good business move, I'd give you dat. It was in the house in Portugal and I kept it and took it all the way to Macao.'

'I really did not want to sell it. I'm very sorry, Paolo.'

'Charlie, now operating as Jack Ray Simmonds, gave Alex the Guia Hill apartment first and his painting, Il Siciliano #1, *The Horse Cart*, just two years ago. Alex is his lawyer and had to stay loyal. Alex was my lawyer too, met him when I was selling the Portugal house. You may recall meeting him that night I hired ya.'

'But that means you can find Jack or Charlie?' Now we were really cooking and was it me or was it getting flamin' hot.

'Why do we want to find him? Li-an, think. Dat letter don't mean nothin'. I sold the Portugal house. The assets are in the family. With me, I mean, goddammit.'

'You don't want to or need to find the artist?'

'Let's see. What've we got? We got Johnny's (OK, I am of the conclusion now dat was a badly chosen name and OK now the partners are running it as a noodle house franchise, wouldja believe it). The mansion in Macao, the apartments in Chicago. Charlie? He just wanted la dolce vita. A few treats, clothes, shoes, spending money. Italian sweeties. Come to think of it, the only things I lost were you and the second painting, which o'course you may not see as assets.'

Was Johnny's named after that Jack/Charlie?

''Course not. We're Italians, remember? It was named after Gianni. You met Gianni on the night we met when Reagan got in. Yep, Gianni the money cat. It was his uncle's niece's second cousin that I had to hire to be the second piano player we had in Macao. The girl. I toldja! Never mind. Forgeddit.'

Chiara was looking for Jack Ray Simmonds, an artist and a con artist, whom she did not know was Charlie Hughes the artist, but she'd never find him. As long as Alex was in charge, the artist was safe.

'She's been lookin' since my uncle snuffed it. And dat's the situation.'

He said 'sit you way shin'. No way he wasn't Italian. Always thought there was something whiffy about him being Jack Ray Simmonds. If he was English, then I was Freddie Mercury. Call it a broad's hunch.

'I can't believe it,' I said, now we were spittin' real fast, everything locked into place. 'You should've told me all this long ago.'

'Dja forget I had a snake bite, a stroke, a friggin' coma? Parlo niente. Zipped. Zapped. Semi-solids for five months!'

I remembered then that Dallas was having her sweet vitamin ZZZs at his place this very moment. What would happen to her plan of keeping him and claiming the Russo reward?

'What about Dallas?'

'Never met a deadline I didn't like. Whaddya think?'

'Well, I'm thinkin', I'm thinkin'!' Just that my brain ain't fast as a frying pan these days.

'C'mon! She just wants to be a pretty tomato. The oil painting that she was. She took care of ya once. Now I gotta take care of her. Capeesh? She don't want no letter. She can't even read Tolstory, ya think she's gonna call New York?'

'It's Tolstoy.'

'See, dat's why I like ya. Ya knew I was just testin' ya, right?'

Outside it was gray as a silky sweater. I didn't come back to Chitown for nothing. Shutter juice filled my quite unexpecting peepers. Bang! Bang!

'Jeet yet?'

But what about she who took care of my every meal? Even took me to the dentist. Gonna be there soon as she wakes up and she won't believe her ruby luck luck. Extra cheese for her. You betcha there was nothing I didn't know about Dallas, especially with regards to food. He was gonna take me to a stand and buy me a 'dog wit everythin' because he knew that was what I loved.

'Know what?' I'd say. 'Make dat three.'

Acknowledgements

Thanks to Unbound, London: Bill Massey for a powerful structural edit, Annabel Wright and her team for the copyedit and proofreading process, Mark Ecob for designing the cover, and Xander Cansell who brought everything together. To my parents, my family and my friends, for putting up with me in fantasyland. I am grateful for your patience, kindness and generosity (not to mention your food, drinks, humour, hugs and chats) in supporting me, my book and my efforts, my dreams and my realities.

Thanks to Beethoven Record House, purveyor of records and tapes, originally in the Heeren Building, a 1931 parade of shophouses (demolished in 1990) on 248-B Orchard Road, Singapore 0923, owned by my uncle and run by my aunt, where I spent every school holiday with my cousins lifting and lowering styluses, making mix tapes, scrutinising album covers, memorising every lyric during my childhood until Uni took me away. What an enchanted time that was.

Thanks to the Unbound Social Club for being there in good times and in bad, for solidarity, for sympathy. To my writing cartel: Penny Faith, Clair Whiteman, Jo Marks, Jane Hoodless, Hamish MacFarlane, Anne Walker, Fiona Parker-Cole and Yvonne Lyon, you have always been there to keep the dream alive for me. To Geoff Davis who thought it was a good idea to keep writing, Bonnie Li for help with Cantonese, Simon Lewis and my mentor Daisy Buchanan for reading *Heart of Glass* and providing me with quotes. Thanks to Isabel White, my first reader.

Lastly, all my supporters and patrons, without whom this book would not exist. Together, we did it. We made *Heart of Glass*.

Who would have thought so many were involved in bringing out just one book? 'It takes a village…'

To all of you, my special thanks.

Patrons

Yasmin Akrum
Saima Alam
Lulu Allison
Sharon Bakar
Jason Ballinger
Tom Bodell
Jessie Bouchot
Emma Bowman
Patrick Broad
Manuela Buggiani
Kate Bulpitt
Charlotte Callister
Amy Carr
Fabienne Carter
Andy Carter
David Chambers
Elaine Chambers
Karen Chay
Gloria Chin
Vera Chok
Helen Cole
Rebecca Davidson
Emma Davison
Jo Dawe
Maria Donoghue
Imogen Drake
Jessica Duchen
S Elliott
Jennie Ensor
Lesley Ewels
Mary Fivey
Anne Fong

Hannah Frankel
Yen Chen Fu
Peter Fuller
Carolyn Gan
Sabine Goodwin
Glyn Goodwin
Hugh Graham
Paul Greenleaf
Lisa Harmey
Michelle Hon Pearson
Ray Hood
Nadege Houlbrooke-Bowers
Jenny Iggleden
Johari Ismail
Paul Johan Omar
Serif Jones
Ania Kielbasa
Jean Kong
Andrew Lee
May Ching Lee
Steven Lee
Alice Lee
Gemma Lloyd-Jones
Kian Low
Serena Lowe
Isha Lowe
Brian McClave
Andrew McDonald
Stephen McGowan
Kate Mcveigh
Simon Miller
Vanessa Moloney
Sadie Nathanson-Regan
Ivan Ngeow
Siow Wah Ngeow
Sean Nowland

Hally O'Brien
Ismail Omar
Rhoda Omar
Josephine Ong
Dephy Oon
Sumira Osman
Severine Pages
Isabella Park
Joy Yee Quek
Lisa Radoje
Marcia Roberts
Jacqueline Sardiñas
Luciana Sena
Naomi Smythe
Judy Stafford
Tabatha Stirling
Kieran Sun
Solitaire Townsend
Nicole Vatanavimlakul
Vanderlinden Veerle
Simon Vrij
Lucy Walker
Philip Ward
Keith Watson
Shireen Watson
Vivienne Woon
Mee Chong Yau